THE
VORTICIST

THE VORTICIST

A Monte Boutista Mystery

Chris Wheatley

Encircle Publications
Farmington, Maine, U.S.A.

Editor: Cynthia Brackett-Vincent
Cover design: Deirdre Wait
Cover images © Getty Images

Published by:

Encircle Publications
PO Box 187
Farmington, ME 04938

info@encirclepub.com
http://encirclepub.com

Acknowledgments

Writing this novel would not have been possible without the support and encouragement of my amazing wife.

For my mother, my wife, and my son.

New York, Fifty Years Previously

Christian Schwarzkopf's most potent memory of his father was this: a tall, black-suited figure, wide-shouldered and powerful, standing, facing away through the window of his office on the fifteenth floor of the building which he owned. A silhouette, framed by the nebulous light of the sun, which burst powerfully forth on this hot American day. He seemed a giant—unmatchable, invincible and terrifying.

Christian knew in his eight-year-old mind that something important was happening, but he did not understand what. Later, he would often recall, with uncanny clarity, the feeling of the thick carpet beneath his feet as he padded nervously to stand next to the towering figure, the feeling of the warm glass against his hands as he leaned against it and looked down onto the street below. Men and women, tiny figures from this height, were leaving the building. They carried boxes and bags. Some stood and milled around, some looked up, gesturing and mouthing.

"Do you know who those people are?" asked his father, kneeling down so that his head was level with the boy's.

Christian trembled. "They work for you?" he replied.

"Not any more," said his father, "they used to. I fired them. Do you know what that means?"

"It means you asked them to leave."

"Yes."

"But why?"

"Because they are weak," said Christian senior, "and if you don't weed out the rot then the rot spreads."

"What happens if the rot spreads?"

Christian's father stood up. His son was torn between regret and relief that the moment of closeness was gone.

"Never pity the poor," said the father, "never pity the weak. A strong man will always rise up. He who does not deserves to be where he is."

One of the tiny men below pulled back his arm and swung it forward. Something small flew into the air and thudded soundlessly against the side of the building.

A thin smile appeared on the face of Christian senior. "They envy us," he said, "and they hate us, because we remind them of what they could have been, if only they had the wit or the will and the courage. They hate us," he said again, "don't ever forget that."

31 October, present day, Cambridge, England

Around nine pm, a man with a knife in his head walked into Parkside Police Station and calmly asked for the Duty Sergeant. Constable Paulsen, behind the desk and not two weeks out of training, struggled to adequately grasp the situation. "I'm having trouble seeing," said the man, slumping to his knees. Paulsen hit the emergency button and yelled for Sergeant Tillison, who appeared in time to see the stricken stranger collapse onto his back. Tillison yelled for the FME and knelt down in the rapidly expanding pool of blood. He was too late. The knife had driven itself further into the rear of the man's neck, severing his spinal cord and killing him almost instantly.

At the same time, across the park, on the corner of Regent Street and Park Terrace, Paula Trasker, a twenty-four-year-old student walking home from her night-shift at Sainsbury's, was knocked flying by a young man in a hurry. This man wore a white hoodie and dark jeans, and came barrelling out of nowhere to leave Paula in a heap upon the ground. He did not stop but kept running. "Bastard," Paula yelled, in a shaky voice, getting unsteadily to her feet and collecting her bag and sundries with trembling hands. Her legs felt heavy and there was something black and sticky upon the sleeve of her coat. It wasn't until she reached the next street-light that she realized it was blood.

Approximately five minutes later, as the FME struggled vainly to administer CPR and Paula boarded the number thirty-one bus home, Daniel Johnston, a pizza-delivery driver on Lyndewode Road, was in the process of handing two Hawaiian Specials to a pretty girl dressed as Wonder Woman, wishing he could get invited to the party. Wonder Woman smiled at Daniel. "Is that your moped?" she asked. Daniel, fishing for change, half-turned and saw a man in a white hoodie straddling his brand new Yamaha Zuma.

"Hey," cried Daniel, thrusting money into the girl's hands and starting towards the bike. The stranger kicked out viciously, catching Daniel in the solar plexus. Daniel obligingly sank to his knees, the engine whined into life, and the machine accelerated away into the night.

"Are you okay?" asked Wonder Woman, kneeling beside him, "Do you want me to call the police?"

Daniel, his muscles constricting in pain, tried hard to look into the girl's eyes and not at her cleavage. "Do you have a phone I can use?" he said, weakly.

*　　*　　*　　*　　*

Detective Chief Inspector Donald Coy got the call at nine-fifteen. He was in his pajamas, with a glass of scotch and a book about Ancient Mesopotamia, when the phone in the hallway rang. Heaving himself out of his favourite armchair, he took the glass with him to pick up the call. "Coy," he said, then listened carefully, raised an eyebrow, drank down the whiskey in one gulp and hung up with a perfunctory "I'll be there in twenty." Putting on today's clothes, he grabbed his keys and badge and wallet and was out of the door in ten. There was no one in the house to say goodbye to.

After a short night-time drive across the city, DS Karen Hardacre met him outside the station, which was now a hive of activity, with flashing lights, uniformed officers, two parked ambulances, and the first of the forensic personnel on the scene. "It's a mess, sir," she told Coy, "literally."

Sergeant Tillison was supervising the scene. There was blood in the doorway and the interior had been taped off. From the entrance Coy saw the Forensic Examiners at work, photographing, cataloguing, and marking the floor.

"We'll need a body on the door," said Coy, "excusing the pun, and rig-lights on the street. There must be a blood-trail on the pavement. Clear everyone back, tape off as much as you can and get forensics to sweep out here once they're done in there. What do we know about the victim?"

"Mr. James Robertson," said Hardacre, "journalist. He had has passport with him."

"Very considerate," said Coy.

"We also have an address. I'd guess that he lives alone."

"How so?"

"Did you see the way he was dressed, sir?"

"Are you suggesting men can't dress themselves, DS Hardacre?"

"I phoned the local papers," she said, "he's not one of theirs."

"Freelance?" said Coy, "interesting. Paying you by the hour, are they?" this last he directed to the plastic-clothed technician who had appeared in the doorway. "I need your boys to follow the blood trail, that's the red stuff we normal people have. I want to know where Mr. Roberston died, preferably this year."

"Sir?" said Sergeant Tillison, "we might need more hands. Can I authorise overtime?"

"Why not," said Coy, "and let's hope Santa is generous this year. Hardacre—bring the car round. Let's go and put your theory to the test."

Hardacre's phone rang. "That was Superintendent Crasp," she said, "he's on his way."

"Praise be," said Coy, "let us mere mortals depart before his majesty arrives. Constable Paulsen—are we arborists? Arborists. Tree surgeons? No? Well then move that damn light onto the pavement where it's supposed to be, man."

As Hardacre left to fetch the car, Coy took one last look through the doorway. *Once upon a time*, he thought, *I'd have jumped at the chance of being shaken out of bed for this.* Now, he reflected, he would give much to be back at home with his book and his whiskey.

Half a mile away, in a restaurant on Mill Road, Tony Perkins wiped his forehead with a napkin and took a deep draft of his wine. Coming out had been a bad idea. He knew something was wrong, but James had insisted they meet. Now he was half an hour late, and Tony was feeling sick. Tony often felt sick. It was the poison they put in the air and in the water, the chem-trails and the chlorine. And *they* targeted him particularly, because he knew more than most and that was the way that they worked. They had gotten JFK, hadn't they, and JFK had known all about the New World Order and that was why they had killed him, had shot him and blamed a communist, of course a communist, because Putin knew also. All the Russian leaders had known, ever since Rasputin told Tsar Nicholas about the Illuminati and they had killed him too, had poisoned him and then shot him and then shot him again.

Tony glanced around the restaurant. A well-dressed couple in the corner stared back and shared a laugh. That was alright, Tony was used to being laughed at, but that wouldn't happen any more. Not once the truth came out. He would be the one laughing then, at their stupidity, at their ignorance. Their pretty mouths would hang open in fear and all those high and mighty people, with their fancy clothes and their cocktails, who looked down on him and shunned him—

well, they would come begging for his help and then he would be the one with all the power.

"More wine, sir?" the waiter, a tall suave-looking man, appeared at Tony's elbow. Tony gave a start. He stood up, and in doing so dislodged the file he had placed upon the table. Tony quickly bent down to retrieve it, knocking chair and table both as he did so. A glass fell to the floor. The waiter bent to help. Tony straightened and stepped back, gripping the retrieved file tightly to his chest.

Out in the night, a siren blared. Tony hastily pulled notes from his wallet and flung them at the startled man. A second later he was outside, making his way hurriedly through the dark.

*   *   *   *   *

Morning came upon the face of the earth with little regard for the birds and the beasts that walked and crawled and flew across it. In Ascension Parish Cemetery, a large crowd of mourners turned their collars up against the cold.

The front strap broke as they were lowering the coffin into the ground. Amidst gasps from the onlookers, the casket slipped slowly forward to rest at forty-five degrees. As the bearers rushed to rectify the situation, Monte Boutista raised his eyes to the slate grey sky. Aunt Penny squeezed his arm. "He couldn't even go to his grave in peace," she said, with a wink.

Later, as the last of the visitors left, they stood together outside the church watching the gathered cars roll away one by one. A light wind stirred the carpet of brown leaves into motion, swirling them this way and that across the path. "All these old friends of my brother's," said Monte, "crooks and thieves the lot. I wonder what they think of me." He inclined his narrow head. "I helped put him away. Twice."

"Sad old men and their haggard old wives," said Penny, "a dying breed of gangster. We should treasure them. The new generation are even more godless. Look at that Roger," she pointed, "three years in

Pentonville. Broke a postman's knee with a jack-hammer."

"I should have been a policeman," said Monte.

"You would never have fit in," said Penny, "they're all black-and-white. There's very little room for nuance in the force. I should know. Talking of which, I see a friend waiting."

Detective Inspector Donald Coy stood at the end of the drive. A grand man, as Aunt Penny described him. In the last few years he had put on weight and grown a thick beard, but had not slowed down one iota.

"Isn't it easier," asked Monte, as they walked toward him, "to see the world in black and white?"

Penny grimaced. "We've too many people like that already. Besides—what a boring existence that would be. Hello dear old thing." Penny gave the waiting policeman a warm hug and then excused herself.

"I'll see you back at the shop," said Monte. The two men walked down Huntingdon Road. It was eleven am. The street was quiet and peaceful. It could have been any normal day upon Earth.

"I would have been here," said Coy, "I got called in."

"On your evening off? It must have been something important."

Coy grunted. "Much as I try getting them to wipe their arses without my inestimable guidance it never seems to take. I guess you haven't read the morning papers? How are you holding up?"

"About Larry?" Monte shrugged. "I am sad for him, in a way. Truthfully it's a complication out of my hair. A niggling thorn removed. Let's hope he finds peace in the next world."

"He didn't have much of a chance with your old man bringing him up. But he had choices like all of us, I suppose. What's so funny?"

"Penny was just telling me," said Monte, "how coppers only ever see things in black and white."

"Was she now. I'll have words with that woman later."

"I don't think she was including you in that statement. You know she's your biggest fan."

"Quite right, too."

They crossed into the open, flat park. More than one couple were out for a stroll. Some children played a game of frisbee. A man dressed entirely in tweed sat upon a bench, reading and smoking a pipe.

"So tell me why they called you in," asked Monte, "I sense it's something big. You have a brisk step back in your legs."

A squirrel scurried across their path and quickly sought sanctuary in a tree. It ran like a sine wave, perfectly balanced and agile.

"Murder," said Coy, "James Robertson."

"I recognise that name."

"I thought you might. Freelance journalist and photographer. Sixty-four, Caucasian, five-eleven, overweight. More so than me. Did some work for the Mayor's office."

"Yes. He called into the shop now and then. Worked a lot from the library. I used to see him there. Are we sure that it's murder?"

"He came into the station on Parkside last night with a hunting knife lodged in his neck."

Monte paused. He looked down at his shoes. They resumed walking.

"Scene of the attack?"

"Bang in the middle of Parker's Piece. No witnesses. We think a woman on Regent might have bumped into our man, literally. She didn't call it in till this morning."

"Theft?"

"Doubt it. He wore that camera around his neck. He also carried a laptop. He still had both when he reached us. Superintendant Crasp is in a hell of a state."

"He doesn't like high profile crimes spoiling his image."

"Neither do I. Mine, that is. I have a very bad feeling about this one."

"You always have a bad feeling," said Monte, "stop kidding yourself—you're going to enjoy this."

"I'm getting old," mused Coy, "What about you? Are you going to take a few days off? How is business anyhow?"

"Slow," Monte looked at his watch, "though I have a client this afternoon."

"That last one was messy. Why don't you take a few days off, get away from it all. That retreat you're so fond of up in Scotland."

Monte shrugged. "I don't feel ready for a break. Did you get a look at the mourners?"

Coy tapped his pocket. "I'll be sending some license-plates to the MET."

"A policeman never rests," said Monte.

"Nor a private investigator. Isn't that why we do it?"

"Very perceptive, DCI Coy."

"They didn't promote me for nothing. Home?"

"I should call in on Sarrah," said Monte.

"Ah, yes," said Coy, "My car's over there, I'll give you a lift."

At the corner they passed a jogger, a young man with a stout chin, blonde hair, and a determined look. The jogger's name was Harold Wainwright. Harry knew he should not be running this hard, even as his feet pounded the asphalt, his body moving in easy rhythm, deep even breaths and pumping limbs. He also knew he was not about to stop any time soon.

"It's hard to accept," his dad had told him only the night before, "when you look in that mirror I know what you see—a young man, indestructible, but you aren't. There are a million other things you can do with your life."

The Doctor had said that also, two weeks earlier at Addenbrooke's Hospital, as Harry and his father sat, with the late afternoon sun streaming in through the window, and listened to the news that would forever change Harry's life. Hypertrophic Cardiomyopathy. Harry had practiced the pronunciation internally, as if by absorbing and studying he could somehow master and thereby conquer the thing. Like at the gym when coach Thompson was teaching him a new combination—intricate footwork or the correct way to pivot when throwing a right cross.

Harry looked down at his feet, watched them push and fall with unstoppable precision, watched the ground sweep past underneath. When he felt the tightness in his chest, he finally stopped, sweating, sat down on a public bench and let his head rest back against the stone. An elderly couple walked past, arm in arm, shuffling painfully slow. They smiled at him. The old man raised his walking stick in greeting.

"Lovely day," he said, "what a lovely day to be young."

London, 1977

Christian could no longer tolerate hotel suites. Vast, empty and impersonal, with their contrived elegance and deathly stillness. He greeted every new one like an antagonistic creature and longed for the moment, each morning, when his father would put down his paper, look to his Rolex and stand. "Entertain yourself, my boy," he would invariably say, or some slight variation on the same, before leaving. Often he would not return until the early hours of the night.

Christian used room service as a tool for his amusement, often ringing down for the slightest of things. They always obliged and never complained, these figures from another world who came and went with silence and smiles, stepping like base-born intruders in the palace. His father's power cowed and frightened them and Christian delighted to see it in their eyes.

Then too, there was the delicious disgust that arose within him when a certain type of being transformed the solitude into a realm alive with possibility. If the servant were a man, strong, large or hairy, Christian would experience both fear and elation—a hunter facing the mighty lion with the surety of a rifle in his hands.

If the servant was a man lithe or slim or a young woman of the same, quite a different effect would result—a terrible, tingling longing. If it were a woman full-figured or matronly, Christian would gag and balk and watch spell-bound as one might find one's eyes drawn to a hideous accident or a dead animal, bloated and rotting and full of infection.

But these diversions could not fill a day and, inevitably, Christian would light a slim cigarette (or simply lodge one between his lips), saunter to wherever his father had left his daily 'stipend' and coolly take out the cash, counting through it in his hands, allowing the tonic of power to flow through his body and twist his lips into a tight smile.

On this bright, spring morning in London, Christian stepped forth around eleven. He stood for a while at the top of the steps outside the hotel, leaning his back against the warm stone, hands in pockets, observing the sharp shadows on the concrete and the softly-sparkling gold of the hand-rail. This had become a ritual, this pause, half-giving himself up to the city, savouring its promises and allowing the merest rub of the masses to contaminate his person.

Boldly (this was part of the adventure) he would take forth his cards from his pocket and slowly and deliberately sift through them. These cards he had taken from phone-boxes on his semi-regular strolls. They were advertisements for prostitutes. Humans that could be bought and sold. Sifting through them made his heart race and his hands tremble, and Christian would often draw out this process for the longest time. He possessed the power and opportunity to own, at least for an hour, whichever he desired, and this feeling in itself was almost enough.

Almost.

Cambridge, present day

The receptionist at Highfields Mental Health Hospital had the signing-in-book ready before Monte reached the desk. They had grown used to seeing his face over the last few months. The investigator took a seat in one of the armchairs sprinkled around the small public entrance. He rifled through the magazines but, finding only the usual uninspiring fare, he left them there on the table. It was a few minutes before Sarrah appeared through the door to the patients' wing.

Monte hugged her, feeling her sharp ribs press against his. "I bought you a hot chocolate," he said, handing over the paper cup. She took it and smiled but did not drink. They wandered out onto the grounds, an expanse of plain grass with old stone walls, and a few low trees here and there. Sarrah hugged her cardigan tight against the cold.

"You're looking well," said Monte.

"No, I'm not," said Sarrah. "How was it?"

Monte shrugged. "Formal. A lot of Larry's friends were there. I didn't talk to anyone and they didn't talk to me."

"Do you think I should have gone?" asked Sarrah, "I should have gone, right?"

"You didn't owe Larry anything," said Monte, "he never did a thing for us. Just the opposite, in fact."

"Still," said Sarrah, "he was our brother."

They sat on a low wooden bench. The grey sky began to spit rain. The trees and the wall sheltered the siblings from the worst of it.

"Did you," asked Sarrah, "did you see him?"

Monte was quiet for some time before answering. "No," he said, "it's not like that."

"We've never really talked about it much." Sarrah gently touched her brother's arm. "We should. One day."

"One day," said Monte.

The rain continued to fall. It spotted the plastic cup in Sarrah's hands, the cup from which she had not drunk a single drop.

Cambridge, 1979

Christian Schwarzkopf took another mouthful of foie gras and swallowed down the rich taste with a mouthful of champagne. Someone thrust a cigar into his hand. The club was full of noise and smoke and the smell of food. In their very best clothes the Student Conservative Club were celebrating—the men in their best tuxedos, the women in extravagant ball gowns.

Confetti flew, showering Christian's plate and dropping into his glass. He roared with laughter. Mattie's hand came down upon his shoulder.

"It's a new dawn," Mattie shouted over the music, "a new era. Our era."

"Our era," said Christian.

"Ladies and gentlemen," shouted Puffin from the end of the table, dear ridiculous Puffin, with his pot belly and his square face. "Ladies and gentlemen," shouted Puffin again. Abruptly the music died away.

"Be upstanding," said Puffin, as party-poppers exploded, the revelers whooped, and yet more confetti rained down, "and toast to our new leader!"

Puffin gestured to the head of the table, where some inventive member had brought in a framed portrait of the lady herself, which sat now, propped in the appropriate seat, smiling thinly. A chorus of cheers ensued.

Mattie beat his fist upon the table, so did Christian, and soon everybody was thumping, drumming with such force that plates bounced and clattered. Then Puffin was on the table, stamping and flailing his arms as the music started up. Laughter and bank notes hailed the hopelessly-out-of-time Club President. Mattie looked at Christian and together they scrambled up to join Puffin, laughing till their sides hurt, wheeling and stamping and howling at the hanging lights.

Later, much later, as the two friends walked unsteadily home through the dark sleeping streets, bow-ties hanging limp and shirt collars undone, Mattie slapped Christian upon his arm. "Nature calls, old boy," he said. Wheeling to one side, he undid his fly, laid a hand upon the ancient stonework and leaned forward.

"Beast," mocked Christian. He watched his friend's back, listened to the splash and gurgle. A shadow, a movement, caught his eye and Christian turned to see a ragged shape, seated just beyond the lamplight upon the ground, with its legs stretched out before it.

Christian moved to investigate, his brogues clicking noisily on the flagstones. The figure looked up, its dirty face half in darkness. It had a beard. It wore crumpled clothes and even at this distance, it stank. A quarter-full bottle of booze lay by the rough-sleeper's side, a shopping bag full of rubbish.

The figure looked up. "Spare some change, sir?" it said.

Christian ran his eyes over its face, the nicotine-stained teeth, the watery eyes and the dirty, broken nails on its hand that scratched under its beard with a disgusting rasping sound.

"Just a bit of change for the night shelter?"

"Christian?" said Mattie, catching up. "What have we here?"

Christian put a hand inside his jacket and pulled forth his wallet. He began to let notes fall, one at a time, ones and fives and then tens and twenties. The rough-sleeper, astonished, eyes wide, groped to catch the windfall. Mattie exploded into howls of laughter. Christian followed suit. They staggered away, arm in arm, doubling-up with mirth.

When they reached Mattie's digs, Mattie sank back against the wall. Christian thought his friend looked perfect in the lamp light. Mattie breathed hard, spat out another gasp of laughter. He put a hand on Christian's shoulder. "Goodnight, old friend," he said.

Christian licked his lips, his breathing fast and shallow. He moved closer and pushed his mouth towards Mattie's.

"Jesus," said Mattie, turning his face and bringing his hand up between them. "Christian, what are you doing?"

Christian stood back, appalled.

"God," said Mattie, "Christian, I didn't realise. I'm not. I mean, what do you think I am?"

"It's okay," Christian heard himself say, "it's okay. A stupid prank. It's okay."

Mattie shook his head. He laughed, but this time there was an edge.

"You're a strange one," he said, wagging a finger, and with that he turned, unlocked the black door, and was gone.

Alone on the street, Christian stood for a long time unmoving, staring at the door, a welcome and bitter barrier. When, at last, he started for home, the darkness had begun to lighten to grey and a cold chill was in the air. He reached the place where the homeless man lay asleep. Christian, standing over him, felt a searing wave of anger rise up from his gut. With his lips curled into a snarl, he pulled back his right foot and kicked hard.

Cambridge, present day

Aabira was outside the shop when Monte arrived. She was looking inward through the large glass frontage and directing Aunt Penny who, on the interior, was in the process of placing large crystal rocks amongst the display of books, board-games and vinyl records. The exterior of the shop was painted dark red, with an old-fashioned frontage and gold-stencilled lettering both on the window and above the awning which read 'Devant's Emporium'.

"Salaam alaykum," Monte greeted the young woman.

"Wa'alaykum salaam," she replied.

"What's with the crystals?" said Monte.

"Penny says they will ward off negative energy."

"Tourmaline and rose quartz," said Penny, coming to the doorway, "although any dark stone will do."

"Are we expecting trouble?"

"Did you not see the sky?" said Penny, "Strange clouds up there today."

Monte stepped back and looked up.

"How was the funeral?" asked Aabira, shading her eyes and following suit.

"Strange," said Monte, "He has peace now, I suppose. I hope. It's not as if we were close."

"Well," said Penny, "you did fine, and as you say, he has peace."

"Inshallah," said Aabira. "Our client is coming at two. Are you sure you wouldn't like me to cancel?"

"No. Thank you. Let's go over the notes."

Their client, Alison Perkins, at that moment stood inside a decrepit flat in Cherry Hinton Road, wondering what amongst the mess of stacks, bags and folders-full of papers, photographs and cuttings she should or could take with her to the meeting. Consulting a private detective seemed at once both ridiculous and only proper. At least no one could accuse her of not doing all that she could.

The flat belonged to her brother, Tony. He had been missing for five days and, as she looked around the small space, Alison could not help but speculate that it may as well have been five years, for all that the dwelling possessed any sense of being cared-for. There was a bare mattress on a spring frame, with two stained blankets to serve as sheets, a battered writing desk, one orange armchair decorated with discoloured patches and tobacco stains and, in one corner, a portable fridge which did not work. She tried to picture her brother here, in the armchair or at the desk, and wondered what must have gone through his mind.

Had he always been this way, she wondered? Had the seeds of what he had become been planted in their childhood? Alison remembered it as a happy time, or at least ordinary. There had been no divorce, no arguments, no money problems, deaths or drama. Indeed, the older she got the more she appreciated what a rare upbringing it had been. Perfectly colourless, safe and practical.

So where had Tony gone wrong? Where had they failed him—his family—that he had come to this—living in squalor, blaming everyone and everything in the world for his state. Paranoid and bordering delusional and, it still shocked her to think, so full of hatred for anyone who was the slightest bit different.

In the end she took nothing but the single photograph she had brought with her, leaving the rest of the detritus where it lay, in the thin sunlight, mouldering with dust and sadness.

*   *   *   *   *

Back at Parkside, DCI Donald Coy sat at his desk with the latest hourly report from the incident room. The slim folder did not contain much, which was natural at this time and did not worry him. By contrast, the photographs spread out in a neat arc on the desk bothered him very much. They represented a real danger that this investigation was about to take him into waters he did not feel adequately prepared for, and Coy was a man who strove always to be prepared.

The solution, he knew, was to concentrate for now on the tangibles. Forensics had completed their job at the station entrance, and were finishing up at selected locations across the street and in the park itself, with the precise scene of attack forming a centre and a half-dozen spots along the route. Calls had gone out on social media and in the local press for witnesses to come forward. They had the student, Paula Trasker, although her description of the attacker ran to a single item of clothing and approximate age. Any DNA from her clothing was likely to be compromised beyond usefulness.

Officers were at this moment going door-to-door along Regent Street. Others were checking CCTV. They knew for sure the direction in which the assailant had immediately fled and something may well come from that. If they were lucky, the combination of drag-net and lab work would turn up something.

The photographs were another matter altogether.

Cambridge, 1979

The sun shone in waves through the open window as the thin curtain flapped and bulged in the breeze, bringing with it sounds of a city in summer. Christian held his hands tightly around the thing's neck (was it man or woman?), savouring the squirming and pulsing of its skin beneath his fingers. He/she had a beautiful face, in a common disgusting way and it excited Christian to see the look of desperate pleading in its eyes. He squeezed tighter and held on until the body went limp and then he sat motionless until the shuddering of delirious pleasure subsided.

Then he half-dressed, brushed aside the beaded curtain and pattered through the tiny flat to the kitchen. He made himself a cup of tea and stood staring out of the window into the playground of the school next door. He watched the children run and play and laugh and scream and wondered what he had thought and felt at that age. He could not remember. It seemed to Christian that he had always been this way.

After a time he returned to the bedroom where the curtain still billowed, and studied the naked hermaphrodite figure stretched out upon the bed. He felt himself both excited and repulsed and as usual, delighted in the feeling. At the moment he/she came to, Christian was fully dressed and sitting in a chair, dozing pleasantly. He turned to regard the thing as it rubbed its red-marked throat and took hold of its senses.

"You bastard," said the thing in a croaked voice, tears welling up in its eyes, "I didn't say you could choke me that hard."

Christian stared at it coldly.

"You're a maniac," it said, "I'm calling the police."

Christian stood up and the creature shrank away. He took out his wallet and stripped out bill after bill, throwing them down upon the end of the bed. Like a timid animal caught between fear and hunger, the thing eventually reached out to scoop them up.

Christian smiled. His father had imparted a great truth. Everyone had a price. Everyone.

Cambridge, present day

By the time Alison Perkins reached the shop it had begun to rain. She looked dubiously at the gold lettering and double-checked the address. A bell rang as she opened the door and stepped into the cramped but welcoming interior. The white-haired woman behind the counter smiled.

"Miss Perkins?"

"How did you know?"

"You look like someone in need of answers. Go on up dear. Can I bring you anything? Tea?"

"Perhaps some water," said Alison, eyeing the narrow stairway. On her way up she noted the framed pictures—mandalas and sunsets, angels and oddities. One bore a quote in what she supposed must be Arabic, with an English translation underneath. 'If you are grateful,' it read, 'I will give you more.'

The door facing the top of the stairs was open, and let into an airy room one side of which was taken up with a large bay window. There were rugs upon the floor, a fine sturdy desk and an ornamental fireplace. The walls were painted white, with blue skirting.

A young lady sat with notebook and pen in hand. She wore a dark ankle-length tunic and head-wrap. The man was of medium height, with tight curls of black hair. He stood and raised a pale hand. "Miss Perkins? I'm Monte Boutista and this is my assistant Aabira. Please take a seat."

"You'll forgive me," said Alison, settling herself into an armchair,

"I've never done this before."

"Not many people have," said Monte, "I have my notes from your email, but why don't you start by telling us again what brought you here?"

"It's my brother," said Alison, "he's missing. At least I haven't seen him. It's been five days now. He hasn't been at his flat. He's not answering his phone. We had an appointment on Monday and another on Wednesday and he's missed both. He was always terrible at remembering but he would at least have phoned me, or left a message. I know that he would."

"Does he work?" asked Aabira.

"No. That is, he's self-employed. It's complicated."

"The more information you can give us," said Monte, "the easier it will be to find him."

"Yes, I understand. I'm not trying to be secretive, Mr. Boutista, it's just…my brother…he has social problems."

"Of what nature?"

"He's a loner. When our parents died they left us both a substantial sum of money. Not a fortune but enough to live on, for a few years at least. My brother Tony doesn't work. He writes, but I don't think it makes him any money."

"What does he write?" said Monte.

"Pamphlets. Articles. Essays. He sells them, at events, or he tries too."

"And the theme of these essays?"

Alison bit her lip. "He's a good man," she said, "he's just misguided. He reads things on the internet." She sighed. "From what I gather he mostly writes about immigration, about," she glanced at Aabira, "foreigners. And conspiracies, all sorts. I never really understood it."

"I see. And he writes these from home?"

"He used to work in the public library but he was banned. I think someone reported him to the police—because of the material he was printing out."

"Was he arrested?" asked Monte.

"Cautioned, I think. He wouldn't really talk about it."

"Is that the only time he's been in trouble with the police?"

"No. He was giving a talking to last year, for distributing pamphlets in the town centre. I told him not to."

"He lives alone?"

"Yes."

"And you've reported him missing to the police?"

"Three days ago. They said they'll add him to the list. They just didn't seem interested. He has a reputation, you see, as a troublemaker. He's not a bad man."

Monte nodded. "Any other relations in the immediate area?"

Alison shook her head.

"Miss Perkins, do you know if Tony has a current passport?"

Alison half-laughed. "I'm sorry. Tony didn't believe in passports, mister Boutista. He felt they were another way for the government to spy on him, or some such nonsense. To tell the truth, I don't think Tony has ever been outside of Cambridge."

"Friends?"

"There was one man. They used to sit next to each other in the library. The last time I saw Tony he told me they were working on something. I can't imagine they were friends though."

"Do you have a name for this man?"

"Yes, James. James Robertson."

Monte exchanged a look with Aabira. "Are you sure about that?" he said.

"Yes. I remember because he takes the photographs for our charity events. I'm in the Women's Institute."

Monte folded the newspaper on his desk and passed it over. "Is this him?"

"Yes," said Alison, "yes. Murdered?"

"Last night."

"Oh. Oh goodness. The poor man. He could talk the legs off a donkey but he was kind. I think he might be, that is he might have been, the only person apart from myself who gave my brother the time of day."

"Miss Perkins," said Monte, "We'll look into your case. Do you have access to your brother's flat?"

"I do."

"And did you bring the documents I asked for?"

"Yes, and I have a photo, the most recent I could find, and a list of anyone I could think of that he might contact. There aren't many, I'm afraid."

"That's very helpful. It's likely we'll need more from you as the case progresses. Aabira will talk you through the paperwork. We'll get started at once."

"Thank you," said Alison, rising, "I'm sure your conditions will be fine. Tony isn't perfect, mister Boutista, I know that, but I haven't given up hope for him. Well one doesn't; does one, when it comes to family. In the end aren't they are all that we have?"

*   *   *   *   *

"If I can't box," said Harry, "then what the hell am I supposed to do?"

"Readjust," replied his dad, "just like you would in the ring."

Harry rubbed his eyes.

"It's just another opponent," said his dad, "you can beat this."

"I can't beat it, dad. This is me now, forever. Don't you get it?"

Harry's dad crossed his arms. "I was in that room too. I heard what the doctor said. There's no reason you can't have a long and fulfilling life."

"I can't box."

"But there are plenty of things that you *can* do."

Harry leaned his head back and closed his eyes.

"Wainrights don't just quit," said his dad, "and I'm not going to let you slump around feeling sorry for yourself."

"Fine," said Harry, "fine. So what am I supposed to do?"

"I've fixed you up with something temporary. An old mate of mine. I owe him and he owes me."

"Doing what? Not painting and decorating?"

"Sleuthing," said his dad, with a smile.

"What?"

"Sleuthing." Harry's dad crossed to the bookcase and took down a dictionary. He threw it to Harry. "Using your mind for a bit will do you good. Now, you want some tea or not, you daft lump?"

"Yeah." Harry took up the book, and without enthusiasm turned the pages. He read the relevant entry with mounting confusion and began to think he had misheard the word.

Cambridge, 1984

Julian Schwarzkopf put an arm round his son's shoulders and smiled broadly for the cameras. Christian smiled too at the assembled masses, the pompous dignitaries—small men and women with a modicum of power, puffed up and preening and ridiculous, sanitised and conservative to the world with a bellyful of dark worms inside— at the press, those buzzing little flies with their glass eyes flashing and words spitting uncontrollably from their dirty mouths.

They all stood, on this autumn day, with dying leaves cluttering the ground and specks of rain blowing as the waning sun fought a last stand for summer, in front of the arched entrance to Highfields Adolescent Mental Health Unit. A blue ribbon stretched between two stands behind them, and, at the request of the mayor and other persons, Julian and his son where handed a garish pair of oversized golden scissors. The glass eyes flashed again as, each with a hand on the instrument, father and son cut through the ribbon, which fell to the floor like a stricken snake, to suitable applause from the crowd.

"Mister Schwarzkopf," a journalist called out as the claps faded, "what made you get involved with this project?"

Julian rolled back his shoulders. "The mental well-being of the students and good people of this beautiful city has long been of interest. Ever since my days here, when I had the pleasure and the privilege to study and to row, I'm proud to say, for one of the greatest teams ever entered into the boat-race…" Applause once again. "…I've wanted to give something back. And my son…" he waved Christian forward "…who himself is a great rower, although not quite as good as his old man…" laughter "…well he told me about this project and he convinced me it was a good and worthy cause…"

Christian lost interest as his father droned on. His eyes scanned the crowd. Off to the left, safely separated from those of importance, stood the group of doctors, nurses and patients who lived and worked here (the hospital having actually been open for some weeks). It was the patients who attracted Christian most. Some smiled, some looked at the ground or stared ahead with a morose blankness in their eyes. There was something about them, all of them. They were marked by an absence, no, an addition. Something indefinable lived inside of them. A fear of what life could do to them and what they could do to life. In this, Christian sensed brothers and sisters, only of course those poor unfortunates were not blessed with his power and his strength. They were defeated.

This was the first time that he saw her, standing with her shoulders hunched, one arm across her chest and the hand of this arm gripping the other. She looked like a boy, but she wasn't. A visceral thrill ran through Christian. She had short dark hair and large brown eyes. She was skinny—wiry. Her face was elfin and androgynous, her body straight and her breasts small. She was beautiful.

Christian was so entranced that it was some moments before he realised that a true rain was falling, wetting his hair and running freely down his face. Someone—the major, put his fat dirty hand on Christian's arm, and pulled him into the atrium, where the babbling crowds had retreated. Julian was still talking, smiling and easy, making jokes about the British weather. A reporter pushed his way to the front, a man with an unkempt mop of brown hair, a beard and large glasses. Christian screwed up his face in disgust.

"Lucas Grundy," said the man, "freelance. Mister Schwarzkopf, I'd just like to ask you... do you have anything to say concerning the town of Plaline, Texas, whose inhabitants are still without clean water after one of your factories illegally dumped chemicals into the Frio river?"

An audible wave of shock spread throughout the crowd. Mutters of disapproval rose up. Christian's heart leapt. He looked to his father, afraid, but Julian's expression had not changed and he did not miss a beat with his answer. "We're doing everything we can to help those good folks up at Plaline after a terrible accident which was not at all our fault. If I may so mister...? Grundy. If I may so, I really don't know why you would bring this up now, instead of celebrating this positive and beneficial step forward in the health-care of your community."

As a groundswell of murmured approval broke out into clapping, Christian swallowed hard and put a hand to his stomach. The man Grundy tried to speak, but was drowned out by those around him, who edged him forcibly back into the crowd. For one brief moment, Christian had been terrified that the very ground on which he stood was about to be torn apart, that the gossamer lie that his father was something beyond mortal, beyond reproach and immune to the judgments of others had about to have been shattered.

It was more than that. Christian was constantly terrified, he admitted to himself, that at any moment his own mask would be torn off, and the bestial face behind it revealed. It was too late now, far too late, to do anything other than fully commit to the public persona he had cultivated so carefully. To be able to live two lives was a burden, not a blessing.

As the formalities ebbed to a stop and the guests began to mingle, Christian once more caught site of the girl. Through a window he saw her, reposed elegantly upon the grass, resting on one forearm, long legs spread before her, that delicate heart-shaped face angled towards the ground.

Temporarily renewed in his vigour, Christian moved to the open doors, and strode across the grass to meet her.

Cambridge, present day

The light was fading from the sky as Monte left the shop, headed right and then turned left down Burleigh Street. He walked past the yellow rectangles of light spilling out from the shop windows and doorways. They were charity shops mostly, with the odd café and the launderette. He was early, and so he slowed his pace, taking time to stare at the merchandise on display behind the glass frontage of Forbidden Planet. Heroes and monsters, spaceships and superheroes.

On a whim he went into Black Barn Records, a spacious two-storey independent. He was surprised that the young girl behind the desk knew the name that he asked for. She showed him to a bin in the corner labelled 'Jazz'. It was a section they were always moving. The poor relation pushed from pillar to post.

In idle moments Monte pondered how the music he loved had become so middle-class and neglected. It had begun as working-men's music, a music of the streets, birthed in nail-sharp nightclubs and pitiless saxophone show-downs. A music of the people, bathed in pain and in striving, with its roots in the slave trade and its arms reaching for the stars. In the same way there was nothing 'easy' about the recordings of Frank Sinatra, Nat King Cole or Nina Simone, which adorned the 'easy listening' rack adjacent. These were works of art which required engagement and rewarded study.

They only had one Eric Dolphy CD—the seminal 'Out to Lunch'. Monte already had this on vinyl, but car stereos don't play vinyl.

Monte paid the seven pounds, tucked the bag under his arm and strolled the rest of the way down to Rose's Tea Room on the corner.

Donald Coy was in the process of taking off his coat when Monte walked in.

"Hungry?"

"A little," said Monte, taking a seat.

"Good," I ordered two all-day-breakfasts. Real meat for me, fake for you."

"You should try it," said Monte, "it's good for you."

"My palate doesn't agree."

"Your blood pressure would."

"You can't do proper thinking with a flat stomach," said Coy, slapping his belly.

"Is that in the manual?"

A waitress placed two coffees on the red plastic tablecloth.

"Want any coffee with that?" asked Monte as the policeman helped himself to several spoon-fulls of sugar.

"How was your client?" asked Coy.

"Interesting," said Monte, "and pertinent. Missing person. Does the name Tony Perkins ring a bell?"

"Perkins," said Coy, "yes. A little toe-rag of the racist variety. We nicked him for breach of the peace a couple of times. His sister's some big-wig in the community."

"She's in the WI."

"A venerable institution. She's also on a few committees and citizens groups and the like. Fancies herself as a benefactor."

"The thing is," said Monte, "during our conversation the name James Robertson came up."

"It did? In what capacity?"

"He and Tony Perkins were friends, apparently, or at least acquaintances. The sister told me that the two of them were working on something."

"Working on what?"

"She doesn't know."

"You think Tony Perkins could be our murderer?"

"I can't see it," said Monte, "but there could be a connection. Maybe they upset someone. Stuck their noses in where it wasn't appreciated."

Coy stirred his coffee. "Bit far-fetched isn't it? I can't imagine those two turning up anything momentous. They're hardly Woodward and Bernstein."

"No," said Monte, "no they aren't, or weren't. Still…"

"Still," said Coy, "I'll open a line of enquiry, unless you want to carry the ball for a day or two?"

"That's fine," Monte shook his head, " but I'm going to check out Tony's flat tomorrow, I'd appreciate a free shot at that. There's something odd about all this."

"Your sixth sense kicking in? Be my guest. I'll send a couple of lads round on Monday. I'm assuming you'll share anything relevant."

"As always."

The waitress returned with two plates slightly steaming. Coy flourished his knife and fork with gusto.

"What is the latest on Robertson?" asked Monte as he watched his friend tuck in.

"Not much," said Coy, between mouthfuls, "I need to sit on this one a little. I'll be able to tell you more tomorrow night."

"I was thinking," said Monte, "I might take a walk after dinner. To Parker's Piece."

Coy stopped eating. "And you're going to ask me as a friend to come with you?"

"Just this once," said Monte, "yes."

Coy shrugged his big shoulders and went back to work on his dinner.

"Well," he said, "just this once."

A little under an hour later the two stood in the grip of night, in the middle of the large open flat green of Parker's Piece, at the point where the four paths which criss-cross its surface meet. Their breath misted slightly in the sharp air as they approached the ornate lamp post which marked the centre of the park. The lamp post was dark green edged in gold. Exotic red-eyed fish entwined themselves above the lettering that read 'Reality Checkpoint'.

"It's a hundred and fifty years old," said Coy.

"I read," said Monte, "that the inscription refers to the point where students leave their protective bubble and meet the real world of the city."

"I was told," countered Coy, "that coppers used to harangue drunks here to make sure they were sober enough to get home."

Monte looked up at the bright lamp.

"Either way," said Coy, "this is where James Robertson received his fatal blow. Swimming pool," he went on, pointing to the distant lights, "too far for witnesses. Ditto the Regent."

They looked to the grand façade of the recently renovated Georgian building that dominated the Western corner.

Coy sighed. "We checked anyway."

"Coach drivers or passengers?" asked Monte, looking back at row of shelters along Parkside.

"We've contacted the relevant companies," said Coy, "that's a work in progress."

"Unlikely, I suppose."

"A peculiar choice of location," observed Coy, "well-lit and exposed on every side."

"Yes," said Monte, "why not further back in the shadows?"

"Spur of the moment. Unplanned."

"Yet carrying a knife and prepared to use it."

"I told you I had a bad feeling."

Monte knelt on the asphalt path where a dark stain was still visible. "Here?"

"Right so."

With some difficulty, the policeman bent down. "You know this gives me the willies every time we do this?"

"I know. And if you don't want to be here…" said Monte.

"I said that it gives me the willies," said Coy, "that's all. What is it?"

"Every time I do this," said Monte, "I expect nothing to happen. And every time I'm disappointed."

"Because it always does," said Coy.

Monte narrowed his eyes and nodded slowly. He focused on the blood stain upon the ground. A peculiar, familiar feeling stole over him—an adrenalin tingle coupled with a peaceful warmth. A certainty. The light of the lamp became blue. The stars increased in brightness and clarity. The image of Coy, on the periphery of Monte's vision, appeared to retreat and at the same time to take on a flat, two-dimensional aspect, like a cardboard cut-out fringed with light.

A large man, pale and ghostly, came out of the night, walking briskly despite his size. A smaller figure, agitated, looking this way and that, followed behind.

"I see them."

Coy licked his lips. "Where?"

Monte gestured slowly. "It's him. Robertson. A young man too. I can't see his face."

Coy stared into the darkness. "Anything else?"

"He's been following for a while," said Monte, "this was his last chance. It only took one blow."

Monte rose and stepped forward. "I can't see his face," he said again, "this was no kid off the streets."

Coy glanced about nervously. "Why do you say that?"

"This boy is educated. Scared. He's never done this before."

"Ask him why?"

"I can't ask, Don," said Monte, "I can only get what I'm supposed to." He took another step forward but already the images were fading. Monte fought hard to retain focus. It was a balancing act. One that he knew he would soon lose.

Coy nodded. "Is there anything else?"

Monte shook his head. "He ran."

They began to walk, slowly.

"This way?"

"Yes."

"Here on the corner," Coy gestured, "this is where he ran into that student."

"He knocked her down," said Monte, "then he went left. Along Regent Street. He was scared."

"Where was he going?"

"I don't know. It's fading, Don."

South-East along Regent. The night was eerily still and quiet. A light mist began to rise. Once or twice Monte bent down to touch the cold ground. Under his direction they turned left onto Glissen Road. At the intersection of Lyndewode they stopped.

"Something happened here," said Monte, screwing his eyes up. "That's it. I'm out. I've lost him, Don. I've lost him."

They turned to survey their surroundings. The nearest house stood behind, right on the corner. A dozen stone steps led to the front door. Two large windows, curtains open, faced the street.

Coy mounted the steps and knocked. A young lady answered, a student, thought Monte.

"Good evening ma'am. Chief Inspector Coy." He held up his ID. "I'm sorry to disturb you at this hour."

"Oh," said the girl, "you're here about the stolen scooter? On Halloween? I was wondering when someone would come."

Coy looked back at Monte. "Do you mind if we come in," he asked, "I'd like you to tell us everything that you know."

Cambridge, 1984

Lucas Grundy jumped at the knock on the door. He looked up to the corner and realised with some irritation that without thinking he had turned off the switch and the accompanying red light which ensured that the 'do not enter' sign was lit up.

"Come in," he said.

Jerry Muller, features editor at the *Cambridge Herald*, half-opened the door. "Are you ready with those photos for the Highfields piece, Lucas?"

Lucas pushed his glassed back up his nose. "Sure," he said, gesturing to an untidy pile on the corner of the desk.

Jerry reluctantly edged his way in and picked them up. He stood looking at Lucas, who pointedly ignored him, turning away and holding negatives up to the light. "There's still that piece on the varsity match needs writing up," said Jerry.

Lucas said nothing.

"So," said Jerry, "you're going to do that today?"

"Yes," replied Lucas, "that's what I said, isn't it."

Jerry crossed his arms. "That's also what you said yesterday."

"Well now it's today," said Lucas, "and I'm saying today."

"Look, Lucas…" began Jerry.

Lucas sighed heavily.

"…you're a good photographer and not a bad writer…"

"Not bad?"

"Not bad," Jerry repeated, "but this business is all about deadlines. You can't always be disappearing off or hiding in here."

"I'm not hiding," said Lucas, "I'm working."

"Well so long as you get that varsity piece on my desk by four. Okay?"

Lucas swallowed his irritation. "Okay," he said, and did not relax until he heard Jerry close the door. Then Lucas wilted, leaning his head against the work-station. "Fucking varsity," he muttered, and began sorting through the remaining photographs. He held up one that intrigued him—that of the son, Christian Schwarzkopf, sitting upon the lawn next to a girl (or was it a boy?). There was something peculiar about the way that the younger Schwarzkopf was reaching out to her (it must be a *her*), and something odd in his gaze, something Lucas could not quite put his finger on. He wondered who the girl was. The spoilt-rich daughter of some dignitary, no doubt. Those sort didn't breed outside of their own gene pool.

Several photos later he saw the girl again. This time she was standing with the group of staff and patients. Her eyes stared down and left, her pale face unsmiling. He placed this one next to the former, and looked from one to the other. What was Christian Schwarzkopf doing with this girl? *Probably nothing, you fool*, he said to himself.

It irked him greatly, the way Schwarzkopf Senior had brushed aside his question with the cloying smoothness of an oil-spill. It angered him more that not one person had taken his side. Not one. Idiots and sheep, all of them.

Once more Lucas held up the two photographs. He looked at his watch. It was not yet eleven. Plenty of time to take a trip out to Highfields and still get the varsity report done. He picked up his jacket, switched off the light and was gone.

Cambridge, present day

Monte awoke with an unaccountable feeling of fear. It took him a moment to understand that as he lay in his own bed, and that the hour was morning and that the sun was bright in the sky.

He was washing his face with cold water when his mobile rang. It was Coy.

"How are you doing this morning?"

"Good."

"You're a lousy liar. That scooter was never reported missing. We talked to the owner of the pizza parlour. The driver was unlicensed and uninsured so they decided to write it off. We're bringing the delivery lad in now. Can you meet me tonight?"

"Sure."

"Take it easy."

"Don't worry," said Monte, "I have a new recruit."

Aunt Penny was waiting on the landing, arms crossed.

"I'm fine," said Monte.

"Hmm," she said. "I'll make you some rosemary tea. There's a young man waiting to see you downstairs."

"Good."

"I'll send him up with the tea."

In the office Monte sat in the high-backed chair behind the desk. Stan Kenton played softly from the stereo. Monte leant his head back and swivelled the seat toward the windows. Sunlight took the slight chill from the room. His throat still felt thick. There was a knock at the door. Harry Wainright entered. They shook hands.

"Harry."

"Pleased to meet you, Mr. Boutista. My dad's told me a lot about you."

Monte turned off the music. "Call me Monte. Sit."

Harry took a seat. He looked around. "That's a lot of books."

"Do you read much?"

"Not really. I'm more hands-on."

"Hands-on is good," said Monte, "although it's never a waste of time to open a book."

"That's what my dad's always telling me."

"Well, reading isn't a requirement. Attention to detail is. The best way to learn is to do. We'll start you off slow until you pick it up. You understand employment is on a case-by-case basis?"

"Suits me," said Harry, "I'm looking to keep my options open. What sort of work do you do here, Mr. Boutista? I mean, I know you're a private detective. Is it cheating husbands and so on?"

Monte shook his head. "We don't take that sort of case. We tend to pick up clients who need help that the police, for one reason or another, can't provide. That sound okay to you?"

Harry shrugged. "Sure."

"Good," said Monte, "Can you drive?"

"Yes."

"My car is the red Audi A6 out back. Penny will show you. I want you to pick up my assistant Aabira and then you'll be driving to another address to do a house search. Aabira will fill you in on the case."

"A house search?"

"Yes. Is that a problem?"

"No. I mean, is this legal?"

"We have the owner's permission. Or as good as."

"What are we searching for?"

Monte smiled. "Any questions, ask Aabira."

"Aabira?" said Harry, "is that Russian?"

"Arabic."

Harry shrugged. "What do we do afterwards?"

"Come and meet me at the library," said Monte, "and I'll buy you both lunch."

When Harry had left Monte switched the stereo back and stood by the window, looking down into the street.

"Tea," said Penny, coming in with two cups.

"How are you, Penny?"

"Oh, I'm fine. And the young man?"

"Harry? We'll see."

"He has a good aura," said Penny, "complicated though. You see those clouds haven't changed much?"

"Are you happy here, Penny?"

"You know I am. Are you?"

Monte smiled.

"Not answering," said Penny, "we'll come back to that. This music is nice. Nineteen-forties?"

"Stan Kenton," Monte nodded. "You know," he said, "Kenton was an alcoholic. He abused his own daughter."

Penny grimaced. She sipped her tea. "He was probably abused himself," she said, "that's how it often starts."

"Karma," said Monte, "does that make it wrong for us to derive pleasure from his music?"

"Nothing either good or bad," said Penny, "but thinking makes it so."

"Richard the third?"

"Hamlet," replied Penny, "that was always my favorite."

"I should read more Shakespeare," said Monte, "but it seems you could twist that any way you want."

"There is only one truth," said Penny.

"And sooner of later all must come to it. Now that's a quote that I do know. And he was right."

"That's what makes you so good at what you do."

Monte sipped his tea. As Stan Kenton played on, he felt the warm liquid working its magic, and thought ahead to what the day was likely to bring.

*   *   *   *   *

Aabira was up early for the school run. She walked her younger sister, Faheema, to St. Matthew's. Her younger brother Bilal, now fourteen, went with them as far as the bus stop to Sancton Wood. It was a cold start to the day, but bright. By the time she returned home, her mother and father had left and the house was blissfully quiet. Aabira made herself tea and toast and sat at the sunlit kitchen table, going over the course notes from her last lecture.

Around quarter past ten a car-horn sounded outside. From the window she could see the familiar shape of Monte's Audi. The driver was a young white man with blonde hair. He was handsome, but his chin jutted aggressively and there was something about his bearing that immediately set her on edge.

She sat down and resumed reading. She read through another two beeps of the horn until finally there was a knock at the door.

"Are you Afeera?" asked Harry, when she opened it.

"No. I'm Aabira."

"Right," said Harry. His eyes flicked up and down. "Monte sent me to drive you. I'm Harry. I beeped the horn."

"I heard. You'd better come in. Would you like tea or coffee?"

Harry shook his head. He took a seat at the kitchen table. "Nice place."

"Thank you. It's not mine. Here's the file."

"What file?" said Harry, picking it up.

"This is our file on Tony Perkins. He's been missing for five days. We've been hired by his sister to find him. You can read through that while I get ready."

"Is this really your day-job?" asked Harry, leafing through the pages.

"I'll be ready in ten," said Aabira.

Fifteen minutes later they were driving through the quiet streets. The sun shone, but the air was chill. Harry found the A6 a pleasure to drive.

"So what else do we know about this Tony Perkins?" he asked.

"He was a loner," said Aabira, "a conspiracy-theorist. Racist. In trouble with the police a couple of times. He had money from an inheritance and he lived alone. No close family except for the sister."

"Lucky him," said Harry.

They drove on in silence.

"I guess that headscarf keeps you warm in the cold weather," said Harry, after a time.

"Are we going to have this conversation now?" said Aabira.

"What conversation?"

"You have a problem with my hijab."

"I don't have a problem," said Harry, "I just don't get it, that's all."

"Perhaps you should read a book."

"You're the second person today who's said that."

"Maybe Allah is giving you a hint," said Aabira, "slow down, we're looking for number one-twelve-a."

They found a space twenty metres from the house. The door to 112a was set into the side-wall of the building.

"What are we supposed to be looking for?" asked Harry as Aabira unlocked it.

"Bus tickets, receipts, travel cards, note books, journals, bank statements. Anything that can flesh out what we already know. Photographs too. Photographs are always good. Anything we take needs to be itemized."

"Here's hoping for drugs or guns or something interesting," said Harry, following the woman up the narrow staircase to the inner door. Aabira produced another key and gave Harry a look.

The interior was dank and odorous. A bed-sit with a couch, small writing-desk and chair, a single bed and tiny kitchen area. The only separate room was the bathroom. The décor was at least thirty years out of date and it was possible the place had not been cleaned for at least as long. There were piles of books and newspapers in one corner, a pile of clothes in the other and some press-cuttings stuck upon the wall, together with an amateurish painting of a sunset.

Aabira pulled back the ragged curtains.

Harry winced. "I think I liked it better in the dark."

"You take the books," said Aabira, "I'll take the desk. Make sure to flick through all the pages. Remember, we're looking for receipts or anything hand-written."

"I remember," said Harry, without enthusiasm.

Twenty minutes later they compared notes.

"Anything useful?"

"Press clippings," said Aabira, "with no central topic. Deaths, hospitals, diseases, cancer, accidents, UFOs, conspiracies, torture."

"Cheery bloke."

"A take-away menu, a broken watch, nail-file, elastic bands. And a notebook, but it's full of gibberish. We'll take that with us. How about you?"

"A lot of grubby James Bond novels," said Harry, "and the 'Bumper Book of Detective Fiction'. Also lots on secret codes and cyphers and all that. And something called 'Tropic of Cancer' with the corners of all the dirtiest pages turned down."

"And you checked through everything thoroughly?"

"Yes, ma'am," said Harry, "couple of book-marks and that's it."

"What about those clippings on the wall?" asked Aabira.

They stood and looked at them.

"Work on New Shopping Centre Delayed," read Harry, "Children's Centre Receives New Funding. Fascinating."

"I'll take some photographs," said Aabira, "you check the bed, under and in."

Harry eyed the yellow-stained duvet. He sighed and got down on all fours. "Nothing underneath but dust and a bit of change. And a pair of sneakers. Nothing up top except…nice…some used tissues and a sock. Jesus, I hope there's soap in the bathroom."

"Alayhi as-salaam," said Aabira, "since your hands are dirty, you may as well check through the clothes. Search the pockets."

"And what will you be doing?"

"Taking some more photos," said Aabira, "and making notes."

"What did that mean?" asked Harry, taking up a pair of jeans and holding them at a distance, "what you just said? Arabic is it?"

"It means 'peace be upon him'," said Aabira, sitting down.

"Upon who?"

"Jesus."

"I thought that was Christians, not your lot," said Harry, pulling some rubbish from a pocket.

Aabira shook her head. "You really do need to read a book."

They searched on. "Okay," said Harry, a few minutes later, "we've got chewing gum, bus tickets and a few receipts. Four of them from the Golden House Restaurant."

"We'll take everything except the gum," said Aabira, "wait a minute. Yes, this menu's from the Golden House too."

"So he liked a Chinese."

"Right," said Aabira, standing up, "I think that we're done here."

"Wait a minute." Harry walked over to the wall. He studied the sunset painting. He took it down and turned it over. There was a piece of paper stuck to the back.

"How did you know?" asked Aabira, her mouth hanging wide.

"Guy reads a lot of spy novels," said Harry, "they always hide things behind paintings. Don't they?"

Cambridge, 1984

The afternoon was warm but overcast, with flashes of sun half-heartedly chasing the shadows. The lawns at Highfields were deserted save for Lucas Grundy and his camera. He had been able to use his press pass to gain access for "supplementary pictures for the article on the opening." A peculiar and melancholic quiet pervaded. Something about the sun-edged clouds made Lucas feel uncomfortable. They resembled those found in religious paintings. The unknown and terrifying majesty of heaven.

He felt drawn to wander a complete sweep of the grounds. Treading softly upon the lawn, from light to shadow to light, then footsteps crunching upon pebbles. Somehow Lucas knew before he saw the girl that he would do so. She stood alone, a vision, one bare arm hanging loose, the other clasped around it. She seemed utterly lost.

Lucas moved to within touching distance and stopped. "Hello," he said, "hello."

The girl turned slowly. Her large brown eyes held something unfathomable.

"What's your name?" said Lucas, but the girl did not respond.

Carefully, Lucas reached down to the girl's wrist and lifted it so that he could read the white plastic tag. *Maria Waters*, it said.

"Maria?"

She appeared to notice Lucas for the first time. Her lips moved but no sound escaped.

Lucas became aware of a presence and turned to see Christian Schwarzkopf, tall and broad-shouldered and tanned, dressed in a light suit, striding across the grass towards them.

"Maria," Christian, said, and the girl's head snapped up obediently. "Come," he held out a hand, "come with me now. This man means you harm."

Maria moved towards him. Christian threw a look back at Lucas. "Go," he said, as if talking to an animal, "don't come back."

Lucas half-lifted his camera, and then let it drop. He watched the man and the girl walk away. He felt profoundly disturbed, as if something of vital importance had just happened but he had no idea what he should do.

Cambridge, present day

"He was a pain in the arse," said Ken, "always rude to the staff. One of those scruffy-looking types. You usually feel sorry for that sort of person but Tony had a nasty streak."

"In what way?" asked Monte.

They were sitting in the coffee shop in the library where Ken worked.

"He hated people," said Ken, "the looks he used to give. He was racist. That stuff he used to print out—we had to handle it, you see. I put in a complaint. A lot of us did."

"Articles from the internet?"

"No. They were things he used to write himself. He used to make them into pamphlets and try to sell them. I didn't read a lot of it— just enough to know it was unpleasant."

"And so the police became involved?"

"Not soon enough in my book. They came to see him in the library and escorted him out. I'm not sure if he was charged with anything, but after that, management banned him for three months. And then he was back, of course, but at least he was more careful. I think he went somewhere else to print. Oh, I'll tell you one other thing," he went on, "lately he'd been asking for old local newspapers from the store. Drove us mad."

"Did he ever say what he wanted them for?"

"No, sorry. He didn't."

"Listen, Ken, I'm sorry to make this a business chat. I'll make it up to you."

Ken waved his hands. "No problem. I've said it before and I'll say it again—of all the things in the world I never expected you to end up in the line of work that you have."

Monte shook his head. "This is the only thing I've ever really been any good at."

"Must make you cynical though. I don't like to think of you ending up as a cynic."

"You don't have to worry. I have Penny to keep me balanced. Listen, I hear Tony used to hang around with James Robertson?'

"That was a shock," said Ken, "him getting killed like that."

"What did you make of James?"

"He was a decent sort. A real bore, though, if he could get you cornered. Told all these tales about how he made a fortune on the stock exchange, and that he used to be in the French Foreign Legion. I'm sure most of it was rubbish."

"Did he ever talk about stories he might have been working on?"

"Not to me. He did photography for some council events, I know that. And he always wore that press badge. I never saw his name in the paper, though."

"Were he and Tony friends?"

"They used to sit together all the time. I think James was trying to steer Tony away from his worst instincts, from the little he used to say about it."

"He ever mention they were collaborating on something?"

Ken shook his head. "I did see them once or twice having dinner together at the Golden House. You know, that Chinese place just off Regent Street."

"Yes, I know it." Monte checked his phone. "I have to go Ken. I owe you a dinner."

"Monte, there's this jazz trio playing at the Hot Numbers next Friday. I can get us tickets if you'd like to go."

"Sure," said Monte, "I'd like that."

On his way out, Monte caught site of a familiar figure disappearing down the escalator. He stood for a moment, rubbing his neck, half-turned away and then, with a muttered reprobation to himself, hurried across and down the stairs. He caught up with the woman as she was heading to the lower floor exit. "Sumiyyah," Monte lightly touched her arm.

Sumiyyah turned and smiled. "Monte," she said, "it's good to see you."

"How are you? How is college?"

"I'm on my way there now," she looked at her watch, "I'm sorry, I have to run. Late again."

"I'll walk with you a way."

"So," she asked, as they headed out into the weak sunshine, "how have you been? How is your shop? And Penny? I like her."

"The shop's fine," said Monte, "I'm fine. Have you been to the botanical gardens yet? I remember you said that you wanted to."

"No, no, I've been busy studying."

"Perhaps we could go together?"

Sumiyyah hesitated. "Yes," she said. They stopped. "Let me give you my number."

The investigator typed the information into his phone and read it back. At that moment, it began to ring.

"It's okay," said Sumiyyah, "I have to go anyway. Call me."

"I will."

"Salaam alaikum."

Monte met Aabira and Harry in the atrium of the Lion Yard Shopping Centre. They had been waiting for ten minutes.

"We need to make copies of everything," he instructed, over lunch at Pret, "and return all of it tomorrow."

"At first glance," said Aabira, "there's nothing obviously helpful. Although we have the notebook."

"Make a digital copy of that too, if you would. You can show Harry how it's done."

"What about my find?" said Harry, "that's something, right?"

Monte smoothed out the piece of paper. It was a single A5 sheet filled with lines of numbers in a repeating pattern, two digits followed by a dash followed by another number, ranging from one up into the seventies.

"Thoughts?" he asked.

"A book code," said Aabira, "also, the writing isn't Tony's—it doesn't match the numerals in his notebook."

"Or the notebook isn't Tony's and the code-sheet is."

"If it is a book code..." said Aabira.

"What is a book code?" said Harry.

"If it is a book-code," continued Aabira, "then it might match one of the books at his flat. I could go through them all, but it will take some time."

"Harry can do it," said Monte, "you're coming with me to the Golden Dragon."

"The Golden Dragon?" Aabira frowned. "There was a menu from there at Tony's. And receipts."

"Can somebody please tell me," said Harry, "what a book-code is?"

Monte tapped the paper. "It's a basic cypher. On each line, one of the numbers, probably the first, refers to a specific page of a certain book. The numbers following give you the line, word, and letter to look for. All the letters taken together spell out the message. In this case, since we're looking at pairs of numbers, one must refer to the page, the other how many letters to count in. Probably."

"So how do you know which book to use?"

"You try them one by one," said Monte.

"And how do I know which number refers to what?"

"You don't. You have to try each possible combination on each book until you find one that works."

"Sounds like a blast," said Harry.

"Let me know how you get on," said Monte, "and try and have the car back by five."

"Wonderful," said Harry, as they stood up. He blew air from his cheeks and gave the waitress a winning smile.

Cambridge, 1984

Nurse Selina smiled as she saw, through the bay window, the polished white mini-bus pull into the parking lot. She ran a hand through her thick black hair, smoothed down the front of her tunic and gave a friendly wave to old Mister Lee, the driver, as he jumped down onto the gravel.

"It's here," said Selina, crossing into the day-room, where the selected patients had assembled and sat, lounged or stood, for the most part chattering boisterously with excitement.

At her announcement they stirred like a swarm of bees. Anna and Julia, the two anorexic girls, perpetually unwilling to sit still, bounced even higher, hugging each other and clapping their hands. Thomas, the germaphobe, with his thick black glasses, round face and pudding-bowl haircut smiled and shuffled forward, attempted to pull on his jacket without letting go of its sleeves. Poor Maurice, rocking backward and forward, made a gurgling sound, only his eyes able to convey any hint of translatable emotion.

Doctor Morton, tall, suave and pleasantly indifferent, began to shepherd his charges towards the door. Selina sought out Maria, who stood apart, as she always did, in this case in the corner of the room, leaning against the wall with her hands behind her, her large eyes staring downward at nothing.

"Maria," cooed Selina, "it's time to go."

Maria swayed a little, and for a moment Selina thought that the girl was not going to move. Slowly, though, as if stirring from a dream, Maria stood and obediently began to follow the others.

Outside in the blustery sunshine, Mister Lee was in conversation with the handsome Christian Schwarzkopf. Selina arrived in time to hear Doctor Morton address the businessman.

"Very much appreciated," he said, "your financing this mini-bus has made a world of difference. I'm glad you can join us for this little trip."

"I'm happy to have a chance to contribute," Schwarzkopf flashed a smile at Selina, "I'll follow behind you in the Jag."

It took less than a half an hour along quiet roads to reach the little leafy town of Ely, which breathed calmly under the gaze of its impressive cathedral. The group spent a happy morning in the cathedral grounds, drawing pictures in pencil and crayon on large white pieces of paper. Doctor Morton smoked his pipe and gazed appreciatively up at the spires, chatting with Mister Lee about sundry matters, while Selina moved from patient to patient, gently encouraging their efforts.

Christian Schwarzkopf stood to one side, his jacket over one arm and his shirtsleeves rolled up. He observed intently, and as discreetly as possible, the curve of Maria's back, neck and shoulders as she sat and scribbled a delicate picture of one large window.

After a bathroom break, they retired to the rolling green slopes of the park. Large blankets were spread upon the ground, sandwiches and drinks laid out. Nurse Selina watched the clouds, broken by the elegant spires of the ancient building, and thought of the only meaningful romance she had encountered during her short life. She wondered, with a small and wistful thrill, if she were ready yet for another.

The day wore on. Doctor Morton read his book. Mister Lee snored loudly under a tree. The patients dispersed a little way around. Christian Schwarzkopf saw his chance. He caught up with Maria on the far side of a large oak, where the girl lay stretched out upon the grass.

"Maria," he knelt beside her, "Maria."

Christian ran his fingers gently up and down the inside of the girls' wrist. She turned her big eyes towards him. He smiled.

"Do you know who I am?" he asked.

"Are you the one?" she replied.

"Which one?" he said, "who do you think that I am?"

"The one they told me would come to look after me."

"Who told you."

Maria drew her arms around her stomach and turned on her side, facing away.

Christian stroked her hair. "Yes," he soothed, "yes I am the one."

Hesitantly she turned back. She half sat-up. There was a pleading look in her eyes. "I'll do whatever you say."

"Good," said Christian, stroking her cheek, "that's very good." He glanced around. "Come with me, over there, among those bushes. Somewhere we can be alone."

Maria rose and followed. Nurse Selina, watching them go, thought again what a nice and attentive young man the junior Schwarzkopf was.

Cambridge, present day

Donald Coy and DS Karen Hardacre stood outside the imposing door to Lloyd's Lodge, a modern three-storey mansion on Cavendish Avenue. The house had extensive gardens, front and back, with a high thick hedge shadowing the six-foot walls. A wide gravel drive led from the road to the pillared entrance, where the two policemen waited.

The man who opened the door wore a cravat, a bright yellow tweed jacket, cotton trousers and polished brown brogues. His face bore an expression of annoyance. He could not have been older than his early twenties.

"Yes?"

"Chief Inspector Coy," declared Coy, "this is DS Karen Hardacre. Is Mr. Christian Schwarzkopf at home?"

"He's out," said the man.

"And you are?"

"Richard Bowers, Mr. Schwarzkopf's personal assistant."

"I see. And may I ask where Mr. Schwarzkopf is now?"

"He's at a meeting in the city."

"London?"

"Of course."

"And when do you expect him to return?"

Bowers sighed. "Is this really necessary? He's a very busy man."

Coy stared. And then he stared some more.

Bowers capitulated. "He has an appointment in Cambridge at four. I expect he'll come here first to change."

"Very well," Coy looked at his watch, "I believe we'll come in and wait."

"If you must. You can sit in the library. But please don't touch anything."

The library was the very cliché of the country house, two walls of floor-to-ceiling shelving stuffed full of identically-bound volumes. Coy felt he knew what they would be without looking. A third wall was taken up with a voluminous fireplace, while the last sported bay windows overlooking the lawn.

"How long do we wait, sir?" asked Hardacre.

Coy grunted. He looked at his watch, ambled over to the desk, and tried the drawers. They were locked. A flash of movement through the window made them both look up. A young lad stood there, half-crouched on the lawn. He wore a blue hoodie pulled low over his head and his stare was fierce. Almost immediately he took a step sideways and disappeared from sight.

"Hardacre," said Coy, "fetch."

Karen Hardacre was almost at the library door when it opened. The man who stepped in was tall and pale, with striking cheekbones, almost handsome despite his thin bloodless lips and heavily-lidded eyes. His pupils were a washed-out green and he spoke with a smooth West-Coast American accent.

"Delightful," he said, moving to one side as Hardacre slipped past.

"Mr. Schwarzkopf," said Coy, "Detective Chief Inspector Coy."

"Inspector Coy," Schwarzkopf smiled, "I'm sorry to have kept you waiting."

"Not at all. Forgive me for dropping in unannounced. Your assistant seemed to think you would be some time."

"My meeting finished early. Drink?" Schwarzkopf crossed to the desk, where stood a decanter, "I've always wondered if it were a myth, you policemen not drinking on duty."

"I'm unhappy to confirm it's a reality."

"Reality is what we make it," said Schwarzkopf, "I'm afraid I'm on my way out again very soon. Will this take long?"

Coy shook his head. "I don't think so. Are you aware of the name James Robertson?"

Schwarzkopf poured himself a glass of whisky. "Isn't he that fellow who was stabbed in your police station?"

"Not in it." Coy folded his arms, "outside it."

"Of course. The devil's in the detail, isn't that what they say?"

"Detail is our business, Mr. Schwarzkopf. Speaking of which—at the time of his murder Mr. Robertson had in his possession a digital camera. On said camera were a number of photographs of this house, taken, it seems, from inside the grounds."

"Good lord," declared Schwarzkopf, "how extraordinary. What on earth do you think he was up to?"

"I rather hoped," said Coy, "that you could tell me."

Schwarzkopf shook his head and took a drink. "I'm afraid I'm at a loss to explain."

"Did you know Mr. Robertson?"

"I never had the pleasure. I never will, now."

"Would you be so kind as to look at this photo?"

"This is him?" asked Schwarzkopf, "No, I don't recognize him at all."

"Do you have CCTV installed here, Mr. Schwarzkopf?"

"I'm sorry, but no. Why would I, after all?"

"You are a very wealthy and well-known man."

"Well again I must apologise Inspector, but no."

"Chief Inspector," said Coy, tucking the photograph back into his pocket.

"Of course. I imagine there's a world of difference. Is there anything else I can help you with, Chief Inspector?"

The door re-opened. Hardacre came in. She looked at her boss and briskly shook her head.

"No, thank you Mr. Schwarzkopf," said Coy, "if there's anything else I'll get back to you. Oh, one thing—is Mr. Bowers in permanent residence here?"

"No, but on occasion his duties require him to stay overnight. I have a room set aside for him at the rear."

"Is there anyone else regularly in the house?"

"I have a cleaning lady, a cook, my housekeeper Mrs Watts."

"I see. I wonder if you would supply me with their full names and addresses."

"I'll have Bowers arrange it. Are you thinking one of them might have seen this Roberts fellow?"

"We live in hope," said Coy, "we live in hope."

Back at the station Coy waved away an approaching constable and went straight to his office. He was surprised to see a stranger occupying the seat behind his desk. The man had grey hair and grey eyes and did not smile as he got up.

"DCI Coy?" he said, "I'm DCI Rivers, MI6 Liaison. I'm taking over the investigation into the murder of James Robertson, as of now. I expect you to brief your team accordingly and to hand over all pertinent documents at once."

Cambridge, fifteen years previously

"Don't you like it here better?" asked Christian Schwarzkopf.

Maria put the blue pill upon her tongue and swallowed dutifully. She sank down lower into the warm fragrant water of the bath. Christian, seated behind her, ran an appreciative hand up and down her arm. "Your Christian will take care of you." He kissed her hair. "One day soon you will be able to stay here forever. I'll get you out of that hospital for good."

Some minutes later he pulled himself up, leaving the girl in the water as he threw on his gown and padded back into his work-room. His newly-acquired abstract paintings decorated each wall and he had not yet lost the thrill of surrounding himself with them— he suspected and hoped that this would indeed never happen. The cutting straight strokes of David Bomberg and Wyndham Lewis gave Christian boundless joy. Their boldness, courage and brashness infused his spirit with vigour. All the better for enjoying the girl when she emerged.

And without prior warning she was there. The slightest of sounds gave her presence away and Christian turned. She stood naked, but she was not looking at him and there was a dangerous expression in her eyes. Her mouth curled back in horror, her limbs held taut and stiff.

Maria was transfixed by the paintings. They leapt out towards her—their sharp lines and crashing colours. They assaulted her like hammers, smashing against her skull, exploding inside her head. They split her skin and dissected her mind. She screamed. She writhed. Dimly she heard someone calling her name.

Christian grabbed at her arm. "Quiet," he shouted, "quiet." The girl twisted and turned and broke free. She staggered from the room, still screaming.

Christian followed. He grabbed her shoulders. She scratched at his face, and to save himself, he let go. Maria collapsed against the kitchen units. Her eyes flashed wildly and her fingers clawed at the wooded surface.

"Devil," she screamed, "devil."

"Shut up," snarled Christian, glancing around as if he could see his neighbours through the walls.

When he turned back, Maria was running towards him with a knife.

By some miracle he managed to grab her wrist and spin her round. She leapt at him, teeth biting. Christian forced his other arm up between their bodies. He pushed with all his strength and, as Maria once more ran towards him, pulled back his arm and caught her square upon her chin with his fist.

She fell, striking her head hard upon the table, and lay prone and unmoving upon the floor.

Cambridge, present day

"What do you think of him?" asked Monte, as they walked.

"Harry?" Aabira shrugged. "I think he's unmotivated, a little close-minded, and uneducated. But then again, he did find that paper, and he didn't put up too much of a fight over the book-search, which is not a pleasant job. Maybe he'll turn out to be okay."

"He's going through a significant readjustment," said Monte, "he'll either bend or he'll break. I think that's why his dad sent him to us."

Aabira shivered, and pulled out her gloves. "Do you think there's really a connection between Tony Perkins' disappearance and James Robertson's murder?"

"What do your instincts tell you?"

"It's possible. Yes, I think that there must be."

"Must be?"

"Not fair," said Aabira, although she smiled as she said it. "I'm to trust my instincts *and* keep an open mind?"

"For what it's worth," said Monte, "I agree with you. I think they were working on something. Whether that's connected to James' death, I don't know, but I think it's likely Tony got spooked and went into hiding."

"But according to the sister," said Aabira, "Tony disappeared days before the murder."

"Yes," mused Monte, "that is curious."

"This is us," said Aabira, looking up at the sign.

The Golden Dragon was quiet at this hour, with just two tables being served. Monte asked at the bar for the manager. She was a youthful-looking woman with a broad smile.

"Miss Zhou?"

"That's me, how may I help you?"

Monte handed over his card. "I'm trying to a find a missing person, Tony Perkins. I believe he was a regular."

Miss Zhou took the proffered photo. "Ah yes," she said, "he is here often with another gentleman."

"This man?"

"Yes, that's him."

"Can you tell me when they were in last?"

"I think it must be several days ago. Ten. Maybe two weeks."

"Were they ever any trouble?" asked Aabira. "Did they argue?"

"No," said Miss Zhou, "they seemed very friendly. This one," she pointed to Tony, "is very scruffy. The other one is a real English gentleman. A very nice man."

"And the last time you saw them," said Monte, "you don't recall anything odd or unusual about their manner?"

Miss Zhou shook her head. "So far as I remember they were perfectly normal."

"Could they have come in more recently on a night that you weren't here?" asked Aabira.

"It's possible. I can ask the other staff if you like. They are not all here right now."

"Thank you," said Monte, "my number is on the card."

"I hope that you find him," said Miss Zhou.

"So do we," said Monte, "so do we."

Cambridge, 1985

When Lucas woke up his head was crooked uncomfortably between the seat and the car window. He stretched, rubbed his neck, and checked his watch. It was five a.m. The sky was mid-way between night and day, a pale starless void. The terraced street was quiet and empty. There was not a single movement from behind the storied curtains.

He undid his Thermos and poured another cup of coffee. The bitter liquid tasted good. A light rain began to spatter the windshield. Yesterday's paper lay on the passenger-seat, atop the manila file in which Lucas kept the notes and photographs he had made concerning Christian Schwarzkopf. From the picture on the front page, which was folded in half, a familiar pair of eyes stared back.

Lucas unfolded the paper. *Girl Missing From Highfields, Police*

Suspect Foul Play—ran the headline. Its stark words were hardly enough to convey the emotion that gripped Lucas by the throat. He folded the paper inward, so that the face disappeared, and once more stared out at the unpromising sky.

The door to number thirty-seven opened so rapidly that it caught Lucas off guard. He ducked low behind the steering wheel. The graceful figure which appeared at the top of the steps was unmistakably Schwarzkopf. Lucas watched him turn the key and descend rapidly and lightly to the street. The man got into his car, a flame-red Triumph, and pulled away.

Lucas got out. The cool rain pattered his shirt. He tucked his camera inside his coat and opened the wooden side-door which he knew led to the communal gardens. This was a large green area, where a gentle slope led down from the back of the building into a wide tree-lined declivity. Not a single curtain was drawn.

Lucas struggled up the slope, crouching low as he made his way along. At his target he stood, hooded his head with both hands and peered in through the window. After a moment he took out the small crowbar that weighted his right pocket. Working the end in between the window frame and the sill, he pushed firmly, testing the resistance. Upping the pressure a little at a time, the frame gave at the last with a loud snap and a small splintering of wood. Lucas paused for a moment. Satisfied there was no response from neighbours, he pulled open the window.

There was a desk just inside, and the journalist pulled himself through, inevitably clattering objects to the ground as he swung round and jumped onto the carpet. The room was a kind of sitting-room-cum-study. There was a sofa, the desk, cabinet, radio, a record player, television, bookcases, and rugs upon the floor. Framed prints hung upon the wall—angular, impressionistic shapes and lines.

Lucas set to work. He tried the desk first. The drawers were largely full of stationery. There were some letters, which he examined and dismissed, and a pile of receipts, which he stuffed into his inside pocket.

The cabinet was full of spirits. The books were largely philosophy with a smattering of anthropology and art. There was a notice-board with names and addresses upon it. Lucas took a photograph of that, and was about to move upstairs when something caught his attention.

Later he would wonder at how unlikely it had been for him to have seen it—a small tangle of black hair clotted together and stuck near the top of one leg of a small round polished table. Lucas knelt down and gently pulled it free. The hairs were stuck to each other and the table by a thick dry red substance. Lucas's heart raced even as his stomach lurched. He cleared the top of the table and up-ended it, searching closely. He found nothing more on the table itself, but behind, on the wall, the faintest stain of red that had obviously been scrubbed clean.

Lucas followed the stains down. He pulled aside the plush rug and found more evidence on the carpet—faded but unmistakable. He took out his pen knife and with effort cut out a small neat square. Then he pushed back the rug, righted the table and stood, breathing hard.

"Get a grip," he said to himself, "calm down."

The journalist crossed back to the window, pulled himself up onto the desk and scrambled backwards and out, scratching himself painfully on the sill. Outside under the lightening sky, he leaned back against the wall and felt the tears come to his eyes. They had to believe him now, the police. He would drive straight to the station, and would not leave until they listened.

As rain began to fall in earnest, he titled his head back, looked up to the infinite grey, and thanked god it would soon be over.

Cambridge, present day

The killer watched the streets from his vantage point, high up on the twelfth floor. When the white van turned the corner and slowed he knew it was trouble. Fighting a sick feeling in his stomach, he pulled shut the curtain and grabbed his bag from the bed.

"Nan," he called out, "Nan, I'm going out, okay."

The old lady emerged into the sitting room as the killer was halfway to the door.

"Are you coming back for tea?" she said.

"No, nan, I'm sorry. I have to go."

"Go where?"

"I have to meet some friends. Don't answer the door," he called back as he fled into the corridor. Down the rear stairwell he took the steps fast, jumping the bottom few and skidding round the turns. At the ground floor exit he ducked quickly out of sight as a face passed the window. Breathing hard, he edged forward, slowly pushed down the handle, and peered out.

Seeing that the coast was clear, the killer darted across the road and into the alley. He did not stop running until his legs could carry him no further.

Cambridge, 1985

"I'm teaching you a lesson," said Christian Schwarzkopf, leaning close to the face of Lucas Grundy, who was bound by ropes to the chair in which he sat. It had been late evening when Lucas had returned home to his flat to find Christian and two other men waiting. They had bound him by force but otherwise not laid a finger upon him. Not yet. The two men, dressed entirely in black, were young and fit. Lucas had not stood a chance.

"You're trying to scare me," Lucas breathed, "I won't be scared."

Christian stood and gestured. The two men began moving behind Lucas' back.

"We're going to kill you," drawled Christian, "you are going to die. There's nothing you can do about it."

Lucas squirmed and strained as hands grabbed his head, forcing it back. Fingers clamped on his jaw and in his mouth, pulling it wide. A bottle was held up. Alcohol poured into Lucas' throat. He gagged and fought but could not help swallowing a great deal. For long tortuous seconds this went on, until Christian signaled enough.

His stomach on fire and his eyes watering, Lucas stared helplessly. "You can't do this," he gagged. He wondered what would make them stop. The files, perhaps. They were safely hidden at his sister's. But even as that spark of hope flared he felt, on some deep instinctual level, that this would not be the case. Christian was still talking, but Lucas was not listening. A sudden wild calmness gripped him. This is right, he understood, this is how it has to end. The monster devours the knight, and in doing so, it is damned.

"Do you understand, now?" said Christian, bending close, "you are going to die. Tonight. Very shortly. We are going to take you to the park and drown you. This is going to happen and there is nothing you can do about it."

Lucas began to cry uncontrollably.

"He understands," said Christian, his voice lowering to a contented sigh. He reached out to brush the journalist's hair back from his eyes.

"Hair," mumbled the journalist, "I have her hair. Oh, you are going to suffer, Christian Schwarzkopf. I pity you." He tried to rise.

Immediately the two other men were on him, shoving him down, pulling and grasping painfully at his mouth.

"Finish the bottle," said Christian, and watched as for endless seconds the pale brown liquid showered in Lucas' mouth and over his face and clothes. When it was over the journalist's head lolled forward onto his chest.

"Lucas," said Christian, with his hands on his knees, "Lucas can you hear me."

The journalist began to chuckle. Flecks of froth appeared on his lips.

"We're going to hold your head under the water," said Christian, "everyone will think that you killed yourself. How does that make you feel?"

From the journalist there came no answer.

"Take him to the car," ordered Christian, "let us free him from his miserable state."

Cambridge, present day

Monte met Lee Macklin on the top floor of the Art Café. Monte knew Lee was in his mid-twenties, but he looked far older, worn and worried, with a vacant look in his blue eyes.

"How have you been?" Monte asked as he sat.

Lee shrugged. His every movement was glacially slow.

"Will you eat today?"

"Just tea, thanks."

Whilst Monte ordered from the waitress, Lee's nicotine-stained fingers worried listlessly at the edge of the menu.

"What can I do for you, mister Boutista?"

"It's Monte, I've told you before, and you could start by taking better care of yourself."

Lee looked up. "I'm right where I want to be," he said.

"I don't really believe that." Monte threw up his hands. "Apologies, Lee, I'm not here to lecture you."

"Forget it."

The waitress returned with cups and pots. One at a time, Lee opened six packets of sugar and emptied them into his brew.

"What's the word on the stabbing of James Robertson?" Monte asked.

"Not heard anything," said Lee, "but I'll keep my ears open. I'm going places this week."

"What places?"

"I'll keep my ears open."

Monte pulled out a photo of Tony Perkins. "Have you ever seen this man? He's gone missing. Could be sleeping rough?"

Lee's fingers brushed the picture.

"Can I keep this?"

"Sure."

Lee took the photo. His hand shook and his movements were jerky and disjointed.

"Have you talked to your mother recently?"

Lee shook his head.

"I think she'll be worried," said Monte, "can I tell her I've seen you?"

"Bird or Pres?" said Lee.

"What's that?"

"Bird got all the glory but Pres played like liquid gold. I like him a lot. How about you, Mister Boutista?"

Monte smiled. "I like Pres too," he said.

"Thanks for the tea."

"Lee," said Monte, as the other man rose, "the offer's always there you know. If you need a place to stay, if you want help."

"I'll see you next week, Mister Boutista," said Lee, as he headed slowly for the stairs.

Cambridge, two years previously

Eddie Dankworth enjoyed everything about the experience of amateur boxing. He liked the sights and the smells and the sounds of the gym, the old one, on Brakes Road, not the barely-adequate college facilities at Downing College. This was a Sunday afternoon, a good time, when only those serious about the craft would turn up. Not that Eddie had any ambitions of ever going pro. He was thankful for the thickly-padded gloves and head guard. Boxing, for

Eddie, was both balm and release from the pressures of studying.

A half-dozen familiar faces greeted him as he left the locker room and entered the training-area. A couple of guys were working the heavy bags, another jumped rope, and two more were sparring in the centre ring, under the watchful gaze of trainer and owner Fitch Felmore.

Eddie began warming up, stretching and bending. He kept half-an-eye on those sparring while he did so, and noticed a stranger on the far side, talking to Spider. Spider himself Eddie knew by sight only. Spider helped out at the ring and was also some kind of handyman at the college. The other person was tall and trim and neatly-dressed, around fifty, but clearly he kept himself fit.

"Hey Eddie," called Malcolm from the ring as the second of those who had been sparring lowered himself down through the ropes, "do a couple of rounds?"

Eddie nodded acknowledgment and walked over to Fitch, who helped him on with the gloves. They boxed for four two-minute rounds and Eddie enjoyed it. His footwork felt good and, although Malcolm was the bigger and more experienced man, Eddie took great satisfaction from the two or three occasions where he was able to slip his opponent's jab and counter crisply with straight rights.

When they were done and Eddie climbed down, Spider and the stranger approached.

"This is Mister Christian Schwarzkopf," said Spider, "he'd like to have a word with you."

Eddie wiped his face on a towel. "Pleased to meet you Mister Schwarzkopf," he said, "and what is it that you do?"

"Well, I help people," said Christian.

"What sort of people?"

"All sorts. Sometimes promising students. From the right backgrounds."

"Why don't you get changed," said Spider, "and we'll talk after."

And so Eddie found himself in the dining area of the five-star

Gonville Hotel, eating salmon and sipping claret, while he listened to Christian Schwarzkopf talk.

"You appreciate the finer things," said the businessman, "and yet you push yourself physically. That is a rare combination."

"You'll excuse my asking," said Eddie, "I don't really understand what this is about. Are you offering me sponsorship?"

"Oh I'm offering a great deal more than that," Christian smiled. He leaned forwards. "How do you feel about paintings?"

After lunch Spider drove them all to Christian's house, an impressive two-story mansion set in its own modest grounds, walled and fenced off from the road. In an oak-paneled room on the top floor, Christian showed Eddie his collection.

Eddie knew some of the names of the artists. Wyndham, of course, and Bomberg and Wadsworth. The works were striking—abstract, machine-nightmares encompassing bold lines of movement and colour.

"Aren't they divine?" said Christian.

Eddie moved to stand in front of the nearest canvas. Christian stood at his shoulder.

"They called their movement Vorticism," explained Christian. "Do you know what they were trying to achieve, Edward?"

Eddie shook his head.

"Freedom," said Christian, and there was an almost bestial quality to the excitement in his voice. "They knew," he went on, "that life is an illusion. War is an illusion. Love is an illusion. They understood that to set yourself on any one side, in any one role or niche or mode of thought or morality is to deny the soul its divine right to freedom."

Eddie stared at the striking lines of the paintings.

"Everything you know," said Christian, "everything you have been told is a lie. In the end there is only one side, one cause, which the intelligent man can take. And that is the cause of one's self. Do you think that you agree?"

Eddie nodded slowly. "Perhaps."

"But you don't," said Christian, laying a hand upon the younger man's shoulder, "not yet. But you will, if you let me be your guide."

"I'm not sure what you mean." Eddie did not move away.

"I sponsor a group," said Christian, letting his hand drop, "of students and former students, from noble lineages such as your own."

"And what does this group do?"

"Call us a brotherhood."

"So what does this brotherhood do?"

Christian laughed. "Why," he said, "we do whatever we damn well please."

This was how Edward Dankworth became part of Christian Schwarzkopf's Brotherhood. He was not the first and he would not be the last and he would, eventually, be partly responsible for the murder of James Robertson. For there was only one way to survive in the Brotherhood and this was to move up the pecking order so that you would be safe from the regular culls and occasional unpleasant duties. Everyone understood this and nobody talked about it. For Eddie the choice was simple—learn to slip the jab or get hit. Eddie became very, very good at not getting hit.

Cambridge, present day

Harry rubbed his eyes and threw the final book back on the pile. "Useless," he said to no one. He crossed to the window and peered down onto the street. Rush-hour traffic was starting to build. The sky was darkening. The little newsagent across the road spilled yellow light out onto the pavement.

His mind felt clogged and grey, but at least having something to do had made him forget, for a while. Harry was pretty pleased with his bit of detective work with the painting. It had been nice to show the girl that he wasn't entirely useless.

"Useless," he said again. On a whim he turned back to the wall of newspaper clippings. Aabira had been right—the topics were all over the place. "Okay Harry," he said aloud, "so why pin these particular ones up? Think like a scruffy dead-beat old man."

Harry scrutinized the yellowing bits of paper again. Different dates, none recent. Different writers and at least three different papers. "What am I doing here?" said Harry, "looking at depressing old clippings about dull stories with dull photographs."

Photographs.

He bent down and looked closer. After a moment he stood up, smiled, wrote down a name and left the flat.

Cambridge, four months previously

The garage door swung upward with a bang, displacing clouds of dust that danced in the hot sunshine.

Janey waved a hand in front of her face and held her nose. "Geez," she said, "it's going to take all day to sort this lot. What time's the skip coming?"

"Eleven," said Geoff, "c'mon babe. We can get this sorted in no time."

Janey scowled. "How come it's always us," she said, "that's why I want to know. Where's your brother when there's hard work to be done?"

Ignoring the question, although he agreed with his wife wholeheartedly, Geoff ventured into the cool interior of the garage, which was piled on all sides with boxes, benches and plastic containers. He laid hold of a tarpaulin that completely covered one corner and pulled it free. Janey came to stand beside him and together they regarded the large tub full of wristwatches, the stack of car radios with their wires hanging out, the dozen or so DVD players, laptops and mobiles which lay heaped in an unsteady pile.

"Geez," said Janey, "do you think uncle Colin was on the rob?"

Geoff sighed, shook his head, and squared his shoulders.

"Let's get going," encouraged Janey, rubbing his back. "We can still make it down to the Lion tonight if we get a move-on."

They worked tirelessly, sorting and shifting under the blazing sun. It was after lunch when Geoff came across the cardboard box laying half-open in the skip. He reached out and flipped up the lid. It was full of typed documents and photos.

"Hey," he said, hauling the box closer, "what did you put this in the skip for?"

Janey put a hand up to shield her eyes from the light. "That old rubbish?"

"It's photos and stuff," said Geoff. He pulled out a file. "Historical."

Janey guffawed. "It's rubbish, love."

Geoff read the name on the file: Christian Schwarzkopf. "No, babe," he said, "someone'll buy this." He heaved the box free. "People'll buy anything," he said, "people'll buy anything."

Later that week, at the grand car-boot sale in a field just outside Ely, James Roberston and Tony Perkins ambled, sweating and uncomfortable. Neither men were built for exertion, especially in such weather. James had removed his customary tweed jacket and carried it in one arm; in the other he clutched a plastic bag in which sat a cheese-and-pickle sandwich and a flask of ice water. His beloved camera hung around his neck. From time to time he reached up to adjust the strap, which had a habit of riding up above his shirt collar to rub annoyingly on his neck.

Tony, for his part, was also down to his shirtsleeves, grubby though they were. He was laden with a large hold-all, a small noticeboard on a collapsible wooden stand, and a weighty canvas bag stuffed full of papers and leaflets. They stopped just inside the entrance.

"There's treasure to be had here," said James as Tony set down his things and began to erect his stand. "What are you bothering with that for? You're not thinking of hawking those here? You are?"

"People need to hear the truth," said Tony, pinning a notice to the board.

With an effort, James bent down to pick up a leaflet. "A treatise on the dangers of inter-racial mixing," he read, "dear oh dear, Tony. They won't let you give these out."

"I'm not giving them out," stated Tony, flatly. "I'm selling them."

"How much for?"

"Five pounds each."

"Five pounds," said James, shaking his head. "Dear oh dear."

"You can help me if you like? I'll give you ten percent."

"Not I," said James, "I'm going for a wander. Take some photos. The good folks of Cambridgeshire enjoying the sun. I can sell them for more than ten percent of nothing."

Tony grunted.

"And," James went on, "I'm going to find some bargains in amongst this lot. Ebay is the way, my friend. Ebay is the way."

James immediately set off toward the lines of shining motor vehicles. He judged it prudent to be well clear of any appeals to him for support, should Tony become entangled, as he surely would, with whatever passed for authority in this beautiful green corner of old England.

He took his time, walking up and down the rows, smiling and greeting folks, pausing to take a picture here and there, coaxing a photogenic face into a pose—a little girl in a princess dress, a charming family with their baby in the shade. He searched patiently and methodically amongst those stalls that seemed promising. One or two old books he snapped up, recognising them as original editions from the fifties. Otherwise, the pickings were scant.

James was on the verge of giving up and wandering back in search of a place to sit down and re-charge when he saw the cardboard box nestled under a trestle table near the end of one of the rows. He bent down on one knee and pulled it clear.

"Historical documents," said the stall-owner, a middle-aged man in a tracksuit.

James smiled and pulled out one of the folders. He recognised the name on the front. Christian Schwarzkopf was an important figure locally. James' first hope was that this might be of some sentimental value to the multi-millionaire, or at least earn him a meal and a connection or two.

It wasn't long before he came to quite a different conclusion. Gripping the box and hefting it with some difficulty, he pulled out his wallet. "How much do you want," he said to the man, "I'll take it."

By the time James returned to his companion, Tony was embroiled in an altercation. A furious looking young black lady stood, arms crossed, as two neon-vested men remonstrated with the red-faced Tony, who stood, looking like an immovable sack of potatoes, a batch of leaflets held stubbornly in one hand.

"So sorry," exclaimed James, bustling up, "so sorry," he repeated to the woman, "we're going, now, we're going."

"I'm not going anywhere," said Tony, shrugging his friend's hand from his arm.

"Yes, you are," urged James, leaning in close, "I've found something that's going to make us money. Real money," he finished, pulling down his glasses and staring into Tony's eyes. "You can print a thousand leaflets from the proceeds of what's in this box. A million."

For a moment Tony stared back defiantly. Then he turned and began to gather up his belongings.

"Don't come back," called one of the men as they made their way out through the gate.

"We won't need to if this pays off," said James, "we won't need to ever again."

Cambridge, present day

At that same time Harry was leaving Tony Perkins' flat, Monte was ordering himself another green tea at the Rose Café. As soon as Coy entered, he knew that something was wrong. The big man eased himself down with a sigh.

"We're off the case," he said, "we being the Cambridgeshire Constabulary."

"What happened?"

"Military Intelligence Section Six, or MI6 to me and you—I'll have a cream tea, thanks."

"Are you going to elucidate, or do I have to guess?"

"It seems," said Coy, spooning sugar into his tea, "that the last pictures James Robertson took were of an exclusive property off De Freville Avenue, a property belonging to one Mr. Christian Schwarzkopf."

"The multi-millionaire businessman Christian Schwarzkopf?"

"The very same. As a matter of course one of my officers punched his name into the computer and lo and behold all sorts of alarm bells start ringing. As if by magic, whoosh, DCI Albert Rivers, MI6 Liaison, whatever that means, appears like the veritable genie, come to grant me three wishes, so long as all of them are 'please let me hand over my files and bugger off'."

"MI6? That's foreign intelligence. I wonder what interest they have in Schwarzkopf?"

"Wonder, indeed. Whatever it is they don't want us yokels spoiling their game over something as trivial as a murder."

"So will they be investigating Robertson's death?"

"My guess is they'll put it on the back burner. A very cold, very distant back burner. They must have something very big on Schwarzkopf if they're willing to quash anything even remotely connected."

"Do you think that the connection is so remote?"

Coy appraised his plate. "This one stinks," he said, "and I'm not talking about my scone. I've a feeling things are going to get messy and I don't like mess."

"We found this," said Monte, pushing a photograph across. It was a picture of the hidden piece of paper with code written upon it.

"Interesting." Coy raised his eyebrows. He lowered his voice. "I've seen one just the same. We found it among Robertson's possessions. What's the betting that our one is in Tony Perkins' handwriting and the one you found is in Robertson's?"

"So they were communicating in code. I don't suppose you have a list of all the books Robertson owned so we can cross-reference?"

"As a matter of fact, I do. What Rivers doesn't know is that I am very very keen on backing up my files. Come to the house, not the station, tomorrow evening and we can compare notes. Bring Aabira if she's free, and Penny too. I'll do one of those rabbit-food roasts you're so keen on."

"Room for one more? Harry, my new leg-man. I'm breaking him in slowly."

"Of course. Listen, this Rivers—from the little I know he isn't entirely incompetent. Wherever you go and whoever you talk to from now on, you'd better have a good reason. If any hint of collusion gets out then we'll both be in the pot."

Monte took out a pen and scrawled onto his napkin: *any news on the scooter?*

"This is the Rose Café," said Coy, "not Mata Hari's boudoir. No, not a single hit on CCTV. I imagine it's locked safely in a garage somewhere, or lying at the bottom of the Cam. Which means our boy isn't a total idiot. Which is another reason to be careful, if you needed one. What's your next step, by the way?"

Monte leaned back, sipped his tea and asked himself the same question.

Cambridge, sixteen months previously

Eddie awoke tangled in the soft sheets of the four-poster bed. A shaft of sunlight penetrated the quiet room. Dust motes swirled ceaselessly in its beam. Eddie pushed back the sheet and patted his stomach. It had been too long since he had hit the gym.

Over coffee he looked out of the window and down onto the street. Winter battled with spring. The sky lulled from sunshine to shadow. Eddie watched the few passersby who were out at this time and in this place. The whole milieu appeared strangely slowed down, like a film playing at the wrong speed. At the same time the outlines of objects and people seemed sharper and thicker than they ought to be.

Eddie knew it was the drugs but he welcomed their effect. They kept him more alert and calmer and the soft fuzz was a welcome filter. He stood in front of the painting that Christian had presented along with this luxury flat. Eddie studied it as he had been instructed, first concentrating on specific areas before stepping back and letting the whole impression itself upon his mind.

Life had been good since he had entered the brotherhood. Pills were as free-flowing as money and sex. Private tutors and the very best resources meant that studies were well under control. For every wild night of debauchery there came a day of quiet work, always with the promise of material reward soon to come.

Today, though, Eddie had a mission, a task he must perform. Dressing in one of his fine linen shirts, beige trousers and half-brogues, he started out on the half-mile walk to Downing College. Traffic and people streamed past at a strange speed, leaving slight traces of themselves in the air. Eddie stopped for a Coke, took a purple pill and, by the time he reached the entrance, the peculiar edge had all but disappeared and Martha stood waiting.

Eddie distrusted Martha. She played the fool very well but had a killer instinct behind her veil of childish air-head. The sex between them was very good. Seeing her like this, in her black dress in the sunshine, stirred in Eddie an eagerness for their next coupling.

"Is he here?" he asked.

She curled a finger, smiled, and began to lead him inside.

In the library they sat, opposite one another, with their quarry over Martha's right shoulder.

"You see him?" she whispered.

"Yes," said Eddie. The man in question sat absorbed in his study, with one elbow upon the table and his chin resting in his palm. He had thick, curly hair and a handsome, round face.

"Nice," said Eddie, "what do you know about him?"

Outside in the fresh air they talked more easily.

"So he's struggling?"

"That's what I hear," said Martha, "he's bright but unmotivated. A loner. An outsider."

"Perfect," Eddie nodded, "introduce yourself but take it slowly."

"He's going to have the time of his life," said Martha.

"Yes," said Eddie, "yes he is."

Cambridge, present day

The Killer was freezing. Jamie's shed was small and dusted with cobwebs. He had managed to sleep during the day but now that the sun had disappeared the cold was beginning to bite. At last he heard the sound of his friend departing. A car pulled up out front; there was the opening and closing of doors.

Warily, the killer pushed open the door and ventured out into the garden, which was neat and well-kept. He looked back at the scooter, which was tucked in one corner beneath a pile of deck chairs, then tried the back door of the house and the windows. All were locked and closed. He was hungry and thirsty. If Jamie or any of the others were to find him he did not think it would end well.

The killer pulled up his hoodie and set off through the back alleys towards Mill Road. He had five pounds in his pocket, enough for a burger and a drink. Later he would slip back into the shed, maybe try and steal a coat or a blanket first, maybe from the café. The empty ache in his stomach overruled his fear. Mill Road wasn't too much of a risk. The others didn't go there, not much, and if the police came he'd just have to run for it.

I should get out, he thought, get far away. But the station was too dangerous and the coaches too visible. He needed a vehicle. Jamie's car? He could break in and get the keys in the morning, be gone before Jamie got up, get as far as the nearest town and then ditch it. Jamie would have money in the house too. He always had cash from selling gear. Or he could come clean to his nan. He wasn't going to steal from her, no matter how bad things got. But she'd give him money. Maybe. He felt a sick churning in his stomach, pulled his hood lower and kept walking. "I can only rely on myself now," he said to no one.

Cambridge, Two Weeks previously

"We can make a fortune," said James, passing the pot of green tea across the table. He and Tony sat in the Golden House restaurant. It was late afternoon and the skies were darkening.

"He should be in prison," said Tony, "that Christian Schwarzkopf. He murdered that woman."

"We don't know that," said James, "we've only got…" he paused as the waiter returned and they gave over their orders, "…we've only this Lucas Grundy's word for it. It might be useless, all this. Some photographs, a bit of carpet. It might be nothing."

"DNA," said Tony, "they probably couldn't test it back then."

James sighed. "Of course they could. Anyway, don't you think the police would have investigated? They've probably seen the carpet. And the photographs. We don't even know that she's dead. I've been investigating." From his bag he pulled forth a handful of photocopies. "I found these in the library. Missing, it says. Her body was never found."

Tony looked at them. Then he sat back and shook his head.

"Are you saying we should just hand this over to the police?" said James. "Schwarzkopf would pay us money. Real money."

"So you keep saying. But if it's nothing to do with him then why would he care?"

"People like that always hate bad publicity. It won't be blackmail. We'll just ask for a finder's fee."

"A finders fee?"

"Why not? And if it bothers you that much, what's to stop us getting the money up front and then handing the goods over to the police? What's Schwarzkopf going to do? Sue us?"

"I don't like it," Tony grimaced. "Suppose we talk to Lucas Grundy first? See what he has to say."

"I tried. He's gone. Skipped the country," lied James. "Look, I'm not going to do this without you. If you don't want the money, we can hand the whole lot over to the cops tomorrow. Today, if you like."

Tony scratched with one dirty fingernail under another. "How much money?" he said.

James sat back and smiled. "Oh a lot," he said, "a lot."

Cambridge, present day

Penny let Harry into the shop around half-seven the following morning.

"You're keen," she said.

"It's the best part of the day," said Harry, breathing hard.

"Running is bad for the knees," observed Penny.

"Is he in?"

"Who's he? The cat's mother?"

"Sorry," said Harry, "Mister Boutista."

"Yes, he's in the office. Knock first."

Harry bounded up the stairs. The office door was partially open. He pushed it wide, began to speak and then fell silent. Monte was kneeling on a small rug, facing away from him towards the window. As Harry entered Monte bent down, hands before him, prostrating himself. He could hear the investigator talking quietly in what sounded like Arabic. Harry quietly pulled the door to and went back downstairs. He found Penny in a little kitchen through a doorway behind the counter.

"He's busy," said Harry, "is he praying?"

"I told you to knock," said Penny, "have you had breakfast?"

Harry shook his head. "I didn't know."

"Didn't know what?"

"That Mister Boutista was…is he Muslim?"

"Eggs and toast?" asked Penny, "we have vegetarian sausages too."

"Just the eggs and toast please."

"Kettle's over there," Penny gestured, "make yourself useful."

Harry filled the kettle and set it to boiling. He found two mugs and set them down.

"What's your birth date?" said Penny.

"My birth date? Why?"

"Astrology," said Monte, from the doorway, "good morning Harry."

"Mister Boutista," said Harry, "I found something at Tony's flat."

"Make that three cups," said Penny.

"I was looking at those press clippings on the wall, the ones Aabira told you about. They're all from different papers, different years, different stories. Then I noticed a connection."

"Connections are our stock-in-trade." Monte took a seat at the small table.

"I'll make the tea then," said Penny.

"Sorry," apologised Harry, going back to the kettle. He talked quickly as he poured water into the cups. "You see," he said, "it's the photographs themselves that are the connection."

"More photos," said Monte.

"What?"

"I'll tell you later. Go on…"

"Well," said Harry, "all the photographs were taken by the same guy. Lucas Grundy. I wrote down the name. Can't be a coincidence, can it?"

"Good work," said Monte, "are you free today?"

"Yes."

"I need you to pick up Aabira after breakfast and drive her to the library. Then you and I are going to track down this Lucas Grundy. Oh, and we're going to dinner tonight."

"We are? Where?"

"An old friend's. You'll enjoy it."

*   *   *   *   *

Hardacre found Coy at his desk, typing an email, one finger-press at a time.

"We've had an anonymous tip sir, concerning the missing scooter. An address on Romsey Road."

Coy laboriously finished typing and turned to face her. "That's MI5 territory now."

"Yes, I know," Hardacre closed the door, "it didn't come in through the hotline. It was reported through one-oh-one. I happened to pick it up from the daily files. Of course I'll need to report it to DCI Rivers, but…"

"…but why don't we wander down there first. Let's call it lending a hand."

"Will Rivers mind?"

"Rivers," said Coy, standing up, "will likely hit the bloody roof, but I'll take the flak and, happily, I have enough brownie points in hand to bear it. Lead on."

As they drove through the rush-hour traffic, Hardacre filled in the picture.

"Anonymous call came in at eight-ten this morning. A male voice. He said he'd seen a lad fitting our description wheeling a white scooter into the back garden of one-twelve, Romsey Road, late last night. Said he was acting suspiciously."

"I do like that phrase," smiled Coy, "it gives one a broad canvas on which to operate."

Romsey Road was a quiet side street of neat-terraced houses. They pulled up a few doors down and got out. Coy indicated a side alley, a narrow strip crudely concreted, with patches of weed pushing up at the edges. Twenty feet in it turned a corner, running along the backs of the houses, garden fences on one side and a thick hedge on the other. The ground was muddy and wet. They counted in and stopped at the rear of one-twelve.

The gate hung partially open. Coy pushed it wide. The garden beyond was a picture of middle-England—an impeccable lawn and neat borders of flowers. There was a shed to one side of the house. They made their way inside.

While Hardacre peered in through the rear window, Coy knocked loudly on the back door. After a few seconds a figure appeared behind the frosted glass. "Who's there?" it said.

Coy took out his ID and held it up. "Chief Inspector Coy, and DS Hardacre," he barked, "open up."

The figure hesitated, but after a moment slid a bolt and opened the door. The lad was in his early twenties. He wore sand-coloured chinos and a crisp white shirt, open at the collar. "Good morning," he said, in an accent that spoke of wealth.

"Sir," said Hardacre, "I recognise that face. This is the man we saw through the window at Christian Schwarzkopf's."

"What's your name son?"

"James," said the man, "may I ask what this is about?"

"What's your surname?" asked Coy.

"May I see your credentials?"

Coy held up his ID. "Name," he said.

"Reynolds. James Arthur."

"Well James Arthur Reynolds. The first thing you can do is show us the contents of your shed."

"There's nothing in there but sports equipment and garden furniture."

"Then you won't mind showing us, will you."

"May I get dressed first," he said, "I'm on my way to a rather important engagement."

"Get out here," Coy growled, "and open that shed."

James slid on a pair of loafers, led them over to the shed and pulled back the door. "As I said." He smiled warmly at Hardacre, who did not smile back.

It didn't take her long to find the scooter, hidden behind a pile of deck chairs at the back.

"That's not mine," protested James.

"We'll discuss that at the station," said Coy, "get yourself ready son. I'm afraid your important engagement is going to have to wait."

*   *   *   *   *

Hunger drove the killer to the outdoor market behind the Beehive Centre. Hood up and eyes down, he managed to swipe a bunch of bananas and some apples. From a Newsagent's in Sidney Street, he took a can of energy drink while the cashier was distracted. Stealing, he discovered, was easy if you held your nerve.

A weak sun shone on the cold day as he walked and ate and normal people swarmed around him. On St. Andrews there was a group of students he thought he recognised, so the killer double-backed and took a side route.

It was a long walk. He finished the can and more of the fruit and was almost feeling bold by the time he reached the Big House. Standing on the threshold of the drive his resolution failed him. He went round the back, to the rear entrance James had shown him. A sick feeling welled up from his stomach. He'd done what he'd been told to. He'd stabbed the old man and the old man was dead and now he wanted to rest. He wanted it over. He wanted someone or something to make it go away. But not so far down in his trembling mind he was scared of what they would do to him now.

He turned round, tears stinging his eyes, and arrived back at James' just in time to see the cops taking him away. For a long time he sat in the garden, trying not think. Then at last he got up. "Come on old fellow," he said aloud and to no one, "the game's not over yet. We'll just have to find another way, that's all."

He set off on a slow walk back to town.

*   *   *   *   *

It took Aabira three hours and two coffees to finish going through everything the library had on Christian Schwarzkopf. She started online, trawling through biographies and interviews, puff pieces and press items, *The Wall Street Journal* and *Financial Times*, cross-checking the bare bones of the life of a man she had never met. Anything verified that she believed pertinent, she printed out or made a note of, even a few comments that jumped out at her from the interviews.

Outside, for some fresh air and coffee, as she leaned against a concrete pillar at the shopping Centre entrance, staring out into the grey drizzling day, she thought about Harry.

"What do you do when you're not doing this?" she had asked him that morning, as he had driven her into town.

"I box," he had replied, "professionally. I mean. I don't anymore. I can't."

"Why not?"

He had been silent for a few moments as they cruised through the traffic.

"I have a heart condition. I can't fight. They won't let me."

She had sensed the resentment in his words, and something else—a hesitancy.

"I'm very sorry. That must be hard for you?"

He had glanced at her, quickly, then back at the road, and had not said a word more.

Aabira took another mouthful of the bitter drink. Some youths were hanging around outside, young boys with hoodies and bicycles.

She didn't like the way they were looking at her and muttering. She wondered what their parents were like, whether they knew what their sons were up to, and if they cared. As she turned to go, one of the boys swept past on his bike, near enough to make her step back with a start. She ignored their laughter and headed back inside.

Then it was on to the local press. This Aabira split into two sections—the last five years since Schwarzkopf had moved back to Cambridge, and the four-year period two decades back when he had been an undergrad here at Downing College.

There was a lot of interesting stuff, especially in his undergrad years. As the son of a famous parent (his father had been a multi-millionaire property developer), the arrival of the younger Schwarzkopf had attracted some attention. He'd proved very popular, rowing in the famous crew that had beaten Oxford twice in eighty-one and eighty-two. He had also made president of the Student's Union, campaigning on social issues not just confined to the college.

The most interesting article accompanied a photograph of the Schwarzkopf's junior and senior, at the opening of the Highfield's Mental Health Unit, an institution senior had helped fund. Aabira checked her notes. Highfield's had come up more than once. It seems junior had kept up a special interest.

The librarian smiled as Aabira returned the papers, neatly stacked. "Is there anything else I can help you with?" he asked.

"There is one thing," she said, "can you tell me how far Downing College is from here please?"

Cambridge, two weeks previously

James was breathing hard and sweating. He could not quite believe he stood where he did and was about to say what he had come here to say. But James was a man who had been through a lot, up and down, in situations where many people would have fallen apart. He prided himself on always rising to the occasion.

"Mr. Schwarzkopf," he said, "I came here to tell you that I know." He nodded slowly, feeling somehow more confident now that the words had been spoken. "I know."

They stood in the marble-floored hallway of Schwarzkopf's home. Christian licked his lips. Adrenalin trembled his body. "Know what?" he asked, as easily as he could manage.

"About the girl. The...murder. Maria Waters. She disappeared. Never found. I have Lucas Grundy's file. Photographs. Evidence."

"I don't know what you're talking about."

James looked down. He sighed, and pulled forth a manila envelope from his bag. Putting the bag down, he opened the envelope and took forth the eight-by-ten picture. "This is a copy," he said, holding it up.

"I see," Christian heard himself say, "and exactly what proof do you think this is?"

"This isn't all that we have."

"We?"

"There are...other things," said James. "I know you do a lot of good work for charity," he went on, "and every man deserves to have his past mistakes forgotten. I'm willing to hand over the materials."

"For a price, no doubt."

"Not a great sum for a man of your wealth," said James. He paused, then "one million," he said, 'that's all."

"I see," said Christian, "you will of course give me time to consider?"

"One week," said James, "one week and I will call again. Once you've agreed we can sort out the paperwork."

"Paperwork?"

"The exchange of materials. I want you to know," James straightened his shoulders, "that I am an honest and fair man. Once this is done you won't hear a word from me again."

"I believe that," said Christian, "I believe that wholeheartedly."

Cambridge, present day

"Can I ask a question," said Harry, who was once more behind the wheel of Monte's car.

Monte, who had thus far sat in silence, stirred from his thoughts. "What is it?"

"Why," asked Harry, pulling out into traffic, "are we driving everywhere? Wouldn't a phone-call be more efficient?"

"You get better results this way," said Monte, "a call can be ignored, forgotten or deflected. A flesh-and-blood person standing before you generates immediacy."

"Generates immediacy," echoed Harry, "okay. Asshole!"

Harry slammed on the brakes as the white Fiesta bullied out onto the road. Harry cleared his throat and stepped gently back on the gas. "Sorry."

Monte smiled thinly. "How was Aabira this morning?"

Harry shrugged. "She seemed fine. I don't think she likes me very much."

"She doesn't know you yet," said Monte, "do you want her to like you?"

Harry frowned. "That's up to her. I mean I am who I am. I'm not changing for anyone."

"Don't we all change for everyone to an extent?"

"Are you a philosopher, boss?"

"Some would say I over-think. It's a matter of regression. People are a challenge."

"I prefer a different kind of challenge."

Monte reached into the glove compartment and took out a small folder of CDs, selected one, and carefully slid it into the player. Albert Ayler's 'Ghosts' began to play, an angular and folksy trumpet phrase, simple and rasping, building quickly to an abstract turmoil of noise.

"This is what you listen to?' said Harry. "Wow."

"It helps me relax," said Monte, "it makes me feel centered. You must have things in your life that do the same?"

Harry shrugged. "I've been meaning to ask. How do you know my dad?"

"I helped sort out some legal affairs for him once."

"You a solicitor as well?"

Monte shook his head. "Your dad can tell the story better than I can."

The offices of the *Cambridge Herald* were an ugly two-story prefabricated block in a trading park on the outskirts of the city. They pulled up in the parking lot and walked through the drizzle into the office. The receptionist, a round-faced lady, smiled up at them over her glasses.

"Can I help you?"

"We'd like to speak to one of your editors, if possible, or somebody in charge of your archive."

The receptionist bit her lip. "I can phone up and see if anyone's available."

"That would be great," said Harry, flashing her his best smile, "very kind of you, miss…?"

"Helen," she said, reddening a little, "why don't you wait over there and I'll see what I can do."

Cambridge, two weeks previously

After his third impromptu turn around, James Robertson became sure he was being followed. He exited The Works stationers, passing his eyes briefly over the well-built, bald-headed man in the brown leather jacket who was rifling through the bargain-bin. The same man James had seen behind him in the queue at Dunkin' Donuts and, before that, in the park at Christ's Pieces. The man with the spider-web tattoo on the side of his neck.

Although naturally disinclined to violence, James was not a man to frighten easily. Three years in the foreign legion and several more drifting through the less salubrious parts of South America and the Middle East had seen to that. He would be the first to admit, though, that he was far removed from the prime condition of his youth.

He's trying to scare me off, he thought now, *Christian Schwarzkopf.* It was a natural enough move—a man didn't get to hold onto that much money without playing hardball.

James turned right, and then right again down Fair Street. He tapped the comforting weight of the camera around his neck. So the man wanted to play? Fine. He would stick to public areas, take his ease, and lead this thug a merry dance. Perhaps he would take a tour bus for the rest of the afternoon and, should the man be persistent enough not to quit, arrange a fast Uber pick-up for his ride home. It was, in fact, a good sign. Evidently Schwarzkopf was desperate for the file.

Just as James was formulating this plan, a handsome and well-dressed young man stepped in front of him on the pavement. The man held a map in one hand.

"Excuse me," he asked, in an upper-class English accent, "could I bother you for some directions?"

"Of course," James began, then his eyes followed the young man's gaze down, to where he held, in his free hand, a large, wickedly-bladed knife. Instantly, the leather-jacket man appeared at James' shoulder. He laid a strong hand around James' wrist and spoke urgently into his ear.

"If you make a fuss," he hissed, "we'll do you here." The voice of this man was lower-class and his accent was local.

"If you stab me in the street," stammered James, "there'll be witnesses."

"To what?" said the man with the spider-web tattoo, "we're a hundred miles away, with a room full of friends and there ain't no CCTV here. You know what my boss can do."

"Christian Schwarzkopf?"

The tattoo-man leaned even closer to whisper. "Hand over everything," he said, "bring it to the house. Tonight. If you go anywhere near the police, we'll know. Then that pretty sister of yours in Ukraine will get a visit from some very ugly people."

"Tell him he can have it for all of the money," said James, "like we agreed."

"You stupid old fuck," said tattoo, "bring it tonight, or we'll come and get it and you'll be a long time dying." The man pushed James roughly against the wall, straightened his collar and cuffs, smiled broadly and walked away, taking the young man with him.

James closed his eyes, and breathing hard, took out his phone and typed in a message.

Cambridge, present day

Downing College was impressive by any standards. Two hundred years old, set in acres of picturesque grounds, the sand-colored edifice boasted six twenty-foot high pillars supporting a triangular-topped entrance, with the magnificent sweep of the building extending out either side. A porter met Aabira at the front gate—a fat, sour-faced man who listened without once looking her in the eye. "You'll have to ring for an appointment," he said, half-turning away.

"Well as I'm here now, couldn't you ask someone?"

The man grunted affirmation and shambled away, exchanging a cheery word with some passing students. Aabira waited patiently for almost ten minutes before his return. He gestured off-handedly. "In there and to the left. Secretary's Office."

"Thank you," she said, loudly and clearly, as she passed.

The secretary was a tall, slim man, young and bright-eyed. "Salaam," he greeted her, and bid her take a seat in the office. "I'm Dalip Andrews," he said, "junior secretary. I understand that you'd like to do some research using our files?"

"If possible," said Aabira, "specifically I'm interested in anything you have on Christian Schwarzkopf."

Dalip smiled. "Ah, yes. We will have some material. Can I ask as to the nature of your research?"

Aabira paused. "It's for personal reasons. I'm sorry. I don't feel I can tell you any more."

The Secretary nodded. He pursed his lips. "Nothing in our archives is secret," he said, "although usually we require a formal request in writing."

"I wouldn't take long," said Aabira, "no more than an hour or two, Insha Allah."

Dalip smoothed his short beard, and took a deep breath.

*   *   *   *   *

"The time is eleven-fifteen a.m.," stated Coy, leaning forward slightly over the tape recorder, "present with me are DS Karen Hardacre, James Arthur Reynolds and Mr. Reynolds' solicitor, Simon Lay. Right," he continued, leaning back, "let's get this interrogation started."

"Interview," said Simon Lay, "surely you mean interview."

Coy smiled. "Quite so. Well, James. That is your name?"

"Yes."

Coy pushed up his glasses and peered down at his notes. "Why don't you start buy telling us about the scooter?"

James raised his eyebrows. "The scooter?"

"The one we found in your garden shed. The one that is stolen. The one that is linked to a premeditated murder."

James shook his head. "I'm afraid I can't help you there. As I believe I said at the time, I had no knowledge of any scooter prior to your arrival."

"So how did it end up in your shed?"

"Logically, someone else must have put it there."

"And who would that be, James? Logically?"

"I believe my client has answered your question," said Lay, "he has no knowledge of how this vehicle came to be on his property."

"Is your name James?" said Coy.

"I beg your pardon," said the solicitor.

"Granted," said Coy, "once. But if you answer for your client again I will have you removed from this room. Understood."

"Answer the question, James," said Hardacre.

"I'd love to help you, really," James shrugged, "but I'm afraid I can't. And by the way you can call me Jim."

"James," said Hardacre, "if the prints we recovered from the scooter match yours then we'll know you've been lying and that will go very badly for you in court."

James shrugged again. A small smile was upon his lips.

"Well," said Coy, "we have officers searching your house as we speak, James. Is there anything they're going to find that you want to tell us about now?"

The solicitor leaned over to whisper in James' ear.

"Hey," bawled Coy, "so that the tape can hear, or I'll have Mr. Lay removed."

The solicitor sat back.

"What is your relationship with Christian Schwarzkopf, James?"

"No comment," said James, crossing his arms. "I'm afraid you really are wasting your time."

"Son," smiled Coy, "you really don't want to mess with me. I'm not impressed by your clothes or your accent. I've taken down smoother and smarter thugs than you over breakfast."

James held his arms open wide. "I wish you the best of luck in your search."

Coy nodded. "Interview concluded." He stood and opened the door. "Take James Arthur Reynolds back to his cell," he said to the officer on duty outside.

"He's very cool," said Hardacre, once they had gone.

"Too cool," said Coy.

"Perhaps because he really doesn't know anything about it."

Coy grunted. "That Simon Lay—he's a snake who doesn't come cheap. If you're a clean, upstanding posh-boy then you don't associate with his type. And what was the man doing in Schwarzkopf's garden? That's a coincidence too far."

"Do you want me to nose around," asked Hardacre, "talk to my contacts?"

"Please do," said Coy, "I'll be in my ready-room."

Just as Coy reached his office, Superintendent Crasp appeared in the corridor. "DCI Coy," he said, "a word please?"

Crasp shut the door behind them. "What the bloody fuck," he said, "are you trying to do here, Donald?"

"Sir?"

"Don't 'sir' me. You know exactly what I'm talking about."

"Ah," said Coy, "James Reynolds?"

"Yes, James Reynolds. You know Rivers is in charge of that case. Do you know how well-connected he is? I've heard rumours that would shake you to your boots. This is from the top. The very top. This is MI6, man."

"It was an anonymous tip," said Coy, "I didn't want to hand it over if it turned out to be nothing."

"Well when it tuned out to be something, then you should have. Immediately."

"I could not locate DCI Rivers at that time," said Coy, "and my professional opinion was that any delay might harm our case by allowing the suspect to concoct a cover story."

"You're an old fool," spat Crasp, "with all due respect to your record."

"Thank you, sir."

"When are you going to learn?" Crasp went on, running a hand through what remained of his hair. "You can't simply do as you like with no regard to your fellow officers."

"Reprimand humbly accepted," said Coy, with a sweep of his

hand and a slight bow.

"Look," urged Crasp, "this is just politics. Keeping our reputation clean is what gives us the leeway to do what we do. And we're on the same side, god-dammit, Rivers is not the enemy."

"Understood," said Coy, sitting down and crossing his hands over his stomach. "I'll pass the suspect over right away."

"Yes, you will." Crasp reached for the door-handle. "How did it go, anyway? Did you get anything out of him?"

"Not a thing," said Coy, "he has balls. And Simon Lay is his solicitor."

"Simon Lay? That's very strange. Does this Reynolds have priors?"

"Not so much as a parking ticket."

"A puzzle then. Well, I'm sure Rivers will follow that up."

"I'm sure that he will, sir," said Coy, "I'm sure that he will."

Cambridge, one week previously

In the fragrant interior of the Golden Dragon, James and Tony gave their orders and waited for the waitress to depart.

"My sister's not even in Ukraine any more," said James, after the girl had left.

"Where is she?"

"Oh, I don't know. I haven't heard from her in months. The point is Schwarzkopf was just bluffing. Anyone doing a half-hour internet search could have found out about Juliette."

"What if they're not bluffing?"

"They are."

"If we get the money…"

"*When* we get the money," interrupted James.

"…Schwarzkopf might not leave us alone," said Tony.

"We can disappear," said James, "we can go anywhere you like."

"I don't know anywhere," said Tony, "but here."

"Then you can broaden your horizons. It'll be good for you. Are you sure the material is still safe?"

Tony nodded. "The important stuff's still with Rosalind. The rest is in my safe-spot."

"Good. Well then, we have nothing to worry about."

"I am worried," said Tony, "if they come after me…"

"They won't. They don't even know you're involved."

"But if they're following you…"

"Look," said James, "here's what we'll do. I'll handle everything. Why don't you disappear for a few days until the payment comes through? Leave Cambridge. Leave the country. Go to France, I don't know…"

"What if there is no payment?"

James scoffed. "Schwarzkopf is a businessman. It's going to be a lot less hassle for him to pay up than to commit murder. Don't you see—sending those goons to try and scare me just shows that he's up against a wall. He had nothing to lose. And if he was going to kill me, why try and shake me up first?"

Tony looked down, then back up at his friend. "You're gambling with our lives," he said.

James sighed. "I'm sixty-five," he said, "I live in a one-room bedsit. I have no savings. I'm only getting older and have no one to look after me." He tapped the top of the table with a forefinger. "I need this money. I deserve it." He sat back. "I deserve it."

Cambridge, present day

"Monte," said the dark-haired man who appeared from the doorway.

"Will?" Monte shook the proffered hand, "I though you'd moved on to *The Times*?"

"I did," said Will, "it didn't work out. Long story."

"Will, this is Harry. Harry, Will, an old friend."

"Come on up," said Will, "and tell me how I can help you."

"Well," Monte began, as they climbed the white-painted stairs to the second floor, "I'm looking for information on a man called Lucas Grundy. A freelance photographer. I'm not sure if he's still on your books."

"Name's not familiar," said Will, "but let's ask Peter. If anyone knows it will be Peter."

Peter, a somewhat hunched and elderly figure with a kind face, sat behind a desk in the far corner of the busy, open-plan office, behind a mountain of paperwork and folders.

"How are you today, Peter?" asked Will.

"Could be better," said the man, rising to shake hands with the newcomers, "I have no help at all here and we're already three weeks behind. Ridiculous."

"Monte Boutista," said Monte.

"Harry."

"These gentlemen," said Will, "are looking for anything we might have on Lucas Grundy. Apparently he works for us, or used to. Freelance photographer."

"Lucas Grundy?" Peter frowned, "yes, I know that name. Sad story. He died about fifteen years ago. Suicide. I still see his sister sometimes, she lives round the corner from me. I went to the funeral. Not a single manager from this place. Terrible."

"What sort of work did he do?" asked Monte.

"He was one of our regulars," said Peter, "a nice chap. Lots of people didn't take to him. Quite reserved. He was a good photographer. We used to call him in on assignments if we were a bit stretched. We only had one of our own then. Photographers, that is. These days we're expected to do it all ourselves. Ridiculous."

"Did he specialize in anything? News? Sport?"

"Local news, mostly. You know, I think we have a box of his things in the archive. I'm sure I saw it the other day. Would you like to see?"

"If that's okay?"

"Can I ask what your interest is?" said Peter.

Monte took out his card. "We're private investigators. We're trying to locate a missing person. We came across some information that connects our man with Lucas Grundy."

"I can vouch for them," said Will, "Monte's a professional."

Peter led them through a double door into the cloakroom area, then down a flight of barren concrete steps to a large, musty store room full of cages and shelves. The shelves were on electric tracks, so that only one row could be accessed at any one time. The motor revved noisily when Peter pushed the red button.

"Here we are," he declared after a minute or two's searching. He took out a medium-sized cardboard box. "I asked Valerie, that's the sister, if she wanted the contents, but she said if it was newspaper stuff then we ought to keep it."

"It's a good job we did," said Will.

The three men watched as Monte sorted through the contents. There were plenty of press-clippings from the stories that Grundy had contributed to. There was a notebook with an index that listed snaps he had taken, next to numbers that Monte assumed were film rolls.

"Would you have a store of his photographs?" Harry asked.

Peter shook his head. "About five years ago they had a cull. Everything more than ten years old was thrown out."

Underneath the notebook were sheets of paper to which were stapled receipts.

"Expenses," said Will. Peter nodded.

"The old dog," said Harry, in response to the stack of photographs underneath.

"Miss Cambridgeshire contestants," explained Peter, reading the notes on the back, "nineteen ninety-five. They'd be as old as your mother, now."

"What's this?' asked Monte, taking up a plain envelope. It was sealed. "May I?"

"Go ahead," said Peter, "if it's anything personal I can pass it on."

Inside were two photographs—a six-by-eight and a larger blow-up of the same picture. The black-and-white snap was of a well-dressed man in his thirties. He was standing in a doorway, looking straight at the camera with an expression of annoyance. His arm was around a pretty young woman, some ten years his junior. She looked uncomfortable and afraid. Her eyes appeared unfocused.

The man was unmistakably Christian Schwarzkopf.

"May I keep this for a while?" asked Monte, "I think it might prove very useful."

"If there's a story in this," said Will, half-jokingly, as he saw them out, "be sure to give me first-refusal."

Monte's phone rang as they were getting into the car. He listened, nodded, spoke a word of thanks and ended with "we'll see you later."

"Anything important?" asked Harry.

"The police have a possible suspect in custody for the murder of James Robertson."

"The fellow who got stabbed at the police station?"

"He died at the police station," said Monte, "he was stabbed in the middle of Parker's Piece."

"He was a friend of our missing guy, right?" said Harry.

"Probably his only friend."

"So couldn't that note I found be from Robertson?"

"I think that's very likely."

"Why did I get the feeling," said Harry, "that you're not telling me everything you know?"

He guided the car out into the road.

"If I'm not completely clued in," he continued, "then I can't do my best."

"Tonight," said Monte, "will be a working dinner. By the end of the evening you'll know as much as I do. One thing I can tell you now is that Robertson, before he died, was taking pictures of Christian Schwarzkopf's house."

"The millionaire Christian Schwarzkopf?"

"Yes, and that photo we just found—that's Schwarzkopf in the picture."

"I don't get it," said Harry, "how does this all tie up?"

"That's what we need to find out."

"So where to now, boss?"

"You can drop me in town," said Monte, "then go and find Aabira. She may need your help."

*   *   *   *   *

The Downing College archive was a series of rooms decked out in classical splendor—deep reds and polished oak, grand windows and pillared doorways. The secretary had been good enough to fetch out the Schwarzkopf files and now Aabira sat, alone in the vast room, with papers and news articles spread before her.

Late afternoon sunlight slanted in golden rectangles, casting a small bright and warm patch upon the surface of the desk where, for a moment, Aabira lay her hands and thought of nothing. A rare moment of stillness, she reflected, between family and study and work.

With a deep intake of breath, she roused herself and began methodically to sort through the various documents. There were academic records, pages taken from the student magazine reflecting Schwarzkopf's sporting and literary achievements, and cuttings taken from publications as diverse and illustrious as *Time Magazine*, *Business Insider* and *Investor's Chronicle*.

Much of this was ground she had already covered, but one file in particular caught her attention—a collection of articles concerning Christian Schwarzkopf's patronage of the Highfields Mental Health Hospital. There were a half dozen puff pieces that she had already come across, but also a color brochure from the hospital itself. On the cover was an eye-catching publicity shot of, according to the legend, 'staff, benefactors, dignitaries and patients.' Schwarzkopf was centre-stage, suited and beaming. Aabira looked about her, even though the room was empty. She pulled out her phone and took several shots of the brochure, including a close up of the front page.

*   *   *   *   *

Monte stood in the fading light at the edge of Parker's Piece, just across from the police station. The cold was beginning to bite at his hands, which held a street map. The traffic was light but increasing— the start of the daily exodus from place-of-work to the varied comforts of home. A few joggers circled the park. The lights in the Leisure Centre glowed warmly. The red light of a construction crane was the only star in the sky.

"Where were you going, James?' said Monte to himself. Far from home or any bus stop leading there. Perhaps the questions should be where had he come from? The restaurant? Monte made a mental note to go back and double check. What else was nearby? Had James been heading for the police station anyway? At nine o'clock in the evening? That made no sense. An assignation? Tony Perkins?

Monte strolled across the road and onto the Piece. As usual, cyclists abounded along the walkways, threading their way with impatience past pedestrians. As Monte approached the lamppost that marked the ground's centre he increased his pace. Standing in the yellow light, before the curious twisted fish marking the 'End of Reality,' Monte bent down as a light drizzle began to fall.

A solitary bouquet of flowers leaned against the base of the post. Monte carefully picked them up. The accompanying card bore no message, but it did bear the name 'Rosie's Roses' printed in swirling golden letters upon the reverse. Monte replaced the bouquet, stood up and turned back to the station.

*   *   *   *   *

"I just don't see the greatness in it," said Harry.

"You don't see greatness," exclaimed Aabira, "in religion?"

After going home to change, Harry had picked Aabira up outside Downing and now they were driving through the night amid the remnants of the rush hour traffic.

"I'll tell you where greatness is," said Harry, "it's in Sugar Ray Leonard stopping Tommy Hearns on his feet in the fourteenth round. It's in Ali coming off the ropes to knock out Foreman."

"Boxing," said Aabira, "is the very definition of pointless."

"Fighting is courageous."

"Using your fists is easy."

"Easy?"

"Yes," said Aabira, "next left. Not using your fists, that's the hard path."

Harry shook his head. "You don't understand." They drove on in silence for some time. "So whose house is it that we're going to?"

"Donald Coy," said Aabira, "he's an old friend of Monte's. A policeman. Detective Chief Inspector."

"That's pretty high up. I didn't think cops liked private investigators."

"Donald and Monte," began Aabira, but then she faltered, "they go back a long way."

The house was a modest detached property at the end of a quiet cul-de-sac.

Coy answered the door in suit pants and shirt, over which was a white chef's apron emblazoned with the words 'kiss the cook'. He embraced Aabira, and shook Harry's hand. There was an unmistakable smell of whiskey on his breath.

"Welcome in," he said to Harry, "and remember—what's said inside this house, stays inside this house."

Monte was seated in an old leather sofa in the large kitchen-dining room, leafing through a book on Mamluk, India. Penny sat next to him, with her needles and wool to one side, stroking a large black cat that had made a comfortable nest in her lap. Many other books populated standing units, shelves, a table or two, and part of the floor. Decorative lamps of Eastern design brought a cozy feel to the space, and here and there scented joss-sticks curled thin trails of smoke into the warm air.

Harry took an armchair, down the side of which he found an old magazine. "*Man, Myth and Magick*," he read the title aloud.

"A vital education," Coy called from the kitchen, where he was busy with various pans and plates.

"Are you sure he's a policeman?" Harry whispered to Aabira. Aabira smiled and shook her head.

"Not just any policeman," said Penny, "he's the best. Isn't that right, Don?"

"You bet."

Dinner was served around the big oak table—homemade soup with homemade bread, mushroom and chestnut roast with vegetables, sweet toffee pudding for dessert. It was, to Harry's surprise, delicious. Harry helped himself to wine. He was on the point of offering some to Aabira before Penny's raised eyebrow made him think again. Nevertheless, the conversation flowed easily and was good-natured in tone.

"More dessert, boy?"

Harry shook his head and patted his stomach.

"All the more for the cook," Coy heaped the last of the pudding into his bowl and poured himself another glass of wine. "Did you see that look—your boss is of the opinion that I am subconsciously eating and drinking myself into an early grave simply to avoid retirement. He thinks I don't know that he thinks that, but I do."

"We can only go by the evidence," said Monte.

"Harry could get you fit," said Aabira, and then blushed slightly. She looked at her watch. "It's time to pray."

Monte and Aabira absented themselves to another room whilst the remaining three sat making small talk and digesting their food. Harry picked up a photo from a table. "This is you and Monte?" he said to Coy, "Wow. How many years ago?"

"Not all that many," said Coy, "that was our graduation ceremony from university."

"Who's the girl?"

Coy took the photo from Harry's hand. "That's Monte's sister Sarrah," he said, and replaced the picture on the shelf.

"Where's she hiding these days?"

"Come and sit here for a moment," Penny patted the sofa next to her, "I've drawn up a few notes on your birth chart."

Upon the return of the others, they all helped with the dishes, washing and drying and storing. After all was done, they once more retired to the table.

"Let's get down to business," said Coy, lowering himself into his chair, "what do we have?"

"We have a dead body, James Robertson," said Aabira.

"Yes," said Coy, "and our man James Reynolds in custody, who may or may not be the killer. At any rate he was found in possession of the stolen scooter which we suspect the murderer made use of."

"Forensics?" Monte tapped the table with a long finger.

"Forty-eight hours," said Coy, "and we'll know if his prints match the moped. There were none on the knife, as you know. Don't forget Reynolds was seen in Schwarzkopf's garden."

"And thanks to Harry," said Monte, "we have a connection between Tony Perkins and Christian Schwarzkopf, although it's a little tenuous—the photographs on Tony's wall, all taken by the same man—Lucas Grundy."

"So who is Lucas Grundy?" asked Penny, squinting down through her bifocals.

"He was," said Monte, "a freelance journalist for the local press. He left a box of possessions in a store at the offices of *The Herald*. Grundy was tracking Schwarzkopf. He took this candid photo, and possibly more than we don't know about." Monte placed the photograph onto the table.

Aabira gave a start. "I think I recognize that girl." She took out her phone. "She's in a photograph in the hospital brochure I found at Downing. She's very memorable. See."

"Highfields," said Monte, and exchanged a look with Penny.

"It's an old photograph," said Penny, "this says 'Staff and patients'. It looks very much to me like our girl was one of the latter."

"Yes," Monte nodded, "all those on the right definitely have the look of patients."

"So Schwarzkopf's interest wasn't merely philanthropic," grunted Coy, going back to Grundy's snap.

"There's an insight into his character, if we needed one," said Penny, "abusing a vulnerable young woman."

"We don't know that he was abusing her," said Harry.

Penny pulled down her glasses. "I'll bet you my last teeth that he was."

"All the same," Harry shrugged, "so what's the link to our man Tony?"

"Robertson and Tony were friends," said Monte, "we know that they communicated in code and that they were working on something together. Tony had Grundy's pictures on his wall. Grundy was tracking Schwarzkopf."

"And the last images on James Robertson's camera were of Schwarzkopf's house," said Coy, "a pretty tangle. Don't forget that Grundy is also deceased, drowned. By his own hand."

"Do we think that Tony was killed too?" asked Aabira.

"He might just be hiding," said Harry, "well wouldn't you? Especially if you were the paranoid conspiracy type and your best friend's just been murdered."

Aabira sighed. "Well, what about Grundy then? Was it really suicide?"

"I'll look into it," said Coy, "I have the time now I'm off the Robertson case."

"What if we're making too big a deal out of all this?" said Harry.

"Then we'll find out," replied Monte, "one way or another. Let's not forget that our chief responsibility is with our client. We need to find Tony."

"Everything points to Schwarzkopf," said Aabira, "and didn't you say your murder suspect was seen in the grounds of his house?"

"At the base of every great fortune there lies a great crime," quoted Coy.

"So what do we do next?" asked Harry.

"Aabira," said Monte, "tomorrow I'd like you to find out more about Grundy. He has a sister still in the area. You should visit."

"What shall I tell her?"

"The truth," said Monte, "or a measure of it—that we're working on a case that may or may not be related."

Penny pulled a face. "People don't take kindly to digging up painful memories."

"I can handle it," said Aabira.

"Oh, I don't doubt that, dear, but perhaps you should take Harry. That handsome smile is a winner."

"Harry's going to be busy," said Monte, "we may have a lead on Tony." He held up the florist's card and placed it before them. "Somebody left flowers where James was stabbed on Parker's Piece. No name or message but the florist might remember."

"Is that everything covered?" asked Aabira, "I can visit the sister in the afternoon. I have an online study session in the morning."

Monte picked up Grundy's photo. "I'm going to try and find her."

"What about the book code?" asked Harry.

Coy crossed to a dresser and pulled open a drawer. He took two sheets of printed paper and placed them on the table. The first contained a series of book titles, the second a photocopy of a hand-written note consisting of seven lines of numbers. From her file, Aabira took out the note from Tony's flat, together with the list she had typed of all the books they had found there.

"Not a match here," said Penny.

Coy rubbed his considerable chin. "If it is a book code, and our experts think that it is, then it was a book that they didn't keep on them."

"Perhaps something at the library?" ventured Aabira.

"Could it be something else," said Harry, "maybe not a book at all?"

"It has to be something they both have easy access to."

"Visit Tony's flat again," said Monte, "See if there's any post, personal or otherwise. I'll ask his sister's permission to open it."

"It's going to be a busy day," said Coy, "a busy day indeed."

*   *   *   *   *

Early next morning Monte found Lee where he said he'd be, sitting on a bench in the middle of Christ's Pieces.

"Did you bring the bread?"

"Yes," said Monte, handing it over.

The sun waxed and waned as they sat, alternately bringing welcome waves of warmth and plunging the park into a grey chill. Lee's hands moved whilst his eyes stared into the distance. Pulling out slices of the bread, he tore it into chunks and threw them to the ground, where five or six ducks soon gathered, squabbling amongst themselves for the treat.

"Lee," said Monte gently, after a few minutes had passed.

"Spider," said Lee, "a man named Spider. Two lads from Romsey mentioned the name and then shut up quick. They said one of Spider's boys stabbed someone on Parker's Piece. They said this Spider used to hang with them but he's moved up. Done well for himself. Some high class big league stuff. Corporate."

"What are the names of these lads, Lee?"

Lee shook his head. "I don't know their names."

"Where was this?"

"Crack house on Samuel Road."

"What number?"

"It's on the corner. Red door."

"Do you know this Spider?"

"Heard of him. Been in the same room as him once."

"And?"

"Nut-case. Hard-nosed. Always fancied himself as something special. A white-collar criminal. Semi-educated. Not from the slums. Spent a year at University, so he says, and then got kicked out for doing some poor bastard in."

"Does he ever come to that crack house?"

Lee shook his head.

"No, this was three, four years back. Don't see him anywhere now."

"Anything else?"

"Not yet. Have you got ten pounds?"

"I'll buy you a meal."

Lee threw down the last of the bread. "If I hear anything else," he said, "I'll let you know."

* * * * *

Hardacre thanked PC Colin Wilkins. They parted ways rapidly as DCI Rivers appeared from around the corner.

"Good morning, sir," she said to Rivers as they passed. She seemed to feel his eyes on the back of her head.

Coy's door was open and the big man sat at his desk, peering through his glasses at some paperwork. At Hardacre's appearance, he removed the spectacles and tossed them to one side.

"What ho, Hardacre."

"Sir," Hardacre closed the door and took a seat.

"Forensics back?"

"Yes, and Reynold's prints are not on the scooter."

"Dammit," said Coy, "too much to ask for. That little brat is involved somehow."

"River's team is running some background checks, just in case."

"And you know this how? Ah…" Coy sat back, "young PC Wilkins was drafted onto the team, wasn't he. Do I see little cherubs flying in the air, Hardacre?"

"Do you want this information or not, sir?"

"You're no fun, Hardacre. What are they up to with Schwarzkopf?"

"Wilkins…that is, I don't know sir," she sighed, "alright, Wilkins is only on the leg work. Whatever else they're up to is very hush-hush. Rivers has a personal secure line and only his team are allowed onto the file-stream."

"Well, Hardacre, such is life. Have you much on today?"

"Only the paperwork on two dozen back cases and at least ten inquiries to follow up."

"Excellent," said Coy, "then you'll have plenty of time to check the archives to see what we have on one Lucas Grundy."

"Sir…"

"Superb," Coy checked his watch, "I emailed you the details. I think. Who knows where those messages end up. I have a check up with the doctor and then the pleasure of an afternoon meeting with Crasp. Phone me if you find anything. Cheer up, Hardacre—it's nearly Christmas."

*   *   *   *   *

Sarrah was in the patient's common room, in a hospital bed which had been wheeled to the window, so that the pale sunlight illuminated her frail form. Monte looked at the tube attached to his sister's thin arm.

"I'm sorry," she said, "I tried."

"I know," said Monte, "you have nothing to apologise for."

Sarrah leaned back into the pillows. "Tell me about the outside world."

"What's to tell?" said Monte. "The usual chaos and disorder and fake news and real news and everyone, more or less, just carrying on as normal. Work, shopping, watching TV, gardening."

"Sounds nice," said Sarrah.

Monte chuckled. "The staff here," he said, "are they…okay?"

"What do you mean?"

"No one troubles you?"

Sarrah shook her head.

"Does a man called Christian Schwarzkopf ever visit?"

"*The* Christian Schwarzkopf?" said Sarrah, "No. Why?"

"He's a patron," said Monte, "he and his father founded this place."

"Oh. Well, I've never seen him. I'm sure I would have noticed."

"Shall I read you some more?" said Monte, taking up a book.

"Please."

He read, but it wasn't long before Sarrah was asleep. Monte stayed for a while anyway, alternately staring at the clouds and the pronounced bones of his sister's face.

*   *   *   *   *

Rosie's Roses sat between a barber's and a news agent on an unassuming little street just around the corner from the station. There was a rustic-style display behind the large window and rows of plastic containers filled with seasonal flowers before it. Powerful scents assailed Harry's nose as he entered.

The woman behind the counter was middle-aged, with a large pile of dark hair and an attractive, if homely, face. "How can I help you, dear?" she asked.

"This is a lovely shop," said Harry.

"Thank you. Is there anything in particular that you're looking for? Something for the girlfriend?" the florist's eyes flickered down to Harry's hand. "Wife?"

"Actually, I'm trying to track down a friend of mine."

"Oh, yes."

"It's for his sister. He's gone missing and he has…some mental health problems."

"Poor dear."

"Yes, only we think he might have bought some flowers from here recently. We found a card."

The woman pulled on the spectacles that had been hanging around her neck as Harry handed over the card. She looked at both sides.

"Well that's ours alright, but without a name there's not much we can do."

"Tony Perkins is the name. Here, I have a photo."

"Yes," said the lady, looking closely, "I think I do remember him. Funny looking chap. He, you'll excuse me saying, smelled a bit, even in here. I remember thinking he looked homeless. Spent a fair bit on the flowers though."

"When was this?"

"Yesterday morning. I remember because he was outside at eight o'clock. We don't open till nine but I felt sorry for him."

"Did he say what they were for?"

"No," said the woman, "I'm sorry."

"I don't suppose he said anything else that might be useful?"

"Well," said the woman, taking off her glasses, "I remember he said he was local. Sorry love, I'm afraid that's all I can tell you."

"Did you happen to notice which way he went?"

"Yes," she said, "left."

"Thank you," said Harry, "you've been incredibly helpful, really."

*   *   *   *   *

The Highfields Adolescent Mental Health Facility stood in its own small grounds, behind a stone wall which ran the length of a busy thoroughfare. There was a generous entrance way, with iron gates that stood open. The facility itself was some hundred yards back, utilitarian two-story buildings connected to the larger, grander main. Large bay windows let into the left-hand side of the nearest face.

In the lay-by opposite, behind the window of his Ford Cortina,

Richard Jarsdel surveyed the building through micro-binoculars. "What do you know about the place?" he asked.

"Not much," Monte lied, from the passenger seat.

"I can see a Simex alarm system," said Richard, "CCTV covering the front, presumably the rear too. Is it a residential unit?"

"Yes."

"Then they'll have night wardens. It's one specific record that you're after? It would be less risk to hack into the database."

"We're talking fifteen to twenty years gone," said Monte, "it'll be a paper file."

"Mostly likely in a locked cabinet. And you're sure that it's in there?"

"Government rules state records be kept for a minimum of twenty years from the last point of contact. I'd say it's likely."

"People on-site," said Richard, "only one easy exit."

"Can it be done?" asked Monte.

"Anything can be done," said Richard, lowering the binoculars, "it won't be cheap. I'll need time to study the schedule, plus at least two other bodies."

"Just let me know what you need."

Richard stoked his chin. "A bit of luck and a full set of building plans would be nice. The last I can get for myself, if you have any sway over the former, please give it your best shot."

*   *   *   *   *

"What have you got for me, Hardacre?" Coy sipped his chai latte and licked his lips.

"Apart from my undivided attention and one hundred percent of my time?" said Hardacre, "nice coffee is it?"

"RHIP," said Coy, "rank hath its privileges. Is that the file on Lucas Grundy?"

"Yes, sir." Hardacre took a seat. "Pretty straightforward. He was found dead in a stream on Davy Road, just next to Coleridge Park. Drowned. Coroner was pretty clear on the verdict."

"Was he indeed."

"Yes. Water ingested into the lungs. He was alive when he went in. Couple of parking tickets. One public disorder offence. Seems he was disrupting a legitimate protest by some pro-Israeli group. Statements from the sister say he was prone to depression and under pressure at work. He was a freelance journalist."

"Like James Robertson."

Hardacre put down the file. "Is that what this is about?"

"Probably nothing, Hardacre. Mum's the word. What's the latest from Casanova on the inside?"

"It's not fair asking me to do this, sir."

"I know. I'll make it up to you."

"You've been saying that for three years."

"Patience is a virtue and so on."

Hardacre sighed. "Nothing new on our suspect. No other connections and his girlfriend is giving him an alibi. They're going to let him go."

"So we're supposed to believe that scooter ended up there by chance. What do you make of the Schwarzkopf connection?"

"That boy being there, and Roberstson's photos? I'd like to know more, but to be honest sir, it's out of our hands and I have a mountain of paperwork."

Coy drained the last of his tea. "I won't detain you any longer Hardacre. You are a free woman."

"Thank you, sir."

"Leave the file, please."

Hardacre turned at the door. "Sir, word is MI6 are taking this pretty seriously."

"You never said a word to me."

"It's not me I'm worried about," said Hardacre, "it's you."

*   *   *   *   *

"Then you're no closer to finding him?" Alison Perkins tried vainly to keep the frustration out of her voice.

"We have a lead," said Monte, who was seated in his customary chair on the other side of the desk. "We think perhaps his disappearance is linked to a perceived threat, either real or imaginary."

"What threat?"

"James Robertson. It seems he and Tony were working on a project together, possibly concerning the death of a journalist some years ago. I think Tony was scared."

"Of what?"

"I don't know yet. My guess is that he went into hiding, and then when James was murdered it drove him deeper underground. I've emailed you a full report."

"I know," Alison sighed, "it doesn't make much sense, Mr. Boutista, and to be frank I'm not sure I'm getting my money's worth."

"I'm sorry you feel that way, Mrs Perkins. We will find Tony."

"Tony is a fantasist," said Alison, "I know that. All that in your email about secret codes and conspiracies. Do you think any of it could be true?"

Monte paused. "That's also part of our investigation."

Alison drew a pile of papers from her bag. She laid them upon the desk. "Tony's post. I picked it up from the flat."

"I had a man going there today," said Monte, "this will save us some time."

After she had left, Monte pulled the elastic band from the papers. Turning to the window, he began to sort through them in the light of the sun. The bank statement he opened at once. He scanned through it quickly, circled a half-dozen entries with his pen, and picked up his phone.

*   *   *   *   *

Donald Coy leaned on the balcony, sipping his sweet coffee and watching the players on the squash court below. The squeak of sneakers and dull thud of the ball grated on his nerves, though he derived a certain pleasure from observing the battling alpha-males, sweating and straining, inevitably looking ridiculous as the small rubber sphere swooshed past just out of their reach.

As the game drew to a close, Coy finished his coffee and ambled downstairs, through the plush reception to a seating area outside of the changing rooms. He took a seat, fished out his glasses and began to read the latest issue of *The Fortean Times*, which he habitually kept in the inside of his coat pocket. He was halfway through an article on 'blank-eyed-kids' when Coroner Leigh Farmoor-Dawley appeared, his kit-bag slung over one shoulder.

"Donald," he exclaimed, "what on earth brings you so dangerously close to physical activity."

Coy carefully folded his magazine and stood up. "I'd say between the two of us, you look the closer to a heart attack right now."

"I take it this is business?"

"Your deduction is better than your back-hand."

Leigh grunted. He checked his watch. "I'm due back in the office in twenty minutes."

"This will only take ten. I'll buy you a carrot juice."

"Make it a latte."

They took a table in the corner of the white-washed canteen. Bay windows looked out onto the lawn, and let in the autumn sunshine. Two young lads in muscle shirts and shorts were the only other occupants.

"It's a cold case," said Coy, "nineteen-ninety-eight. I took the liberty of requesting the file that your office supplied us."

Leigh fished out his own glasses, balanced them on his nose and peered down at the manila folder.

"Ah, yes," he nodded, leafing through, "Lucas Grundy. Yes, he was one of mine. Pretty straightforward case from what I see here.

Suicide. Diatom test was conclusive. Lung distension. Non-specific lesions. Blood-alcohol very high. I really can't see what else I can tell you."

"Why suicide? Why not 'death by misadventure' or 'accidental'?"

"Well," said Leigh, taking off his glasses, "I really think you chaps should know more about that."

"How so?" said Coy.

"I don't believe there was a criminal investigation. This file says that witnesses were examined. I presume that you chaps came to the same conclusion that we did."

"You," said Coy.

"I beg your pardon?"

"The same conclusion that you did."

"Well. Yes."

"The file also mentions bruising on the shoulders and wrists."

"Does it? This really was a long time ago." Leigh checked his watch.

"There's nothing else you remember about the case?"

"Like I said," said Leigh, rising, "it really was straightforward. May I ask why you are enquiring?"

"His name came up as part of an ongoing investigation," said Coy, closing the file, "I'm sure it's nothing. Like you said—it all seems straightforward."

As Leigh left, Coy rose and crossed to the corner of the window. There was a small gap from between where the curtain hung and the edge of the frame. He watched Leigh throw his bag into the boot of his crimson Rolls and climb into the driver's seat. Leigh held his head in his arms for a moment, before dialing a number on his mobile and holding it to his ear as with one hand he guided the car out onto the driveway.

*   *   *   *   *

In the taxi, Aabira took a moment to gather her thoughts. *I can handle it*, she remembered saying, words which now stung as the butterflies rose in her stomach. She realised that the driver had been speaking.

"Excuse me?" she said.

"I said I bet you're glad of that headscarf in this cold, luv."

Aabira smiled thinly. This was not what she needed.

The sister of Lucas Grundy lived in an unexceptional cul-de-sac; her house was semi-detached and modest.

I'll never be able to afford anything like that, not on my own, was Aabira's first thought, as the taxi drew to a halt. Alone on the pavement, she took a couple of deep breaths and ran through some opening lines in her head. She could see no signs of life through the window. She pressed the bell, half-hoping the sister was not at home.

There was movement behind the frosted glass pane. The woman who opened was in her fifties or early sixties. Her hair was long and dark with flashes of white. She wore a plain cardigan and a woolen skirt.

"Lucille Grundy?"

"Yes," said the woman.

"My name is Aabira. I work for a private investigation firm. I was wondering if I could have a chat with you about your brother, Lucas."

*   *   *   *   *

Tony Perkins' flat was as dark and dank as Harry remembered. *How could anyone live like this?* he thought as he stood and surveyed the scene. It disgusted him—people with no drive or ambition or self-respect, living like pigs, with no dreams, nothing to separate them from anyone else, their lives empty and without purpose. *Isn't that you now*, he thought, staring into the filthy mirror on the desk. He was keeping himself busy for a reason, he knew, but the truth was always there. Without boxing he was just another Tony Perkins.

He turned away. There was no post, not even circulars. Not even junk mail could be bothered with this place. On the way out, Harry's phone rang. It was Monte.

"Alison Perkins just dropped off Tony's post, she collected it last night," he said, "Tony still gets his bank statements on paper. The only entries for the past week are a cashpoint in the co-op on Brookgate, off Hills Road. Use that smart phone of yours and get a list of B-n-Bs within a mile of there. Visit them in person. Are you okay?"

"I'm fine," said Harry, "why wouldn't I be?"

As a light drizzle began to fall, Harry turned South and began to walk.

*   *   *   *   *

The interior of Lucille Grundy's house was light and airy and very neat, full of hand-crafted cushions, polished wood surfaces and shelves adorned with animals in glass and porcelain. Lucille took a photo from the mantelpiece and passed it to Aabira. It was of a young Lucas in fishing gear, standing thigh-deep in a river and smiling broadly.

"This is how I like to remember him," she said.

"He was very handsome," said Aabira.

"I was never happy with the verdict. Suicide. Such an awful word."

"You think that the coroner got it wrong?"

Lucille sat and smoothed down her dress. She reached for the pot of tea and began to pour.

"Milk?" she said, "sugar?"

"No sugar. Thank you."

Aabira waited patiently for the woman to compose herself.

"There were bruises on his shoulders and arms when they… That was never explained."

"Was he upset about anything at the time?"

"Lucas was always upset about something. Politics, injustice, the state of the world. He was a socialist. We both were. I still am, but I was never as committed as Lucas."

"Miss Grundy…"

"Lucille."

"Lucille, did your brother ever mention a man called Christian Schwarzkopf?"

Lucille put down her tea. "Yes," she said, "he talked about him a lot. He didn't like him. He said he was a criminal, the worst of the worst."

"Did he ever explain that?"

"I suppose he did. Yes, probably. I'm afraid I never listened enough. Lucas liked to talk. Why have you come here now? You mentioned an investigation?"

Aabira passed over Monte's card. "My employer. We're working on a missing person case. The man in question kept a lot of press photos taken by your brother."

"Oh. So, you're just checking? I thought perhaps…"

"If we find anything new about Lucas, anything at all, then we'll let you know. I don't suppose…do you have any of his work? Files, clippings…"

"I lost them all," said Lucille, "not long after he died my house was burgled. After Lucas's death I kept some of his things. There was a, what do you call it? A strong box. I always meant to get a locksmith, but it didn't seem urgent. Whoever broke into my house took it. I suppose they imagined that there where valuables inside. They must have been very disappointed. My brother was not a rich man."

Outside on the street, Aabira called Harry's phone but he didn't answer. She rang for a taxi, and as she waited, she thought of Lucas Grundy. A crusader for justice, that was how Lucille had described him. Despondency crept over her. *Isn't it true*, she thought, *that none of us do enough?*

*   *   *   *   *

DCI Rivers found Donald Coy in the saloon bar of the Trout and Whistle, hunched over a plate of salmon, a pint of ale to one side.

"Have a seat," said Coy, "drink?"

Rivers eyed the surroundings with distaste. He squeezed himself into the booth.

"Donald…" he began.

"Ah, first names. This must be serious?"

"I'll be frank," said Rivers, "I need you to stop interfering with my investigation."

"Part of my job," said Coy, taking a sip of his beer, "is to monitor all ongoing cases conducted by personnel in my station."

"Don't give me that nonsense," said Rivers, "I came here, informally, because I'm told you're a good copper."

"Doubly serious," said Coy. He chewed a mouthful of salmon. "How about we collaborate?"

Rivers looked puzzled. "Donald, if you have any information I don't know about, you have a duty to share it."

"Who said I did? But my insight could prove valuable."

Rivers shook his head. "I can see I'm getting nowhere," he started to rise.

"James Reynolds," said Coy, "I saw him myself at Christian Schwarzkopf's place."

Rivers sat back down. "Go on."

"Reynold's solicitor is as dirty and as slick as they come and I'm betting he also works for Schwarzkopf. I am assuming that you've looked into this?"

"I'm not as inept as you seem to believe."

"A man died in my station," said Coy, "I'm not about to let that go."

"We are actively investigating the murder of James Robertson."

"So, are you shielding Schwarzkopf? Or are you using him?"

Rivers ran a hand through his hair. "You need to let this go," he said.

"I would like to help you," said Coy, "but first I need to know your intent."

"You're making a mistake, Donald."

"Stop calling me Donald, for christ's sake. And get down from your high horse."

Rivers stood. "If you persist in butting heads, this is not going to go easy for you."

"Money talks, Rivers. Does it talk to you?"

Rivers was already moving away, and a second later he was gone.

*   *   *   *   *

The killer awoke with frozen limbs and pain in his legs and back. It took a while before he realised he had been woken by the sound of the bin-men. He had lain all night under a hedge in a narrow alley that ran through the backs of a dozen houses on Cowper Road. He lay for some moments, trying to clear the fog in his mind. He'd had a plan for today, a purpose. What was it? London. That was it. He was going to hitchhike to London, he was going to get away. Once there he'd head towards the universities. Maybe there was work there, cash-in-hand. They'd see he was bright. Educated. Maybe he could get something going. Be a bag-man. There must be plenty of drugs going around.

There were sounds from behind the garden fence of the nearest property. The killer struggled to pull himself free from the branches in which he had become entangled. One of his shoes came off in the process. The sounds in the garden grew closer. The killer, balanced on one foot, swore. He put his socked foot down in a puddle and reached to grab the errant trainer. He was jamming it back onto his foot when the garden gate opened.

The killer stumbled away. A man's voice called "hey," and then "hey," again, but the killer did not stop.

*   *   *   *   *

Harry was standing in the queue at the co-op, impatiently staring out of the window when he saw Tony Perkins. Harry did a double take. He fished out the photo from his wallet, looked at it and then back at the disheveled man who was making his way towards the door. The man disappeared from view behind a poster but then reappeared in the doorway, where his sunken eyes met Harry's. For a moment they both stood still. Then Tony turned and ran.

Harry pushed his way through shoppers. By the time he was out on the pavement Tony's dumpy form was some way down the street and moving fast. Harry began to run. "Tony," he called. Perkins looked back over his shoulder as he crossed a side street and increased his pace. Harry nearly ran into the car that screeched to a halt just in time. He made to cross again but the driver, misinterpreting, or perhaps not caring, lurched forward, cutting him off.

Harry swore and ran on, earning a blast from the car's horn. He pushed his way angrily through a crowd who were exiting a cafe. "Tony," he shouted again, although he had no hope of making the man stop. At the corner he stopped and looked round wildly. He went east, swiveling his head to scan the street. Then he saw his target, some fifty metres away, leaning over with his hands on his knees. Tony saw Harry at the same time, gave a start, and set off across the road, towards the train station.

By the time Harry reached the plaza, Tony was at the entrance. Tony turned. Harry stopped and raised his hands. Tony took a folder from his battered leather satchel and dropped the bag. As Harry began to walk towards him, Tony looked round in desperation. Harry took advantage and began to sprint. Tony jumped and ran into the station. When Harry reached the entrance, Tony had already run through an open barrier and was standing on the platform looking back, the folder clutched tightly to his chest.

Harry nodded his head, slowed to a walk, and moved purposefully forward. Tony licked his lips, closed his eyes and, a second before the incoming train reached the platform, he let himself fall backwards onto the track. Someone screamed, the train's horn blared, and Harry, eyes wide, sunk to his knees.

*   *   *   *   *

Monte had the taxi drop him at the entrance to Wandlebury Park. It was a fine day, sharply cold but sunny. Monte felt relaxed as he walked up the gravel path onto the mud track. Yellow shafts of late afternoon light shot through winter-bare branches, a large patch of snowdrops shone humbly, nodding their heads in the breeze. Monte thought of Harry. "It's not your fault," he had told him, "Tony was already running, and not from us. I am to blame for bringing you into this."

In truth, though, Monte knew it had hit the boy hard. He planned to speak to him again, as soon as this day was over. Monte felt uncomfortable for not feeling worse about Tony Perkins, but he knew the real villains were out there, he felt it. Whatever Tony and James had stumbled upon was real enough to get them both killed. What was needed now was to push on through and discover the truth.

It was a fifteen-minute walk to the large open declivity, a wide patch of grass surrounded by moderate slopes, with long wooden tables and benches in its centre. Richard sat at the end of one of these, separated from a group of adults and children who were enjoying tea and snacks, all of them wrapped up against the cold. Soon the weather would be too unseasonable for picnics.

Richard wore sunglasses and a hiker's grey jacket and hat. He rose to greet Monte and together they walked on into the woods.

"Plans were easy to find," said Richard, "and from observation we can guess the rest. The big unknown is where the files are. Depending on time there's no guarantee."

"And no second chance," said Monte, "I understand. When can you be ready?"

"There's a slight delay. One of my men is out of action. I'm looking for a reliable replacement."

"Is it something I can do?"

Richard shook his head. "Nothing personal Monte, but I never take my clients into the field."

"It's a beautiful day," said Monte, "what do you do, when you're not doing this?"

"Work is my hobby," said Richard, "I enjoy it."

"You find it fulfilling?"

"Yes."

"Spiritually?"

Richard laughed. "I'm not sure what that means."

"Perhaps you should take some time to find out."

They walked on in silence.

"Are you trying to convert me, Monte?"

"I'm not so sure of myself as to play the role of anybody's guide," said Monte, "I don't know anything more or less than any other soul."

"Somehow," said Richard, "I doubt that."

By this time, they had reached the car-park.

"Can I drop you somewhere?"

"Back at the office, and then on to Coleridge Road, if you would. There's someone I need to see."

*   *   *   *   *

Aabira called at Harry's dad's place around noon. Harry's dad answered the door.

"Hi," she said, "I'm Aabira. I work with Harry."

"Come in luv," he smiled, "I'm Frank. Harry's mentioned you."

I wonder what he said, was the first thing that ran through Aabira's mind.

The house was modern, but with a homely, lived-in feel. Aabira sat in one of the comfortable armchairs, looking out through patio doors to a well-kept garden. Rain pattered the windows and all else was quiet.

"I'll fetch him down," said Frank, "then we'll have a cuppa."

Minutes passed. Aabira was beginning to doubt that she should have come when Harry finally emerged, dressed in sweatpants and a gym shirt. There was stubble on his chin and his hair had not been brushed. He took a seat on the sofa.

"Hey," he said, without meeting her eyes. "How's things?"

"Harry," said Aabira, then she stopped, stood, and moved to sit beside him. She placed a hand on his arm. "I came to see how you were."

Harry shook his head. "I shouldn't have chased him. He died because of me."

"No."

"You don't understand. I was…frustrated. Pent up. When I saw him and he ran I was angry. I looked angry. That's what he saw. That's why he didn't stop."

"He was paranoid. Normal people don't throw themselves under a train."

Harry ran a hand through his hair.

"Tea?" asked Frank from the doorway.

Aabira took her hand from Harry's arm and moved back. "Thank you."

"Be nice to the lady, lad. She came because she cares. Ain't that right?"

"Yes."

"How's Monte?" asked Harry.

"He's following leads today. He's concerned about you."

"I thought the case was closed. We found Tony, right?"

"We're not going to stop. Not until we find who killed James Robertson, and who Tony was really running from."

"I still don't see much of a connection."

"Lucas Grundy. Robertson. They were all investigating Christian Schwarzkopf. Tony was holding a file, right?"

"Yes."

"Well, what if that was the same file that was stolen from Grundy's sister?"

Harry crossed his arms. He sighed.

His dad came in bearing a tray with three cups and a jug of milk.

"You cheered him up, yet?"

"I'm trying, sir."

"Frank."

Aabira wrapped her hands around the warmth of the proffered cup.

"It's not his fault," said Frank, "that's what I keep telling him. He was doing his job, that's all."

"Dad…"

"Dad, nothing. You pick yourself up, lad, you learn from your mistakes and you carry on. Right, miss?"

"Yes."

"I'll leave you two to it," said Frank. He gave Aabira a warm smile before he left.

"You should come back to work," said Aabira, "when you're ready. I think it might do you good."

"Everyone has ideas," said Harry, "about what's best for me."

For a while they sat and listened to the rain.

*   *   *   *   *

The Twenty-two Club was seldom open at this hour, but when Donald Coy knocked loudly on the sub-basement door and flashed his ID through the partially-frosted glass the door opened to reveal a young woman in a red top and slacks. She wore large hoop earrings and an uninterested expression.

"Is Stan in?"

The woman rolled her eyes and stepped aside. "He's in the office. Stan," she called out, "some copper's here to see you."

Stanley Unwin was in his early fifties, tall, thin and balding, and dressed fashionably for the nineteen-seventies. The top three buttons of his shirt were undone, and a large gold medallion nestled in the thick, dark hairs of his chest. He poked his head out of a side door, made an audible sound of disgust and then waved a thin arm. "Come in."

Coy surveyed Stan's office. It was expensively decked out, but untidy. Overflowing ashtrays jostled for room next to billiards trophies, half-open boxes, drink bottles and executive toys. Stan sprawled in a chair behind his desk, hands behind his head. He yawned.

"Keeping you up?"

"Hard at work," said Stan, "what the hell do you want?"

"I'm here to check your receipts," said Coy, "I've been seconded to the IRS."

"Give over." Stan screwed up his face.

"Alright," said Coy, "do you keep an up-to-date list of your members, mister Unwin?"

"Course I do, but you ain't seeing it."

Coy nodded. "That carton of fags come with an invoice?"

Stan stared. "Fuck you," he said. He opened a drawer and took out a leather-bound book. He opened the book and passed it over.

"Good boy," said Coy, putting on his glasses. "Well, well. Coroner Leigh Farmoor-Dawley. Does he still come here every other Thursday?"

"Regular as clockwork."

"And Christian Schwarzkopf?"

"Man's a gent. We put on something special for him." Stan grinned.

"What would that be?"

"I'll be having that book back now. Unless you got a warrant."

"What about a man named Rivers. A copper. Tall, bald. He would have been a recent guest."

Stan shook his head. "Nah."

"Does Schwarzkopf come alone?"

Stan sniffed and brushed an imaginary speck of dust from his desk.

"When was the last time this place was audited?" asked Coy. "I can get people down here so fast you won't have time to say, 'license rescinded'," he threw the book on the desk, "you weasely little worm."

Stan lit a fag. "Alright," he said, "Alright. Mr. Schwarzkopf comes in with his best boy, cocky fella, not tall, but built. Crazy fucking eyes."

"He have a name, this best boy?"

"He don't need a name," grinned Stan.

"What do you mean?"

"You can't miss him," Stan made a motion across his face, "he's got this big spider's-web tattoo on his neck."

"On his neck?"

"That's it."

"Do you have CCTV?"

Stan shook his head. "Complete privacy here. It's a selling-point."

"I'll bet it is," said Coy, "I'll bet."

*   *   *   *   *

Monte stood in the twilight on a patch of grass at the western side of the Coleridge Recreation Park. The rectangle of dark water had once been a swimming pool. Long since abandoned, it now stood as a bleak monument to failed community projects. Monte knelt down at its side, picturing the scene when they had found Lucas Grundy's body, face down and lifeless.

He removed a glove and lowered his hand into the chill water. For ten minutes he knelt, meditating, hoping for the feeling to arrive, until his fingers were numb past the point of pain. Finally, he stood up. Whatever had happened here was too far removed in time. All he could get was a distant feeling of confusion.

He understood that there had been a struggle though, and for a moment the unmistakable sharp haze of a hangover stabbed through his head, together with the strong smell of spirits. It had been a long, long time since Monte had drunk, but he recalled the experiences clearly.

Sitting, for a moment, on the abandoned swing, he took out his phone and scrolled down the list of contacts. His thumb paused over the entry for Sumiyyah. For a long while it paused. Twice he started to dial and then disconnected. "Fool," he said to himself, and put away the phone.

Monte regarded the houses opposite, a row of expensive white-faced flats, glowing with warm yellow light. The bare trees before them were stark shadows against the darkening sky. He did not at first notice the hooded figure standing motionless by the railings. When he did the teenage boy pulled down his hood, revealing his shaved head. The youth grinned widely and, with his eyes fixed on Monte, made a slow cutting motion across his neck.

Monte narrowed his eyes, looked left and right, stood up and started walking towards the boy. When he was fifty feet away the boy turned and jogged across the road and into a narrow alley. Monte lifted himself over the railings and followed, feeling in his pocket for his torch. At the entrance to the alley he paused and was about to turn back when the sound came as of somebody scrambling over a fence. Monte flicked on the torch and started forward.

The walls of the alley were around six feet high, in places brick, in others wood, with garden-doorways at regular intervals. Monte walked halfway in. The boy was nowhere to be seen. He turned to go back. At the entrance there now stood three figures, hooded and shadowed, hands held low and grasping long, thin shapes that might be blades or clubs. There was a scrape from behind. Monte knew before he turned what he would see. Another group of figures stood at the far end. He was trapped and even as he cursed himself the figures on either side began to laugh and whoop and walk towards him.

Monte tried the nearest door, gripping the handle and pushing his shoulder against it, but it stood firm. He began to shout, calling for help. His breath misted, the boys cried louder and their footsteps sped up to a run. Monte tried the next door and then the next, shoving with all his weight.

Finally, one gave, just an inch or two. He was acutely aware of the voices growing louder and louder. He took a half-step back and kicked. This time the door gave a good eight inches and Monte pushed himself through, panicking for an instant as his arm became trapped, but at last managing to pull it free with a tearing sound.

Monte slammed the wooden door shut and leaned his weight against it as heavy, jolting blows threatened to explode the entire thing inward. He knew he couldn't hold them for long. The light in the back window of the house whose garden he was now in was on. He called out. Something sharp smashed through the wood above his right shoulder. Monte lunged forward and ran towards the house. He heard a loud smash and pursuing feet.

The back door opened, letting forth a pool of yellow light. A figure stood framed against it, large and imposing. "What's going on?" it shouted, "hey!"

Monte stumbled at the figure's feet and pointed backwards. "They're trying to kill me," he said.

"Get out of here," cried the man into the shadows.

A hand grasped hold of Monte's arm, helping him up.

"Come in brother," said the man, "you're safe now. You're safe."

*   *   *   *   *

The killer hitched his first ride up on the ring road. Scowling and sticking out his thumb, it had been an hour before a car had slowed down and pulled onto the hard shoulder. It was a blue Nissan. It looked new. The killer was shivering when he got into the passenger seat. The driver was a middle-aged white guy, with thin blonde hair and glasses. He wore a suit and a bowtie and smiled curiously.

"Hello," he said, "where to?"

"London."

The man nodded and they pulled out into the traffic. "I can take you some of the way," he said, "my name is Nathan."

The killer said nothing. Nathan licked his lips. "Cold out tonight," he said.

"Yes."

"You look freezing." Nathan reached into the glove compartment and pulled out a half-bottle of whiskey. "This'll warm you up."

The killer stared at it for a while. Then he screwed off the cap and took a deep swig. He coughed, wiped his mouth on his sleeve, and took another drag.

"Warm you up, eh?" said Nathan.

The killer looked out the window at the charging lights and at the painted lines on the road as they raced in and out, a crazy geometry to match the crazy world. He began to feel the warmth of the whiskey spreading up from his stomach.

"I'm going to see my sister," he said, "thank you."

"Family problems?"

"I lost my rail-card," the killer took another swig from the bottle.

Nathan reached out a hand and placed it on the killer's thigh.

"We could go somewhere and get really warm," he said, in a thick voice.

The killer squirmed away. "What are you doing?"

"Come on," said Nathan, "I'm giving you a lift. I gave you whiskey. Don't tell me you didn't know when you got in."

"Fuck you," said the killer, "stop the car."

"Don't be a bitch. I'm not asking much."

The killer banged his fist against the window and the windscreen. "I said stop the car."

"Jesus," said Nathan, "alright you little prick." He swerved the Nissan onto the hard shoulder and brought it to a halt.

"Little prick," he shouted again as the killer opened the door and leaped. Bottle still in hand, he disappeared into the night.

*   *   *   *   *

"Thank you," said Monte. He took another sip of the sweet tea.

"Must have been quite a shock," Shahid, the man who had opened his backdoor, was tall and sturdy, with a fine black beard and a soft voice. His wife, Gayatri, round-faced and welcoming, sat beside him in their living room. "Are you sure you don't want to call the police?" she said, again.

"My friend is a Detective Inspector. I'll report it straight to him. And I want to pay you for your garden door."

Shahid waved a hand. "Don't worry about that. I'm just glad it was already broken enough for you to get in. What do you think they were after? Money?"

Monte shook his head. "I don't think it was that," he said, "I promise my friend will investigate. And I really do want to pay you for..." he was interrupted by the sound of his phone ringing.

"Speak of the devil," he said, "it's my policeman friend. Do you mind...?"

"No, not at all."

Twenty minutes later Coy's car pulled up outside the house. The detective shook hands with Shahid. They briefly inspected the garden. "I'll have a team here in the morning," said Coy, "we may be able to get some prints."

On their way back to town, Monte told the story in detail.

"This was planned," he said, "they must have been watching the shop."

"I'm going to put Hardacre on it, first thing," said Coy, "they must have used two or three cars, or a van. Are you sure you didn't see any van?"

Monte shook his head.

"How's the kid?"

"Harry? I spoke to him last night. He's not doing good."

"Perkins didn't throw himself under a train for no reason. I spoke to the coroner about Lucas Grundy. He said there was nothing suspicious. He was lying. He also frequents the same club as Schwarzkopf. Did any of those youths have a spider web tattoo on their neck?"

"I didn't get a close look. They were wearing hoodies."

"Hmm. The club owner described this spider web man as Schwarzkopf's best boy."

"Shouldn't be too hard to find with a marking like that."

Coy absently chewed a nail as he drove. "Maybe you shouldn't go back to the shop."

"I don't want to leave Penny on her own."

"If these are the same people who did for James Robertson, they're not playing around."

"I think they were just trying to scare me off."

"You want to drop this and lay low for a while."

"No," said Monte, "I want to know the whole story. I want to find out who killed James and Lucas Grundy. I want to find out what they had on Christian Schwarzkopf."

Coy nodded. "Well," he said, "then let's do it."

$$* \quad * \quad * \quad * \quad *$$

Penny Trasker knew trouble when she saw it and she saw it often. When you have your eyes open, you do. It was a perfect cliché, only at least this time the van was blue, not white. It had pulled up opposite the shop at six o'clock that evening and remained motionless ever since. It had no business being there. No one got out or in. From time to time the man behind the shaded windscreen talked on his phone.

Penny shut the shop at seven and went upstairs to watch the vehicle from the window. Around fifteen minutes later a scooter pulled up and the helmeted driver exchanged words with man in the van before accelerating away with a high-pitched whine up the street.

Five minutes after that Penny phoned one-oh-one and reported the suspicious activity to the police. Then she made herself a cup of jasmine tea, pulled a chair up to the window and continued to watch.

*   *   *   *   *

"Barney," the killer hissed, his breath streaming up into the night air.

Barney, in his early twenties, with a shock of jet-black hair, stood up from where he had been squatting in the open doorway, taking a long drag on his cigarette. He peered into the dark of the garden. "Who's there?"

"It's me," whispered the killer, coming closer.

"Jesus," said Barney, glancing back at house, "where have you been? Spider's been going mental."

"I did it, Barney. I stabbed that man, just like they told me to. I killed him."

"Yes, I know. It's been all over the news. Why didn't you meet Spider and Eddie like you were supposed to?"

"I did," said the killer, "I heard them talking, about how they had to get rid of me. They said I was a liability. They said I was weak. That's why they chose me to do it."

"No," said Barney, "you must have heard wrong. Eddie wouldn't do that."

A figure inside the house passed by the window. The killer slunk back into the shadows. "Listen. Can you help me? Tell them they don't have to kill me. Tell them I'll go away. I just need some money. Not much. Just a bit. They can give it to you for me. Or just get me my bank cards. And my passport. I need my passport."

"Okay," said Barney, "okay. But why don't you come inside. Lorro's here now. You can talk to him. I'll back you up."

"No. Don't tell them I was here. Tell them I phoned you. Make something up. I'll come back another time."

"Alright," said Barney, "do you need anything? You got a place to stay?"

The killer shook his head.

"You'll freeze."

"I'll be fine. Just talk to them."

Barney nodded. "You're still one of us," he said, and with a last look back, he disappeared into the house.

Bending low, the killer snuck closer to the window. Despite the cold, it was open a few inches and he could hear voices from within. Spider, he recognised, and Lorro and someone else, maybe two. The killer listened as they talked. He listened a long time, and then with a heavy heart and a knot in his stomach, he slunk quietly back into the night.

*   *   *   *   *

Aabira had the taxi stop when the fare reached five pounds, for reasons of economy as much as anything. Besides, it was only a ten-minute walk and she wanted time to think before reaching home. Home was not always a good environment for deliberation.

It was late, cold and dark, although the streetlights were bright and clear. Aabira walked unhurriedly. She said an inward prayer for clarity and tried to clear her mind. Just as she was about to step out into the road, a scooter sped past, whining loudly, making her heart jump. The scooter sped on, uncaring, then slowed to a stop further along the street. Aabira crossed to the other side and took a right down Walnut Avenue. The scooter's engine revved loudly. Another answered it like an animal-call.

Aabira tried to shake off her irritation. A light snow had begun to fall and as she walked, she held out her hand to catch a flake or two, which glistened in the street light as they melted upon her palm. More engines started up, ahead of her this time. Two more scooters, headlights blazing, turned lazy circles thirty meters down the road. Feeling uneasy, Aabira crossed again and took a left down Hinton Lane. It was darker here. Big chestnut trees lined both sides of the road, their great bulks glowing a soft brown in the lamplight.

Engines revved louder. Aabira quickened her pace. Her phone rang; she dug it out of her pocket and answered.

"Hi," said Harry, "listen, I just wanted to say…"

"Harry," Aabira interrupted, "I think I might in trouble."

"What do you mean?"

"Right now. I think I'm in trouble right now." A motorbike whizzed past, close. The helmeted driver looked right at Aabira, slowed down ahead of her and turned.

"Where are you?"

"Hinton Avenue. Please come."

The engine's roar was loud and near. The motorbike mounted the pavement and headed straight for Aabira, who staggered back. Her phone dropped and skidded out into the road. She turned and fled, back the way she had come. Horns blared. The houses here faced immediately onto the pavement and Aabira hammered on someone's front door, but she was forced to run on as the motorbike again launched itself in her direction.

Back to the junction she ran, and on across, wheels clipping at her heels, horns blaring, voices shouting. They were playing with her, she realised, herding her, but there was no way out. She saw the alleyway entrance, a dark tunnel half-hidden by branches and turned sharply, leaving the engines behind, running blindly. For a moment she thought they wouldn't follow, but then light surrounded her. She glanced back—one of the machines filled the alleyway, roaring after. Her legs ached but she willed them on. The lit rectangle that marked the way out seemed impossibly far, but at last she reached it, stumbling and falling heavily as the motorbike crashed through behind, skidding out onto the tarmac.

Aabira scrambled up and ran past it, across the road, onto an open flat park of grass. She stumbled again over the roots of a tree and pulled herself upright against it. More engines sounded. The other riders had caught up and they spread out, in a loose semi-circle, revving and laughing and shouting.

One of them dismounted and swaggered towards her, raising his visor and glancing back at his companions. His eyes narrowed as he neared Aabira. He pulled out a flick-knife. The blade glinted sharply in the streetlight. Aabira waited as long as she dared and, with the man just few feet away, pulled out her cannister of self-defence spray and let loose a stream into his face. As the man screamed and doubled over, clutching his head, Aabira turned and ran across the field. Almost immediately, the bikes followed.

Across the black grass she ran, and out onto the pavement, but at last her aching lungs and legs gave out. Collapsing against a bin she slid to the ground. Lights flashed across her eyes. There came the screeching of tires. She looked up to see the scooters surrounding her, circling dizzyingly. A dozen helmeted faces leering and calling. Then a deeper noise sounded—a white pickup truck roared to a halt in the road. Two men jumped out, shouting and swearing. The bikes scattered like roaches. As the noise of their engines receded, Aabira looked up. Harry and his dad grabbed an arm each and helped her slowly to her feet.

*   *   *   *   *

Penny was standing in the shop doorway, talking to Constable Paulsen, when Coy's car pulled up to the pavement.

"Sir?" said Paulsen as the big man got out, closely followed by Monte, "I didn't know they were sending you down."

"They didn't," said Coy, "this is a social call. Hello Penny, what's occurring?"

"I was just telling Constable Paulsen about the suspicious van," said Penny, "a blue transit that's been parked opposite since six o'clock."

"It was gone by the time I got here," said Paulsen, consulting his pocketbook. "No one got in or out, but a rider on a moped stopped to talk to the driver twice."

"At seven-fifteen and again at twenty-to-nine," said Penny.

"Very good," Coy nodded approvingly, "and being a bright young constable, you ran the plates?"

"I did, sir," said Paulsen, "it's registered to a mister Colin Moony, of Halstead Avenue. He has previous for aggravated assault and disturbance of the peace."

"Disturbance of the peace, eh," said Coy, tutting, "we can't have that now, can we, Constable Paulsen."

"No, sir."

"Run along then, lad. Make sure you write it properly and send me a copy."

"Coincidence?" asked Penny as Paulsen headed back to his car.

"I'll pay mister Moony a visit in the morning." Coy grunted.

"What's wrong, Donald?"

"Too many lose ends," said Coy, "someone is running rings round us."

"Time to take the velvet glove off the iron fist?" said Penny.

"Yes, indeed," said Coy, "yes, indeed."

*   *   *   *   *

Harry sat in the kitchen of Aabira's home, holding his cup of tea and watching Aabira's mother, Fayruz, tend to her daughter. Aabira sat with her back to Harry, her bruised and scratched leg in her mother's lap, while Fayruz bathed it gently with warm water and lotion. They talked in Arabic.

Fayruz looked up at Harry and spoke to her daughter. Aabira turned her head. "Mum says thank you again."

Harry held up a hand. "It was nothing."

"Boys these days," said Fayruz, in English, "have no rules. Would you like something to eat?"

"No, thank you."

"Your father would have thrashed them," said Fayruz to Aabira, "this is what you get for walking home alone."

"Mum, please. I'm fine."

"You wouldn't be," said Fayruz, "if it weren't for this young man."

Fayruz finished wrapping a bandage and gently lowered Aabira's leg. "Excuse me," she said, and left, carrying the bowl of water. Aabira turned round.

"How are you feeling?" asked Harry.

"Angry."

"That's good."

"Is it?" said Aabira.

"It's better than letting them intimidate you."

Aabira shook her head. "It was probably just their idea of fun."

Harry's eyes glanced to the table. He gestured towards a folder that lay open upon it.

"You're still working on this?"

"Yes."

Fayruz's voice came from the other room. She spoke in Arabic and Aabira replied in the same tongue. "I'll be back in a minute," she said, rising.

Left alone, Harry put down the tea and pulled the folder towards him. He rifled slowly through the papers. A photo of Tony Perkins stared him in the face. He rubbed his forehead. Beneath it was the list of books they had found at Tony's flat, and beneath those the menu from The Golden Dragon. Harry picked it up. He squinted and looked closely. Tiny indentations peppered the plastic-coated page beneath the words, and some of these small marks bore traces of ink.

"A book-code," he said to himself, "Aabira," he called out.

Aabira appeared in the doorway.

"The book-code," said Harry again, "the note we found at Tony's. I don't think they were using a book at all. Look," he passed the menu over, "it's the menu. They were using the menu. Line-number and letter."

Aabira took the folder and searched through it. She found the copy of the note Harry had discovered.

"Do you have a pen and paper?" said Harry.

Aabira took her notebook from her bag and side by side they set to work.

*   *   *   *   *

After morning prayer, Monte ate a light breakfast and then retreated to his office. He slipped an Alice Coltrane CD into the player and sat before the window, with his feet up on the sill, feeling the warmth of the new sun and looking down upon the early risers—deliverymen, cleaners, builders and others, as they went about their business.

He let his mind drift, setting up in his thoughts nodes of connections—Lucas Grundy, Schwarzkopf, the dark-haired girl, James Roberston and Tony Perkins. Alice Coltrane's piano washed through the air like an abstract water colour. Monte mentally noted the personnel—Pharaoh Sanders casting lightning sheets of saxophone, Jimmy Garrisons soft and supple bass, the only man to stand by his mentor as he had drifted further and further towards the outer reaches of the musical galaxy. Ben Riley and Rashied Ali, on drums, threw a shimmering, dancing veil around them as fine and as rich as spun gold.

Monte was only dimly aware of the sound of the doorbell, of footsteps on the stairs. At the knock on his door he turned and called out. Penny led the way, and behind her came Aabira and Harry.

I want to see you played on the stereo.

*   *   *   *   *

"Colin Moony," said Hardacre, passing the file through the half-open car window before climbing into the driving seat.

Coy opened the file and squinted down. "Well, well, well," he said, showing Hardacre the photograph—a white male in his late twenties, with an elaborate spider-web tattoo visible on his neck. "Spider," said Coy.

"Sir?" Hardacre strapped on her seatbelt and started the engine.

"Hardacre," said Coy, "turn that off a moment."

Hardacre obeyed.

"I'm well aware, Karen, that for too long I have kept you in the dark. I've asked you to do things without explaining the reasons, and for that I apologise."

Hardacre narrowed her eyes.

"You're right to be skeptical," said Coy, "I'm a bullish old man with little give, but my motives are forever pure."

Hardacre pursed her lips.

"I think there is a connection," said Coy, "between the deaths of Lucas Grundy and James Robertson. And that connection is Christian Schwarzkopf."

"How?"

"If I tell you," said Coy, "it may go the worse for you in the long run."

"You've started," stated Hardacre, "you might as well finish."

"Lucas Grundy had information on Schwarzkopf. He kept a file, which was stolen from his sister's house after his death. I think James Robertson and his friend Tony Perkins found that file, or somehow stumbled upon the same information. And now all three are dead. I also think that the coroner in Grundy's case was paid off or intimidated by Schwarzkopf to grease the procedural wheels. I also suspect there may be colleagues among us who have their hands in the same pocket."

"But MI6 are investigating Schwarzkopf."

"Are they? Or are they protecting him?"

"Sir," said Hardacre, "there may be perfectly legitimate reasons why Rivers took over the case. If MI6 are working on something bigger, we could totally bugger it up if we keep on messing about."

"I'll make you a deal, Hardacre. In fact, I'll make you two. If we discover the truth, then we review all the facts and implications before taking another step. We'll go to Rivers, tell him everything we know and let him decide. Secondly, if you want no part of this, then you can leave now and I'll handle things on my own."

Hardacre sat back. She chewed her lip, took hold of the wheel and started the engine. "Where are we going?" she asked wearily.

Coy smiled. "Colchester Road, to talk to Colin Moony, aka 'Spider'. Not only is he the registered owner of the van, which was acting suspiciously last night, he is also often seen in the company of one Christian Schwarzkopf at the Twenty-Two club."

"How is your friend the private investigator involved in all of this?" asked Hardacre.

"Who?"

"Monte Boutista. I checked the address on the van complaint. Also, I'm not blind, sir, or stupid. Well, I'm still in this car, so possibly I'm the latter."

Coy chuckled, sat back, and closed his eyes.

*   *   *   *   *

"Harry worked it out," said Aabira, "and he was right. They were using the menu as a code, not a book."

Monte lowered the notebook. "And this is what it says?"

"That's it."

Penny peered over. "Rosalind. Corpus Christi. Second from left. Well what does that mean?"

"This is the note we found in Tony's flat," said Monte, "what about the other. The one that the police found in James Robertson's apartment?"

"That one doesn't make sense," said Harry, "it's just numbers." He turned the page in the notebook. Fourteen digits."

Monte stared at the page. "Could be a bank account," said Monte, "listen, it's not safe for us to meet here anymore. Aabira wasn't the only one attacked last night. A gang of masked men tried to…well who knows what they were trying to do, either kill me or intimidate me off the case."

"Not to mention," said Penny, "the shop was being watched. There was a blue van parked across the road."

Aabira threw up her hands. "That means we're getting close. I'm not backing down now."

"If they know where you live," said Monte, "then your family could be at risk. Coy will do what he can. I'll ask him to set up a watch, but I'm also going to organise a safe-house. Somewhere I can work from. We'll close the shop for a while, Penny, and you should come too."

"What about me?" asked Aabira.

Monte shook his head. "If you want to carry on," he said, "then you should come with us, but this could last some time. Harry?"

"It's the least I can do," said Harry, "after what happened. Besides, what the hell else is there for me?"

"Okay," said Monte, "let me set this up. Harry, Aabira, how do feel about checking Corpus Christi College?"

Aabira looked at her watch. "I have a study group at the library at ten. I could cancel."

"No, that's okay," said Monte, "Harry and Penny can go to Corpus. I'm going to find us a place to stay for a while."

As he was seeing her out of the front door, Monte urged Aabira to caution. "Stick to the main streets," he said, "and make sure to check in with us when you get there."

*   *   *   *   *

"Expensive neighborhood," said Hardacre as she guided the squad car to a halt.

"There's the van," said Coy, gesturing to where the blue transit was parked, "and there's our boy."

It was unmistakably Colin Moony who just then stepped out the front door of the large, semi-detached house.

"Sir," Hardacre grabbed Coy's arm, "look who's behind him."

"James Reynolds," said Coy, "our innocent scooter-boy. Beginning to believe in conspiracies, Hardacre?"

The two men looked up as Coy and Hardacre approached. They exchanged words. With a last look at Moony, Reynolds stepped forward and held out a hand. "Detective Inspector?"

Coy looked down at the hand.

"Colin Moony," said Hardacre to the man standing behind, "is this your vehicle?"

"Yes."

"Can you tell me what it was doing parked opposite fifty-four-A Regent Street between eighteen-forty and twenty-one-thirty hours last night?"

Moony shrugged. "I don't know. I let a friend borrow it."

"What friend?" asked Hardacre.

"I don't remember. I have a lot of friends."

"James Reynolds," said Coy, "how do you come to know Colin Moony?"

Reynolds began to speak but Moony cut him off. "We met swimming," he said, "we hit it off."

Coy stepped up close. "Anything you want to tell me, Mr. Reynolds? Anything at all? You just give me a ring."

James glanced quickly at Moony. "No," he said, "like I told you the other day. I have no idea what any of this is about."

"Alright. Let's have a look in the van, Moony," said Coy.

"Where's your warrant?"

"Reasonable suspicion," said Hardacre, "open the van."

"Ain't nothing in there but building gear."

"Then you won't mind us looking," smiled Coy.

They stood back and watched as Moony fished keys from his pocket, unlocked the rear doors and pulled them open. Inside were a ladder, a sheet of tarpaulin, and a single bucket of paint.

"Business slow, is it, Moony?" said Coy, examining the unopened bucket and the clean tarpaulin.

"It is a bit, yeah."

Coy slammed the doors shut. "Next time you're at the club," he said, "tell Mr. Schwarzkopf I said hello."

*　*　*　*　*

"I appreciate the extra caution," said Richard, after the waitress had set down his order.

They sat in a small café-diner on the outskirts of town. It was the sort of place where the menus were dog-eared and fading, with price updates handwritten in marker pen. A self-reflective gloom seemed to permeate the interior, muting colours and cloying the air.

Monte sipped his tea, savouring its warmth. "I have to assume I'm being followed everywhere."

"If their van was spotted," said Richard, "then these are amateurs."

"Right now," said Monte, "I don't know if they are trying to scare us off or if they're more serious than that."

"You're right not to take chances," said Richard, "the safe-house is yours. You'll take my advice on how to get there?"

Monte nodded. "What do you know about criminal gangs in this area?"

Richard shrugged. "Even in the nicest places there are people operating. It's just easier to hide in the big cities."

They stared out at the passersby.

"There are too many dead places in the world," said Richard.

"Would you call yourself a cynic?"

"I'd call myself a realist," said Richard, "I'm lucky—I can pick and choose my clients. I have a morality I can live by."

Monte was not so sure that he agreed. "Are we still set for tonight?".

"All being well," said Richard, "we'll have what you need by tomorrow."

*　*　*　*　*

Harry and Penny walked the grounds inside Corpus Christi. The sun was bright but the air was cold and sharp. Students passed, huddled up against the chill, clutching folders or with backpacks slung over their arms.

"It's a different world," said Harry.

"You never wanted to study?"

"Never saw the point. Besides I could never sit behind a desk for long. I need fresh air and sunshine."

"Well," said Penny, "a formal education isn't everything. There's a lot they won't teach in any University that everyone should know."

They walked on.

"How are we going to find this Rosalind?" asked Penny. "If we start asking questions then we're going to attract a lot of attention."

"We might as well try reception, first," said Harry, "wherever that is."

"I don't think they're going to be very helpful."

"Well, you were right," said Harry, twenty minutes later. They stood in a corridor of the ancient building. The secretary they had spoken to had just departed. "I'm afraid we can't give out personal details of our students," she had told them, "under any circumstances. Feel free to enjoy the grounds, and if you have any more questions, you can contact our press office. Details are on our website."

They wandered back outside.

"We have nothing to lose, now," said Harry, "let's see if anyone knows that name."

They had stopped half-a-dozen students, with no success, before the secretary reappeared in the doorway in the company of a large middle-aged man in uniform. She pointed towards Harry and Penny and the man started forward, speaking into a walkie-talkie as he did so.

"Time's up," said Harry.

"Hello," said Penny, approaching another group of students, "excuse me, but do you know a Rosalind who studies here?"

"Come on," urged Harry, gently grasping her arm.

"Did you say you were looking for Rosalind?"

The woman who approached them was in her late fifties, primly dressed, with greying hair tied back in a bun. She smiled warmly. "You don't mean the clock?"

"Clock?" said Penny.

"Dear old Rosie," said the woman, "Rosalind. The Corpus Clock. On our outside wall. Why, you must have walked right past it."

"Can you show us?" said Harry.

"I'd be delighted," replied the woman, "follow me."

*   *   *   *   *

"Miss."

The boy approached Aabira on the corner of the street. He was in his early twenties, handsome in a way, with thick curly blonde hair and blue eyes. He wore dirty track suit trousers and a grey hoodie. His voice bore the smooth, polished tones of the educated and upper class.

Aabira stepped back, looking left and right. The street was busy. She fished in her bag. "I have pepper spray," she said, loudly, "don't come any closer."

"Miss," said the boy again, taking his hands from his pockets, "I saw you talking to Monte Boutista in the shop. I need to see him."

What do you want?"

"I stabbed that man, James Robertson," he said, "and I want to talk to your boss."

*   *   *   *   *

"You have to be joking," said Harry.

They stood in light rain at the corner of Bennet Street and Trumpington Street, outside the Taylor Library. Framed in a seven-foot-high arch in the façade of the old building, behind a sheet of glass, 'Rosalind' glowed golden in the pale light.

"The Corpus Christi clock," the woman had told them, "to give it its proper name. Stephen Hawking himself unveiled it."

The clock was a dazzling sphere of concentric circles of gold with no hands or conventional dials. Squatting atop it, a black, insect-like creature, something like a locust, stared impassively to one side.

"It's magnificent," said Penny, "I've seen it before of course. I never knew its nickname was Rosalind. Two pillars to either side. That must be what the note refers to."

"Idiots," said Harry, "they thought they were playing James Bond."

"Will you look," said Penny, "or shall I?"

Harry stepped up to the arch, peered at the second 'pillar' closely, and began to run his fingertips up and down at the place where its form met the surrounding concrete. There were slight cracks here and there, and in one of these his fingers pressed against something that gave and then sprang back. He tried to grab hold of it.

"Do you have tweezers?" he asked Penny.

She took out a small purse from her back and obliged.

It took a few attempts before Harry managed to successfully catch the corner of whatever it was and pull it free. He took it over to Penny—a small, thin, plastic bag, inside which was a note and what looked like a fragment of cloth.

*   *   *   *   *

The girl could have been anywhere between fifteen and twenty. She was crying and there was blood on her hands.

"Please sir," she said, "it's my dog. He's hurt really bad."

Coy took the key from the lock in his front door and turned round to face her.

"Where is it?" he said.

"Down the alley," she pointed, "I think he's dying."

"Show me," said Coy.

"What happened?" he asked as the girl led the way into the narrow passage at the end of the cul-de-sac.

"I don't know," she said, "he ran into the wood and came back injured."

Flecks of rain splashed into Coy's face from the overhanging trees, whose leaves bent down as if to block the way. They emerged onto the old playing field—an uncared-for square of open grass surrounded on all sides by trees, with a solitary muddy track running down one end.

"Where is it?" asked Coy, and the girl pointed towards a tree stump a few feet into the middle of the park, beyond which a shallow ditch sloped downward. When Coy reached its lip he saw nothing. He turned around.

"I'm going to watch you die, pedo," said the girl, and stepped back as five balaclava-clad men emerged from the trees. One held a baseball bat, another a small black cudgel. At least one sported a knife.

Coy nodded, reached behind his back to press the emergency button on his radio and then into his pocket where he kept his unauthorized telescopic baton. He flicked it out to its full extent, planted his legs apart and held the weapon level with his hip.

"Alright then lads," he said, looking from one masked face to another, "who's first?"

*   *   *   *   *

The killer, whose name was Charles Addington, jumped at the sound of the door. Monte held up a hand, motioning Charles to sit. "It's alright," he said, "it's the rest of my people."

Harry and Penny followed the voices into the back room, where Monte, Charles and Aabira sat round the table.

"This is Charles Addington," said Monte, "the man who stabbed James Roberston."

"Son of a bitch," said Harry, "are you kidding?"

"Well," said Penny, after a moment, "I suppose I'd better put the kettle on."

Harry looked at Aabira, his arms wide.

"Charles found me on the street," she explained, "he wants to turn himself in."

"Just like that?" said Harry. "And you believe this guy?"

"I believe him," said Monte. "He is what he says he is."

Harry stared at Charles, who averted his eyes.

"Now that we're all here," said Monte, "why don't you start at the beginning."

Charles took a deep breath and began to talk.

Cambridge, eight months previously

Charles Addington loved Abigail Deschamps from the first moment he saw her, in the college library, her lean frame slightly bent and her mane of wavy dark-blonde hair tumbling down past her shoulders. The half of her long, narrow face that was visible to him was pockmarked. She had a delicate nose, full eyebrows, and thick lips, and was absorbed in looking at the art books. She ran a long finger across their spines, occasionally pulling one out for further inspection. Charles thought that she was the loveliest woman he had ever seen.

When she turned toward him their eyes met and he felt something. A physical and spiritual jolt. And he had seen that feeling reflected back in her eyes. To his dying days he would swear that he had.

They introduced themselves. They talked a little of art. She was on a fine art undergrad course. He was completing a doctorate in ancient history. They went for coffee and continued chatting, sat outside the café hunched under an umbrella as the rain fell. Charles felt more alive and excited than he ever had, though he doubted very much that this showed.

Abigail was married, she told him, but Charles' hopes were not dented. It seemed appropriate, rather, that his first grand romance would bear shades of tragedy. They exchanged numbers.

They saw each other again. And again. They went for walks in the park. She wore a short dress of many colours, a colourful beaded necklace. Her hair smelt of orange blossom tea. Little by little their lives became enmeshed. It was not long before they began to converse of weighty matters with the lightest of ease. They became intimate confidantes. She did not love her husband, she told him. He did not love his life.

The affair was consummated in room twelve-A of the Lexington Guest House, on a sweltering humid afternoon, with the curtains drawn, the window open, and the television in the next room turned up too loud. That was the last time Charles ever saw Abigail.

She left a letter in his post tray. She had gone to Saudi Arabia with her husband. She had been foolish, she said. She was sorry.

For a long time Charles drifted. Like a leaf upon the wind. His studies failed him. For long days he sat, staring from the window, unmoved by thirst or hunger or life. He lost weight. In the evenings he drank and talked little. He borrowed money from friends and relations. He began to gamble, not because he desired to win, but simply because it was another way of throwing himself into the gutter.

He met his next woman as he sat on a park bench, smoking. She was everything Abigail had not been—short, curvy, with dark hair and eyes, flirtatious, talkative and unreserved. She too was an undergrad. "I've been watching you," she told him, "you're not like the others." His eyes found her thighs, and a cold dead feeling crept into his heart.

He walked with her because she asked, and because he found a certain alluring quality to her air of easy privilege and freeness. Her name was Martha and she told him of a club, a very special club, which could fill any emptiness and salve any wounds. It was for privileged people, she said, educated, from the very best stock. More, these people must have an uncompromising spirit of adventure, an anarchist's appreciation of the material world. They must be willing to cross any boundaries and smash any taboos. She was sure, she said, that he would be welcome.

On the evening of that first day Charles met some of the others—Alice and Barney and Eddie and Spider. In a pillow-filled room in a student-house, with rugs upon they floor, they talked and they drank and they drank and Charles felt a glimmer of something reawaken within him. Uneasy at first, he enjoyed the attention which the girls lavished upon him and which the other men seemed to mind not at all. In fact they greeted him just as warmly.

And so they drank and they ate good food and they played board games and they smoked weed and Charles loosened his collar and the drugs loosened his mind and he felt a kind of family around him. This was an unfamiliar feeling and he liked it. He laughed, and he could not remember the last time he had laughed.

The night waxed and the games turned more flirtatious until, almost before Charles had noticed, clothes were being unbuttoned, unzipped and abandoned. Charles had laughed again at their nakedness, his too, but he had not laughed when Martha came to him, and afterwards Alice, when the room had turned into a blurred kaleidoscope of flesh. When they all lay afterwards, Charles felt a sense of peace descend upon him. And Martha, as she lay once more in his arms, told him of their society, their 'band of brothers and sisters' and of Christian Schwarzkopf—the great man who made it all happen.

It wasn't long before they all met again.

This time they took him to their outfitters in the West End of London, a cavernous, white-walled emporium with racks upon racks of costumes and lines of sweet white bliss upon a marbled table. There were no dressing rooms. The ladies changed shamelessly with the men. Martha and Alice fussed constantly over Charles, dressing him, styling his hair, making him try on this outfit and that. They settled upon a mock-pirate look, with slim red-striped black trousers and an open white shirt with a frill collar. Martha put a black beauty spot upon his cheek. Alice, in a leather corset and with her face painted white like a mime, draped her arms around him and smiled.

They drank champagne, and as the chauffeur drove them back in a limousine with ample room for six, they laughed and told tales of outrageous exploits. They teased and they joked and they treated Charles as one of their own.

They reached Schwarzkopf's house as the sky was darkening. A path lined with lanterns set into the ground led to the open front door. A raucous, pantomime tune spilled out. Lights flickered behind drawn curtains. Spider linked his arm through Charles' and together they led the suddenly sombre procession inside.

There were servants here—impossibly good-looking young men and women, dressed in black from the waist down and nothing from the waist up, except that they wore plain white masks to hide their faces. The double doors to the dining room swung slowly back.

This was the inner circle they had talked of—the Brotherhood. This dark oak-wood chamber, with its sinister, contorted, sexual carvings, its flickering, chandelier light, smoke curling, table groaning with overflowing silver goblets and golden plates piled high with food. There were others here, men and women in flashing colours, sparkling jewels, costume of all variety. Christian Schwarzkopf sat at the table's head. He too was naked from the waist up. He wore a red cape about his shoulders and a slim golden crown upon his head.

Charles had never seen anything like it. They ate carelessly, frivolously. Unwanted food was thrown on the floor, rivers of wine ran across the table. Plates were upended in fits of sudden demonstration. They laughed. They kissed. All was free and all was simple. A hand caressed Charles' thigh as the woman in the peacock mask on his other side poured wine onto their conjoined tongues.

There was no jealously here, no competition, they were comrades in arms. They were one. And Charles felt, for the first time in god-knew-when, a release, magnificent and mighty. Whether it was the food, the pills, the drink—he felt like he knew what it meant to be alive and he abandoned himself to it fully.

Over the next few weeks, a whirlwind of sensual debauchery had followed. As a group they drank and they gambled and drugged and fornicated, in a dozen different hotels and mansions up and down the country, so that it seemed to Charles that he lay forever half-entangled in bed sheets in a stranger's luxury abode, drifting in and out of clarity, waiting for the next warm body or cold drink to arrive. They hunted too, they shot and killed rabbits and pheasants and foxes and life was a never-ending beautiful intoxicated fog of pleasure and blood and numbness. In all this time money was never needed and never mentioned. Somewhere, in the back of his dulled mind, Charles realised Christian Schwarzkopf must be bank-rolling them all.

He knew too, somehow, that the time would come when he would have to pay the price. When Spider put it to him that Charles must kill a journalist called James Robertson, Charles received the instruction with puzzlement, a flickering excitement and, deep down in his stomach, a black pit of fear.

"It's just like killing anything else," Spider had said, "a life is a life. This is the final test. Your chance to prove yourself. You want this to continue, don't you? We've all done it. It will liberate your soul and afterwards… afterwards you can have whatever you like."

How many days had passed between then and the night of the murder, Charles could not recall. In that time he had thrown himself headlong into all that the imagination and wealth of Christian Schwarzkopf could offer, and it could offer much. When the appointed night finally arrived, he stood, clothed as Spider had instructed, in track suit leggings and hoodie, stripped of all his possessions, his wallet, his passport.

They had given him a last potent shot and Eddie had placed into his hands with smiling solemnity the shining wicked blade. They knew exactly where James Robertson was and had driven Charles to a place nearby and had left him to follow the old man.

And Charles had followed as the night had fallen into slow motion, as all around became pin-point sharp—the stars, the grass, his fingers, the knife, the rolling rhythmic pattern of the old man's back as he walked. On and on as if for forever, as if this were his destiny. He was Sisyphus reborn and this was his punishment.

Yet unlike Sisyphus there was a way to end it. A thing he must do. But at the last, at the very last, wild and weary beyond measure, Charles realised that killing was not in him. But he knew that the knife must strike. So he aimed for the swaying shoulder blades, for the fat and the muscle and the bone. And as he lunged the old man began to turn and the knife had slid into his neck.

*   *   *   *   *

"In that moment I wanted to do it," said Charles, "so that one day, she would see—Abigail—she would see my face, in the newspaper, or on the television, or on the internet, and she would see what her leaving had made me become. She would know that I had done it for her. She would know that I am the one."

He ran a hand through his, hair.

"After I'd done it," he said, "I started to go where they had told me to meet Spider. I knew somehow. I think I knew all along that they were using me. I hid in the bushes and I saw them. Spider and Eddie and another man I don't know. Spider had a bottle of whiskey but nobody was drinking. I heard them discuss how they were going to kill me. I thought I could run and disappear but they have my bank cards and my passport. And next day I saw the headlines—that the old man had died. I didn't know what to do.

I couldn't turn myself in. They have no fear of the police. None at all. The one time I mentioned it Eddie laughed. They're playing on another level. He told me Schwarzkopf is protected all the way up. I went to Barney's place and I heard them talking. I heard Spider. They mentioned your name, Mr. Boutista, and a policeman. I can't remember the name of the policeman. They said that they would have to kill you. That's when I decided to come here. I don't know what I expected you to do. I just thought somehow, if I warned you, it might go some of the way to setting things right."

For a few moments an uncomfortable silence reigned.

Harry shook his head. "We're turning him in, yes? We're calling the police?"

Aabira looked at Penny, who remained staring at the floor.

"Settle down," said Monte, "he came to us, remember."

"He's a killer," said Harry. Aabira looked him in the eyes, then quickly glanced away. Harry flushed, swore and moved to the back door, running a hand through his hair and staring out into the garden.

Monte put a hand on Harry's shoulder. "Settle down," he said again. The phone rang. Penny answered, and passed the handset to Monte, who listened quietly, asked "when?" and "where?" before ending the call.

"Coy's in Addenbrookes," he said, "he's been attacked."

*   *   *   *   *

Waking up was not a pleasant experience for Donald Coy. His head felt like it was experiencing the worst hangover ever, sickness welled in his stomach, his vision was blurred and there was a sharp pain in his side. Through misty eyes, he observed the white blankets and the tubes sprouting from his left arm. He moved his hands down slowly to push himself a little upright.

Karen Hardacre lifted the glass of water her boss was groping for and placed it carefully into his hand. Coy nodded, took a sip or two and forced his voice to function. "Get a pen and paper," he growled, "I want to make a statement."

*   *   *   *   *

Christian Schwarzkopf lowered himself into the warm, foaming waters of the king-sized hot tub. He laid his head back as the pleasant heat penetrated the muscles of his body. A long, lean leg caressed his own and he looked over at Spider, whose smiling face bobbed above the gentle lapping waves. Spider's eyes were closed.

"Are you feeling good tonight, Mr. Schwarzkopf?" he said.

Christian reached down to massage Spider's calf. "I have a nagging little anxiety."

"Charlie-boy," said Spider, his eyes still closed. "He'll surface soon enough."

Christian's hands tightened a little around Spider's leg.

"You're a fool not to worry."

Spider opened his eyes. "Nobody would ever believe him."

Christian pulled so that Spider's shoulders slipped slowly from the side of the bath and his body floated closer. "Do you know what you're here for?" he said.

Spider laughed, a little nervously.

"You're here," said Christian, "to make sure that I have no concerns."

"I'll find him," said Spider.

"And then?"

"You know what."

"Say it."

"I'll kill him," said Spider, "just like we killed Grundy. I'll kill him."

"You said you would kill that policeman too and the detective."

"The cop is going to be in hospital for a long time. If Boutista doesn't back off then we'll make him disappear. Whatever was in the file that fat fuck had is gone and even if it isn't there's no way your friends are going to let it surface. There's nothing left to worry about. We've done good."

"Then why do I still fear?"

Spider pulled his leg free and eased back to the edge. "Why don't we pick up some shit," he said, "and make a night of it."

"I want you to kill that boy, like you were supposed to. I want you to kill him and then I want you to come back and use me while his blood is still on your hands."

"I will," said Spider, "you don't have to worry. I will."

Christian pushed himself across the water. He put his forehead against Spider's and laid a hand upon the other man's cheek.

"You love me," he said, "don't you?"

"You know that I do."

"Say it. And keep saying it."

Spider ran a hand through Christian's hair. "For you," he said, "I'll do anything that you want."

*   *   *   *   *

Visiting hours were over by the time Monte reached Addenbrooke's hospital. Nevertheless, the staff let him in, on condition under no circumstances should he disturb the patient, who was sleeping soundly. Monte sat in the corner of Coy's room, listening to his old friend snore, watching the rising and falling of his chest and the slow drip of clear liquid from the IV bag on its metal stand.

When the call came from Richard Jarsdel he answered and spoke quietly, with one eye through the door-window into the corridor.

"I've got a safe-place for you," said Richard, "I'll send the address on secure line. Can you get there tonight?"

"Yes."

"Good. I'll meet you tomorrow. Everything okay?"

Monte looked at Coy's sleeping form. "Not exactly," he said.

"I'm sorry to hear that. Take care."

Monte sat a half-hour longer, ruminating. Then he prayed, checked his Signal account, and ordered a taxi back to the shop.

*   *   *   *   *

Aabira woke in an unfamiliar bed, feeling anxious and disorientated.

My parents are going to kill me, she thought, wondering, as she had on the previous night, what possible excuse she could make which would not make things worse. The safe house was an unassuming and large detached property in the quiet suburb of Trumpington, a mid-eighties build with four bedrooms in one of which, Aabira was acutely aware, slept a known murderer.

When she reached the kitchen-diner, Harry, Penny and Monte were already having breakfast. Outside in the large garden, Charles sat on a bench, his hands stuffed into his jacket.

Aabira helped herself to a cup of tea and sat down.

"How's he doing?" she asked.

"He's fine," said Harry, "it's the rest of us who are stressing out."

"Coy suspects Schwarzkopf has a man on the inside," said Monte, "Charles seems to back that up. He says he heard this 'Spider' saying so. I don't know if handing him in is the right thing. Not with Don laid up."

"What else are we supposed to do with him?" said Harry.

Aabira took some toast. "Will you see Donald today?"

"Am I the only one who thinks this is a really bad idea?" asked Harry. "You do realise we're committing a serious crime right now."

"I realise I'm asking a lot," said Monte, "if anyone wants out then you should go. You can get away for a while. I'll pay."

"Aabira," said Harry, "if you get a police record it will appear on any job application you ever make."

Aabira sighed. "I don't know," she said.

"What is there to know?" Harry gestured, "this is insane."

"It's alright," said Charles, from the doorway, "I'll hand myself in. I'm ready."

"Just hold on," said Monte, rising, "I'm going to talk to my friend today. The policeman. Let's see what he advises. Okay?" He looked around the room.

"Sit down, son," said Harry, stroking his chin. He looked at Aabira and shook his head.

"Charles," said Monte, "James Robertson left us a clue, something connected to Schwarzkopf."

Harry picked up the sealed bag he and Penny had discovered. He shook the contents onto the table. There was a tiny fragment of thick cloth, beige with deep crimson stains, and a piece of paper with the name 'Maria Waters' written upon it.

"Do you have any idea what this is?" asked Monte.

Charles shook his head.

"Did you ever hear Spider or anyone else mention that name?"

"No," said Charles, "no, I'm sure that they didn't."

Monte checked his watch. "I have to see Don."

Harry began to get to his feet. "I'll drive you."

"I'll get an Uber," said Monte, "I'd like you to stay here."

"We'll be fine on our own," said Penny, "Charles is no danger to anyone."

Harry gestured in exasperation. "How can you possibly know that?"

"Look at him," said Penny, "this boy is no killer. Any more than you are."

Harry's gaze fell to the floor.

"Keep me posted," advised Monte, on his way to the door, "and don't use anything but Signal. No names and nothing incriminating. I'll sort this out. I promise."

"I'd better phone my parents," said Aabira.

"What will you tell them?" asked Penny.

"That a friend of mine in London is ill and I'm staying there for a while."

Harry watched her as she left.

"She'll be fine," said Penny.

"We're putting a lot on the line for you," said Harry to Charles.

Charles said nothing. He exited the door back into the garden.

"A sad story," said Penny.

"He had a choice," said Harry.

"He was manipulated."

"How do we even know that he's telling the truth?"

"Does he seem like a killer to you?" said Penny. "He didn't have to come to us."

"He could have handed himself in to the police."

"He handed himself in to us. To warn Monte that Schwarzkopf plans to have him killed."

"Two weeks ago," said Harry, "I was just driving a car, having a little fun playing detective. Two months ago I knew exactly where my life was going."

"None of us asked for this hand," said Penny, "but now we have it we've got to play it. Not by the rules of the law of the land, by the rules of what we know in our hearts to be right." She stood and looked through the window. "That lad made a tremendous mistake. He's going to pay for it. There's no escaping that and he knows it. The life that he knew is over. Donald Coy is in hospital. Before we hand Charles to the police he's going to help us do the right thing."

"And what's that?"

"We have to stop Christian Schwarzkopf," said Penny, "if it's the very last thing that we do."

*   *   *   *   *

"He could be a hundred miles away," said Eddie.

Colin 'Spider' Mooney put his hands on his hips, screwed up his face and crossed one leg over the other. Through his sunglasses he watched the Sunday afternoon footballers going through their motions on Parker's Piece. The two men sat on a bench on the edge of the field. Not twenty feet away a group of students sat in a loose circle, smoking and talking. The day was edging towards cold.

"The boy doesn't have his passport," said Spider, "I do."

"Has anyone checked his folks' place?"

"Do I have to do everything?"

Not for the first time, Eddie felt a flush of irritation towards the boss' favourite. He knew though, the danger of ever letting that show. The best way to counter was to leap ahead.

"Why don't we report him as missing to the police?"

Spider gave him a sideways look. "Are you fucking joking?" he said.

"No. Why don't we send Martha to the folks' place. If he's not there then they report him missing and we get Martha to do a piece for the papers, or if they're not interested, an advert. 'Wherever you are, you can call me in confidence'. Charles would believe her. You know that he would."

For a time Spider said nothing. The students, feeling the increasing chill, gathered their belongings and made ready to leave.

"Hey love," Spider called out, and motioned to the brunette amongst them.

"Me?" she said.

"Yeah, do us a favour?"

"Pardon?"

"Do us a favour? Take your knickers down."

The girl turned away in disgust. Spider laughed loud and long. One or two of the men among the group threw menacing glances at Spider. Spider drew his sunglasses down his nose. "Yeah?" he said, "you want some?"

Eddie sighed.

"And gods walk among us," said Spider, as the group moved away. "Alright," he sat forward and slapped Eddie's thigh, "drive Martha down to the folks' place and get her to charm the pants off them. If Charlie-boy's there then we're sorted. If he's not but they know where he is, that's great."

"And if neither is the case?"

"Then we'll do it your way. Now go pick up that tart and get going."

*   *   *   *   *

Agent Buchanan enjoyed his job. He liked the responsibility and concordant respect that it brought him. Plus he was very good at it. Professional, with the huge bonus that, unlike so many other of his colleagues, he knew the key to avoiding burnout. Four times a year, winter, summer, spring and fall, Jerry Buchanan took a week off and went fishing. He stayed in a log cabin, self-sustained, near a wide blue lake very far away from any man or woman. One day, when his duty was done, Jerry fancied he might retire there for good, driving back, once in a while, and at Christmas and Thanksgiving, to see his family, his nephews and nieces, his sister and his brother.

Not today though, he thought, as he guided the rented BMW up the gravel driveway, Jerry pushed all such pleasant thoughts aside. You could show no weakness dealing with informants and 'collaborators'. Jerry knew that the best way to get results was to treat every one of them the same, from the lowest hood to the grandest and most rotten, like the man he had come here to see.

Christian Schwarzkopf's distasteful secretary let Jerry in, and ushered the agent into the study where he sat, waiting, for the best part of ten minutes, before Christian entered, dressed in smart trousers and shirt and smiling broadly.

"Agent Buchanan."

"Don't ever jerk me around," said Jerry, "if I give you a time, I expect you to be ready."

Christian's smile narrowed. "I will forgive you your crudeness," he said, "you've come from a far more barbaric place than this."

"It's your country too."

"That it is. However, I was referring rather to the circles of company in which you move. Spies. Criminals. So uncouth."

"What is it with guys like you," said Jerry, fishing a packet of cigars from his coat-pocket, "Anglophiles. It's as if you regret we ever gained independence."

Christian eyed the cigar. "Much as I enjoy our little chats," he said, "I've a lunch appointment at two. Perhaps we can make this quick."

"You're not going anywhere," said Jerry, lighting his cigar, "until I've finished with you."

"How very alpha-male."

"It really rubs you, don't it," said Jerry, "your being American. You wish you were English, don't you? With a coat of arms and a family tree back to Adam. You can't fool those lords and ladies, though, they know what you are. And what you aren't. So you have to compromise and try and be something in between."

"Don't pretend," said Christian, "that compromise isn't your stock-in-trade."

"Let's get this straight," said Jerry, "anything I do I do for a reason, and that reason is the advancement and stability of the greatest country in the world, the United States of America. Do I break rules? Would I commit a crime if it resulted in the greater good for my country? You're god-damn right I would. And that makes me proud of what I do."

"Small-minded thinking," said Christian, "I despise it."

"My 'small-minded thinking'," replied Jerry, "is the only reason you're enjoying your five-star lifestyle and not getting forcibly screwed by some ape with halitosis behind bars."

"Don't threaten me, Agent Buchanan. You get plenty of value from me. I know exactly what I'm worth to you."

"Okay," said Jerry, "but you have to see things from my side. Now our friends in MI6 are playing ball, but when a man gets stabbed, in a god-damn police station, and then the detective investigating that murder gets knifed himself it causes a fuss, and that makes life difficult for everyone."

"Nothing of that," said Christian, "has anything to do with me."

"Bullshit. That fellow Robertson had photographs of your house in his camera. CCTV right across the road has him coming out of your driveway. He kept a frigging diary on his computer, which thank Christ our boys got their hands on first."

"And what did it say, this diary?"

"You're going to tell me the initials 'CS' don't refer to you? And it's a coincidence that Roberston spent the last two weeks of his life looking up retirement homes in Spain, even though his bank account says he's poorer than a rat in a woodpile? And then his friend Perkins throws himself under a train with a folder full of papers referring to you by name."

"I'm afraid you can't pin that one on me, at least."

"This is all a game to you, ain't it."

Christian laughed. "The entire world is a game. Haven't you figured that out yet, Buchanan. Is your imagination really so limited?"

Jerry shook his head. "It was blackmail, right? Why the hell didn't you come to me first?"

"I took care of everything."

"You made a bloody mess is what you did. Now tell me what they had on you and is there anything left I need to know about?"

Christian sniffed his wine and took a small sip. "It's all done," he said, "there is nothing else."

"Stabbing that cop was very stupid."

"Perhaps I don't feel the same level of confidence in my protectors as you do."

"I don't give a shit how you feel," said Jerry, "This is housekeeping time. You are going to give me the name of whoever killed Robertson, whoever stabbed the cop and the names of everyone else who knows what you've done."

"Everyone?"

"Everyone."

"What will you do with them?"

"What do you think?"

Christian sat back. He took another sip of his wine. Then he pulled open a desk drawer and took out a writing pad and pen.

*   *   *   *   *

"How do I look?" asked Donald Coy, his voice rasping.

"Like you've been stabbed," said Monte.

Coy half-lifted his arm and with it, the tubes inserted into his wrist. He let it fall again.

Monte took a seat. "What happened?"

"Ambush. Nice young girl to distract me. 'Please sir, I've lost my dog'. I fell for it like a rookie."

"Like a person not expecting to be attacked in broad daylight, you mean."

"Christian Schwarzkopf."

"Yes."

"Get me up to speed," said Coy, gingerly pushing himself up on the pillows.

"Developments," said Monte, "evidence. I'm wondering if I should turn it over to the police."

"Can it wait till I'm back on me feet?"

"This evidence walks on two legs and is in my possession."

Coy rubbed his chin. He grunted. "Pass me that water."

Monte obliged.

"Way I see it," said Coy, "Schwarzkopf isn't going anywhere. But we can't have you and your evidence sitting round in the open."

"I'm not. I had a friend find me somewhere safe."

"And you throw that away by coming here?"

"These aren't experts," said Monte, "these are kids. And I know about shaking tails."

"Oh you do, huh?"

Coy winced and lay back, cradling the cup of water in his hands. "How solid is this evidence?"

"Pretty damning, but it would be one person's word against another."

"It's probably not enough."

"I'm still working on acquiring more."

Coy rubbed his brow. "Monte," he said, "getting yourself killed is not going to help."

"What if we get far away, me and the evidence, and stay below radar until you're recovered. You are going back?"

"Of course."

"This witness thinks our man has friends high up in the force."

"That's all a bit pulp fiction," said Coy, "I think," he pointed a thick finger, "I think back in the day a few faces from the club looked away at the right time, and now MI6 have other uses for Schwarzkopf. That's not the same thing as all-out corruption."

"Okay," said Monte, "let's say Schwarzkopf is on some kind of government payroll. Let's say he's giving them info on something big. If that is the case, then how far would MI6 go to protect him? Would they let him get away with murder? With arranging the stabbing of a policeman?"

Coy bit his lip. "Who the hell knows how high up this goes? We could turn this over now and make a stink and some of it would surely stick. Schwarzkopf gets his fancy lawyers to draw it out, maybe he spends a few months behind bars in a cozy little open prison on conspiracy charges. What about James Robertson and Tony Perkins? If our theory is right then we need to find out what they had."

"Well," said Monte, "I'm working on that too. Don't you want to take this guy down?"

"Oh," said Coy, "don't think for a moment that it wouldn't give me the greatest pleasure. Bang up a businessman and screw over the establishment? My memoirs would pay for my retirement. Have you considered, though, that if we're not dealing with bent coppers, and Schwarzkopf really is giving useful intel to the secret services, forcing him out might result in letting even bigger fish off the hook?"

"I've never been a big believer," said Monte, "in the means justifying the ends. If you let one criminal get away with murder in order to bring down another, what does that make you?"

"Admirably moral," replied Coy, "in my policing life I've made deals. I've turned the other cheek in exchange for a bit of information from a narc."

"Hardly on the same scale. I hope."

"No," said Coy, "no. And I would never ignore a serious crime. But things get complicated higher up. How many mob informants are living new lives. How many crimes have been prevented by their testimony?"

Monte sat back. "I thought we were on the same side."

"We are," said Coy. "You want to tell me more about this witness."

"His name is Charles Addington," said Monte, "he says Schwarzkopf, through Colin Moony coerced him into stabbing Robertson."

"He confessed to the murder?"

"Yes."

"And he told you this willingly?"

"Don," said Monte, "he came to me for help. He wants to do the right thing. I just don't want it to be wasted."

Coy spent a few moments in thought, then: "Go away," he said, "go away for a while and take your witness with you. Find out what you can, if you can, but if there's ever even the slightest sign that you're in danger, phone Hardacre. No, screw that, just phone triple nine and tell them everything. Jesus. Morphine's wearing off."

"Want me to fetch a nurse?"

"I have this handy button," said Coy, pressing it. "Stay in touch. Don't phone my old mobile. I'll need a phone."

"I'm ahead of you," said Monte. He took out the newly purchased smart phone and began to unwrap it.

"Maybe we can write our memoirs together from prison," said Coy.

"Don't pretend," said Monte, "that this isn't the most fun you've had in years."

Coy laughed, and swore as his stitches pulled tight at his side.

*   *   *   *   *

Eddie drove the blue BMW Christian Schwarzkopf had gifted him.

He picked Martha up outside the shops just past the roundabout on Cherry Hinton Road. She wore black jeans, a snow-white jumper and a dark coat. Eddie opened the boot so that she could deposit her small wheeled suitcase inside.

"This isn't a holiday," he said as she slid into the passenger seat.

"Ha ha," she said, "it is for me. Some of us have to study hard to get by."

Eddie steered the car back into traffic and headed for the ring road.

"What is it I'm supposed to do?" said Martha.

"Charm Charles' parents. Find out if they know where he is."

"What's going to happen to Charlie if they find him?"

"What do you think?"

Martha struggled out of her coat. She threw it onto the back seat. "Poor Charlie," he said.

"Never mind Charlie. It's yourself you should worry about. Me too."

"What do you mean?"

Eddie pulled out onto the dual carriageway and accelerated hard.

"We're all accomplices," he said, "that makes us liabilities. So you'd best keep your mouth shut and behave."

"I always behave," said Martha, "unless I'm not supposed to."

"You want Christian to order you to stab somebody next?"

"I couldn't hurt a fly."

"I've seen you do far worse."

"Stop being beastly. Anyway, I've been here from the start. Spider likes me."

Eddie shook his head. "You have no idea, do you."

"Yes I do. I know you think that I'm stupid. Well I'm not."

"I think," said Eddie, "that you are whatever you have to be, depending on the situation."

"You're very cruel," said Martha. She sat up and leaned close to whisper into Eddie's ear. "It's a good job that I love you."

Eddie tightened his jaw. A faint sickness swelled in his stomach.

Martha sat back and played lazily with her hair, looking out of the window. "Poor Charlie," she said again, after a while.

*   *   *   *   *

"How's the house working out?" asked Richard.

"It's complicated," said Monte.

They sat in his car in the parking lot outside Cherry Hinton Hall Park.

"Complicated is good," said Richard, "I don't do commonplace."

Monte opened the envelope. "I take it all went well," he said.

"In and out in five. They probably won't even notice for a while."

"This is her alright," said Monte, pulling out the file, "Maria Waters. Paranoid Schizophrenic. Personality disorder. Poor woman."

"Skip to the end," said Richard, "it will interest you."

"Patient went missing?"

"I took the liberty," said Richard, "of doing a little digging. No extra charge."

"What's this?"

"Newspaper reports. Maria Waters disappeared twenty years ago. There was a full investigation. Even made national television, but she was never found."

"This makes a lot of sense."

"If you need someone," said Richard, "for protection…"

"I'll be fine," said Monte, "you'll excuse me. I need to make a call. Thank you again."

"You know where I am," said Richard through the window as Monte climbed into his own vehicle.

"I do."

Richard watched Monte drive away. He picked up his phone, stared at for a long while, then made the call.

*   *   *   *   *

Bradley Crawford had long since learned to bury his real name deep down into his psyche. He prided himself on embracing each new identity he adopted, down to giving them a proper back-story, little nuances and physical ticks. If I hadn't been an assassin, he thought, not for the first time, as he waited patiently by the baggage carousel at Heathrow, I could have been one hell of an actor.

Customs was as straightforward as ever. Bradley was a man with the confidence that came of having an entire nation's espionage resources behind him. And not just any nation. The greatest. That was one hell of a blocker to have on your side.

He took a taxi to King's Cross, making sure not to pay too much or too little for the tip. In the atrium he bought a coffee and a sandwich and took a seat at one of the round plastic tables. It was twenty-three minutes until his train. He sat and watched the passersby. Ordinary people with ordinary lives. Their world worked according to forces that they only barely understood. Forces of which he was a part. The coffee was passable. The sandwich was not.

On the train he unwrapped his new phone and inserted the micro-sim which he had kept in his wallet, texted the number he had memorized with the right code and waited patiently for the reply. It didn't take long. He read very carefully the destination and time at which he would pick up his equipment, removed the sim and discreetly dropped it into the remains of the plastic cup of coke that stood before him, to be flushed shortly.

Bradley sat back and opened the paper, the *Metro*. After a moment though he flicked it shut again and folded it neatly upon the table. London rolled past. A city like any other, gray, sprawling and teeming with life. Cities were the greatest statements of human civilization, but too few among them were great citizens. How many strove to do their best? How many served their time in the military? How many contributed and how many were just along for the ride?

Bradley had read a paper once, in a circular he had subscribed to, some draft of an idea which he had felt strongly at the time, and still did, was essentially *right* in its thinking: that only those who had served in the military should be allowed to vote. Of course that was only proper and just. If you were prepared to make the greatest sacrifice for your country then that ought to put you right at the head of the queue. Instead, you had to watch the land that you loved being dragged down by soft-hearted liberal elites, college kids, and pacifists whose willful naivety was incomprehensible.

The assassin bit his cheek. This thinking was not for mission-time. It was a distraction, a liability. Something had felt wrong, he reflected, even since before takeoff at JFK. The train had reached the outskirts of London now. Patches of green had begun to pepper the landscape. An attractive young woman took the seat opposite. No older than twenty. She carried a laptop. A student, Bradley thought. The girl caught his eye for a second, looked away, smiled and blushed.

Bradley took out his micro MP3-player and wireless headphones and fired up his favorite playlist. It was good old country from the classic years. George Jones, Merle Haggard and Johnny Cash. Something about those tales of lovesick hearts and hard lives entertained but did not move him. Theirs was not a world he could relate to, and perhaps that was why he enjoyed them. He looked at the girl again and idly speculated how easy it would be to seduce her. People, thought Bradley, as the train rolled on, were largely fools. He would feel much more settled once he picked up the gun.

*   *   *   *   *

Coy sniffed and took the mobile phone from beneath his pillow. Monte answered after the fifth ring.

"Are you driving?" said Coy.

"I just pulled over. How are you?"

"Never mind that," said Coy, "I have Maria Waters' file in front of me."

"That was quick."

"Thank heavens for obedient underlings."

"So?"

"The day she disappeared, Maria was supposed to go and visit her uncle. The hospital gave her a day-pass and a nurse saw her to the train station. The uncle was supposed to meet her at the other end."

"But he didn't?"

"The uncle says that he didn't know anything about it. Whoever called and spoke to the hospital, it wasn't him."

"They never tracked down the call?"

"Too long ago for that. There was a witness, saw her getting into a dark-coloured sports car. That was the last anybody saw."

"Is the case still open?"

"Officially she's classed as a missing person."

"Thank you," said Monte, "I'll call you tonight."

"I'll look forward to that," said Coy. He hung up, replaced the phone, and pressed the button for the nurse. She appeared a moment later. It was Sheryl, the brunette.

"Everything okay?"

"No," said Coy, "I need a whiskey. I'm bored out of my considerable mind."

New York, eighteen years previously

"Relax," said the man, "you're not in any trouble. We both have your best interests at heart."

Christian did not know what to make of this. He did what he always did in these situations—to fall back on the superiority of one's breeding. To buy himself a few seconds with which to gain composure, he slowly and carefully removed a cigarette from the box upon the table, flicked on the lighter next to it, cupped his hands and inhaled deeply, letting the nicotine cloud billow outwards in one long, drawn-out breath. He gestured vaguely to indicate his semi-nudity. "It seems you have me at something of a disadvantage," he said.

The man smiled. "Would you like to get dressed."

"I think I'm quite comfortable as I am."

"We know all about you, Christian," said the man, "we know about your dealer Maurice. We know about the Half-Note club where you get your girls from. And your boys."

"Men," said Christian, "I hope you won't be so vulgar as to accuse me of…"

"Of…?"

"Men," said Christian, again.

"We're not interested in you, as such," said the man, "we've no gain in embarrassing you. Or the memory of your father."

Christian looked away.

"Your father was a good man. A good American. A wealth-creator. The name Schwarzkopf still means a lot in certain quarters. It would be a shame to undo all of that work."

"What do you want?"

The man looked down. "Information," he said.

"What information can you possibly want from me?"

"There are certain people," said the man, "influential people. Rich people. Who move in circles such as yours. Now these certain people we would like to keep an eye on."

"You want me to spy?"

"It would be easy. We wouldn't ask you to do anything dangerous. Our men are the best and we'd support you all the way. Unless of course…"

"Go on."

"Well," said the man, "we could hand our dossier on you over to the police. I've read it and I have to say, Christian, it looks very bad for you."

"Are you saying I would go to prison?"

The man shook his head. "Possession of class-A drugs. Sex trafficking…"

Christian snorted.

"…sex trafficking, prostitution, conspiracy to pervert the course of justice, aiding and abetting of a criminal enterprise. We have photos, tapes. It's not pretty reading."

"You've been very busy," said Christian, "I hope you've had your fun from it."

"This gives me no pleasure at all," said the man.

Christian laughed.

"You'll be looking at twenty-five years minimum. I'm afraid my superiors would insist."

Christian closed his eyes. He took another deep drag on the cigarette. "Well," he said, "it seems I don't have very much choice do I?"

"You'll do it then?"

"I just said so, didn't I?"

"We'll guide you every step of the way." The man sat forward, balancing his elbows upon his knees. "This isn't the end of your life," he said, "you know there are even certain benefits to this arrangement."

"It's hard to see them," said Christian, "from where I'm sitting."

"We don't want you to change a thing," said the man, "we want you to carry on just as before. The drugs, the women, the men. You just carry on."

"I'm afraid I don't understand."

"Don't you? We need the rest of your associates to believe that nothing has happened. Nobody is going to suspect a man like you of being a mole if you carry on as you are."

"How do I know you're not going to prosecute me further down the line?"

"Now why would we do that?" said the man, sitting back. "Think about it. Do you really think that the government wants its dirty linen washed in a public court? Christian, we don't care what you do, just so long as you play fair."

Christian flicked ash upon the sheet that covered his nakedness. "So what happens next?"

"Nothing," said the man, "not for a while. You live your life. In a few weeks we'll start you working. Nothing strenuous. Just a name here, a place there. People we'd like you to meet. People we know you can get access to."

"Will I have to wear a wire?"

The man waved his hands. "No, no. Nothing so crude. This is not about getting prosecutions, Christian."

"Then what is it about?"

"Why the only thing that matters," said the man, "protecting America."

"Protecting America," echoed Christian. He took another deep draft on the cigarette, and watched the smoke curl up in slow intricate spirals towards the ceiling.

"Call me Agent Buchanan," said the man, "I'd like you to think of me as a friend."

Ely, Ten years previously

The great cathedral was almost empty. It was a cold blustery day and very few had come to visit. The under-employed guides were quiet as mice, sensed rather than heard as Christian sat, in a middle pew on the left-hand side, beneath the dizzying heights of the vaulted wooden sky. The geometry was beautiful. It was almost an insult to think that human hands had made this place.

Christian did not understand why he came here. It was a masochistic experience, a mixture of pleasure, pain and emptiness, and he always left feeling melancholy. Nevertheless, he visited often, and had, of course, made a generous financial contribution which ensured him freedom at all times.

The serried ranks and columns drew the eye endlessly inwards toward the great glass window over the font. It made Christian feel powerless and perhaps that is what he wanted. The stillness and quiet were as enervating as they were terrifying, like the gallery-room in his newly-acquired Cambridgeshire house.

Christian had no relationship with god.

For some time he sat, thinking of nothing, letting the filtered light into his being as dust-mites slowly tumbled. At last he rose and headed for the door that led to the Octagon tower. It was off-limits to normal visitors, except for paid guided tours but no one would stop him, he knew, this kindly benefactor who came to sit in quiet reflection. How little they understood of the wolf's nature beneath his sheep's clothing. It was hilarious, thought Christian somberly, a great cosmic joke, how one's character could so easily be masked.

He knew he would never relinquish his power, would never conquer his addictions to sex and drugs and the control over his fellow beings that his extreme wealth enabled. Why should he? Why indeed.

There must be something in me, he thought, as he mounted the narrow wooden stairs, which twisted endlessly upward around the great stone pillar, something *worthy*. How could one cultivate an appreciation of the arts if one were entirely bestial in nature?

Christian climbed without pause. By the time he neared the top he was breathing quickly and sweating slightly, calves throbbing gently and thighs warmed by the strain. He was a fit man who knew that those half his age would struggle to match in physicality.

He stepped out into the cold, sharp embrace of the air. The sky was billowing crisp white-azure. Clouds moved at pace. The masked sun glimmered and glittered and lit up their edges like halos on paintings of saints. The land unfolded below in greens and browns and blues.

Christian grasped the balustrade and stared out fierce and unblinking, as if challenging the very demons themselves, Satan, God or his angels. "Come and get me," he shouted into the wind, "I'm here."

Tears began to fall freely from his eyes. "I'm here," he said and then again.

At length he turned and slumped to the ground, his back to the ancient stone. It was past dusk when he began the long descent back to earth.

*   *   *   *   *

Charles, Harry, Aabira and Penny were playing cards around the dining room table when Monte returned to the house. The smell of cooking was in the air.

"I saved some for you," said Penny, rising, "I've been trying to teach this lot to play poker. Charles is a natural."

"It's simple probability," said Charles.

Harry grunted, stood up, stretched. "I need a coffee. Anyone else?"

"He wanted to go for a run," whispered Aabira, once Harry had left, "Penny told him no."

"He's not used to being cooped up," said Monte, "none of us are."

"It's like he can't sit still for five minutes."

"I expect," said Monte, "right now he'd rather be doing than thinking."

"Is something wrong?" asked Charles, "with Harry? Is there anything I can do?"

Monte looked at Charles. "No."

In the kitchen Penny was serving up. Harry stood by the kettle and stared out of the window. Monte put a hand on Harry's shoulder. "How are you bearing up?"

Harry shook his head. "I don't really know what we're doing. I mean what's our goal here?"

"We go as far as we can," said Monte, "just a few more days. Then we turn over everything that we've got."

"Okay," said Harry, "but what chance do we have of achieving anything?"

"Forget results," said Monte, "to a certain extent that's out of our hands. This is about doing what we can and what's right."

"You want a coffee, boss?"

Back in the dining room Monte placed Maria Waters' file upon the table. "This is everything I could get on Schwarzkopf's girl."

"Maria Waters," said Aabira, "so she went missing. And we have that piece of carpet with blood on it. Do we think that it's her blood?"

"Tony Perkins and James Robertson obviously thought so."

"So," said Harry, "they were going to go to the police? With a bit of old rag?"

"They must have had something else," said Aabira, "maybe the same photos we found, of Schwarzkopf and Maria together."

"Seems a bit thin."

"What if they weren't going to the police?" said Monte. "From what I remember of Robertson he was always searching for a line, an angle. For money."

"You think," said Penny, "they tried to blackmail Schwarzkopf? That's one hell of a move."

"Do you have anything you can add to this, Charles?" asked Monte.

Charles, who was absorbed in studying a photograph from the file, looked up. "She's not missing," he said, "and she's not dead."

All eyes turned to the young man.

"I've seen her," he said, "I went there with Schwarzkopf once. He wanted me to help carry some things."

"Are you sure?" said Monte.

"Perfectly. That's the girl. Schwarzkopf called her his princess. I know where she is. I can take you."

*   *   *   *   *

Albert Rivers was a man who hated anything not done by the book. Primarily, he understood, because exactly following the rules was the one thing that could protect you when shit hit the fan, and shit always did hit, not matter how carefully you tried to steer clear of choppy waters. These particular waters, he reflected, as he steered his car through the evening traffic, were the choppiest he had ever encountered.

He looked wistfully at his DCI's uniform, which hung in a plastic bag from the handle above the rear-left passenger door. He had been expressly told not to wear it, and that, Rivers considered, was a very bad sign. A car behind beeped loudly. Rivers jumped, swore, and set his car into motion, swinging out into traffic and off at the second exit.

When the order had come to meet with Agent Buchanan, Rivers' well-developed survival instinct had kicked in. Instantly he had envisaged holding the meeting at police headquarters, with plenty of others to absorb the flak and, crucially, at least one officer of higher rank present. That afternoon's phone call had disabused Rivers of that notion in the cruelest of ways.

Now he was in a place that he had always dreaded—out on his own, where protocol and rules faded and blurred into obscurity, with no one there to corroborate, no superior to hand-off to and no idea what he was supposed to be fucking doing.

It took him two turns up and down the street to find what he thought must be the right driveway. Rivers steered the car slowly up the gravel rise. High hedges cut off the view of the road. He parked the car next to a black SUV, turned off the engine and stepped out.

The house was in darkness save for one lit window, the curtains of which were half-drawn. Rivers felt ridiculous, scared and affronted. He took a deep breath, raised himself up and reached for the doorbell. There was none. He sighed, and gave the knocker a smart rap. He waited. After thirty seconds he knocked again. He felt his anger rising steadily. He knocked again, but still it was long moments before the door swung inwards.

"You must be Rivers," said the smiling American, "well come in old chum. I'm Agent Buchanan. Cup of tea?"

Rivers felt instantly wrong-footed. He smiled, raised a hand but the American had already dropped his and turned away, leaving Rivers to trail behind uncertainly.

"Have a seat," said Agent Buchanan as they entered the lit front room. A single armchair was placed in one corner, a couple of collapsible chairs opposite. There was a low wooden coffee table in the room's centre. A bare bulb hung from an exposed wire in the ceiling.

Rivers stared at the third man present, a swarthy, broad-shouldered fellow who stood, suited and motionless, leaned against the wall. Rivers nodded to him. The man remained stiff and expressionless. Agent Buchanan gestured again at the armchair. "Please sit."

Slowly Rivers sat. He licked his lips. The big man turned to face him but said nothing. There was the trace of a smile on his lips.

"Who is…" began Rivers.

"Tea?" said Buchanan. "I'll be back in a moment."

Rivers was left alone with the stranger. He tried staring back, then flustered. "This is…" he said, then failed. He made himself as comfortable as possible but could not decide where to put his arms and legs. He became aware of how exposed he felt, sitting with the back of his head facing the window.

Buchanan returned, holding a steaming plastic sealed cup of the type only obtained from coffee shops. The agent put the cup on the table and gave the whole a gentle shove in Rivers' direction. Rivers reached for it, then hesitated.

"It's not poisoned," said Buchanan, grinning. The man in the suit laughed and shook his head. Rivers did not know how to respond.

"Let's get down to business," said Buchanan, pulling up a chair. "Relax, Rivers. We're all friends here."

Rivers cleared his throat. "I'm not certain what you require of me."

"Yes you are," said Buchanan, "we have a situation here. Now my people and your people up top, they're all on the same page, but you, Rivers, you're the, how do you Brits say it? You're the Johnny on the ground."

The man in the suit laughed again.

Buchanan took a piece of paper from his pocket, unfolded it and set it down upon the table. "You've done well so far," he said, "and all we need you to do, if anything untoward happens involving any of these names, in any way, is to bury it. You know how to do that. Tie a neat little bow on it, stamp it shut and drop it into a deep dark file somewhere."

"Who are these people?"

"You don't want to know. Just keeping doing what you do best."

"What's that supposed to mean?"

"C'mon Rivers, I've read your file. I've talked to your superiors. Why do you think you got this gig? It's a..." Buchanan waved his hand in the air, "...a compliment. Now our guys are going to do some cleaning up. We need to know that you'll hold up your end."

Rivers licked his lips. "I'll need orders," he said, "official ones."

Buchanan leaned forward. "What's the matter with you?" he said, "didn't you get your orders? Didn't they tell you to come here tonight?"

"But there's nothing on paper..."

"Well why the hell do you think that is?"

Rivers looked from one man to the other.

"Answer the question," said Buchanan, raising his voice, "why?"

"Security?" said Rivers hesitantly.

"Security," said Buchanan, sitting up and smiling at the man in the suit, "you see, he does get it. Great. This is going great. So you'll do your bit, huh?"

"What if," Rivers licked his lips, "what if this comes back to me? My superior..."

"It's not your superior you should be afraid of," said Buchanan. He stood up. The man in the suit came to stand next to him. They stared down at the policeman.

"You know who you should be afraid of?" said Buchanan. Neither of them were smiling.

Rivers made to stand up but Buchanan leaned over him. "You know who you should be afraid of?" he said again.

Rivers shook his head.

"The Russians," said Buchanan. He stood up and began to laugh. The man in the suit joined in.

Rivers did not know whether to smile or laugh or cry.

"You see," said Buchanan, to his companion, "I told you these Brits were good eggs."

The man in the suit went back to his place by the wall. Buchanan sat down. "Off you go," he said to Rivers, without looking at him. "Don't forget your tea," he continued, as the policeman stood up, "you might want to drink it on your way home."

*   *   *   *   *

Eddie drove for an hour and a half before they stopped, at Martha's insistence, at a dismal motorway service station. The ugly grey buildings squatted solemnly under the morose sky. This was a nowhere-place, with no connection or community, where humans stopped and suffered themselves with the homogenous food, bland atmosphere and shops which promised to disappoint.

They ordered coffee and breakfast and took their trays to a featureless white table by the window. Martha preened and adjusted her top, for the benefit of a nearby gang of bikers who sat, polished helmets at their feet, and exchanged knowing words and nods.

Eddie eyed her with distaste. "Is there real anything at all in your soul?" he said.

"You promised me you weren't going to be nasty anymore," said Martha, "and what's so good in your soul, whatever the hell that is? What have you done that's so noble?"

"At least I don't shop myself around like a cheap rag."

"It's easier for you boys," said Martha. She sipped her Coke through a straw and looked up at him from under her fake lashes. "I actually like it when you're mean to me," she said. "It shows that you care."

Eddie rubbed his temples. "Don't you ever stop?"

"What do you want from me?" said Martha. She rolled her eyes coquettishly at the bikers.

"Some humanity."

"Like you even know what that means."

Eddie reached out to grab Martha's wrist. He yanked so that her ribs pushed up against the table-top. Martha winced.

"I didn't know that's how you like it?" she said.

"Shut up," said Eddie.

"Is everything alright here?" It was one of the bikers. He stood now at Eddie's left shoulder.

"Everything's fine," said Eddie.

"I wasn't talking to you," said the man.

"Tell him it's fine," said Eddie to Martha.

Martha smiled. She drew the moment out, then looked up at the biker and smiled sweetly. "Everything's fine," she said, "I like it when my boyfriend treats me rough."

The biker man snorted, shook his head, and rejoined his friends at their table.

"You see," said Martha, sitting back with her coke, "I have power too." She sucked on her straw.

Eddie looked out at the parking lot. It was going to be a long trip.

*   *   *   *   *

Harry drove, with Aabira in the back seat and Charles next to him, directing. Ominous clouds were choking the sky, the light was grey and dim and the threat of rain hung heavy. None of this could dampen the beauty of the little town of Ely.

"It's actually a city," observed Charles as the famous spire came into sight, "because it has a cathedral, irrespective of size."

"Is that right?" said Aabira.

"Where now?" said Harry.

"Just circle the centre," said Charles, "it's a little road out. I'll remember when I see it."

"You'd better."

"Just take your time," said Aabira, pointedly, "if anything looks familiar then shout."

It took twenty minutes of circling and two false ventures before Charles pointed to the left. "Try there," he said, then, "that's it, straight ahead."

"We're leaving the village," observed Harry.

"I told you it was a little way out," said Charles, "keep going. No, wait. Reverse it. On the left here. Wait. Sorry, no. Try up ahead."

Harry caught Aabira's eye in the mirror. She looked concerned. A heavy rain began to fall so suddenly that it was disconcerting. With wipers on full they crept on, away from the houses down close, hedge-lined back-roads.

"Up the hill," said Charles, after a time, "this is it. See that little track on the right."

"Can we get the car up there?' asked Aabira.

"Yes."

Harry looked at Charles, sighed, shook his head, and nosed the car onto the track—little more than a worn strip of grass with high banks of undergrowth on each side. The rain had ceased but with the further darkening of the skies he flicked the headlights on. The car bumped and scraped its way forward.

"This is it," said Charles. There was a note of fear in his voice.

The house was small and squat and made of old stone, with a little wooden porch, a log-store outside and to the left an unkempt garden. Brown leaves swirled over the grass around the feet of a rusted swing with seats for two.

"You'd best stay in the car," said Harry, "Aabira and I will go in."

He took the keys from the ignition, opened the door and stepped out into the battling elements. A wind had gotten up. It grabbed at Aabira's headscarf and dress. They shielded their eyes and walked up to the house.

*   *   *   *   *

Spider couldn't sleep but it wasn't the storm that kept him awake. He looked at Christian, who lay next to him, snoring softly upon the Emperor-sized bed. Spider looked at the gold watch upon Christian's wrist and at the dark hairs around it. After a while he got up, wrapped a towel around his waist and padded into the study.

He poured himself a whiskey and took one of Christian's one-hundred-dollar cigars from the humidifier. Then he sat in the big chair and put his naked feet up on the shining mahogany desk, letting the glass hang idly in one hand and looking around. He saw the antique candelabra that hung from the elaborately frescoed ceiling, the William Morris wallpaper, gold-and-silver ashtray, leather writing square and silver pen holder. This luxury gave Spider a deep feeling of satisfaction and peace. How he wished, oh how he wished, that all this was his and his alone.

Even the writing pad was monogrammed, he observed, as he lifted the glass to his lips and let a few drops of precious liquid fall down his throat. He grunted and let the glass fall and it was then that his attention lit again upon the writing pad. The topmost square of paper was clean but bore indentations from whatever had been written on the torn-off page that had preceded.

Spider looked toward the bedroom and listened a moment. Opening a drawer and rummaging about until he found a pencil, he pulled the pad across and began to rub the edge of the pencil-lead lightly across its surface. It was an old trick he remembered from school. Something to entertain your friends during a dull lesson.

Quickly the writing from the previous leaf became clear. It was a list of names and addresses, in Christian's unmistakably neat handwriting. When Spider uncovered the first name he was curious. Upon outlining the second he was further puzzled, but it was when he witnessed his own name appear before him that he began to feel an icy coldness run down his spine.

His hands shook and his brain felt numb. He swung the chair round and pulled out the computer keyboard on its retractable shelf.

Spider knew the password of course, even if he did not understand its significance. Once in it was easy to access the CCTV. Swallowing hard Spider pulled up the latest recordings for the study in which he sat. Christian taped all his meetings, Spider knew. There was a secret button underneath the desk—a feature in which Christian delighted.

Spider watched a previous version of his lover write out the very list he had uncovered, and watched him hand it over to the man who Spider had seen only a hand-full of times before. Only a hand-full of times, yet Spider recognized that this man was important. He was, so far as Spider knew, the only person other than his father who Christian was afraid of.

It might not mean anything, Spider thought. It might be routine. He sat there for long minutes but he could not convince himself. In the end, self-preservation won out. Spider re-entered the bedroom as stealthily as possible. He picked up his clothes, wallet, and watch, and took them back into the study to dress.

As a last act he took five hundred pounds in cash from the mini-safe in the bottom drawer. Spider was two miles away in a taxi when he remembered that he had left the pencil-covered note in plain view upon the desk. "I need to go home first," he said to the driver, thinking of his passport, "and then back to the station."

*   *   *   *   *

"Is that really Charles' house?" Martha leaned across Eddie to peer out of the window.

"Charles' parent's house," corrected Eddie. He held the car in neutral with the engine thrumming comfortably as they sat and stared at the mansion—there was no other word for it. A low stone wall fronted the lawn. A neat row of sculpted poplars behind it was spaced far enough apart that the three-story edifice was in plain view.

"I should have been nicer to Charlie."

"Get out," said Eddie.

"Aren't you going to park the car?"

"I'm not coming with you. It's better if you go alone."

"Well where will you be?"

"I'm going to find us a place to stay tonight."

"A double room?" asked Martha, holding her face close to Eddie's.

"Get out."

"No," Martha sat back and crossed her arms, "it's raining."

Eddie stared at her.

"Fine," said Martha, at last, and opened the door.

"Tell them you got a taxi."

Martha screwed up her face against the wind and hugged herself. "What?"

"Tell them that you got a taxi," yelled Eddie. He reached over and yanked the door shut, gunned the engine and pulled away faster than necessary. In the rear view mirror he saw Martha, looking absurd in her scant clothing, flip him a finger. For the first time since the trip began, he smiled.

Derby was a city Eddie knew well. He had been born not far away, in much more humble circumstances than Charles. He found the Travel Lodge without difficulty. Like all such buildings it was little more than a squat rectangle of concrete that promised nothing further than numbing familiarity.

He booked two single rooms (they were next to each other), ordered a roast meal from the chain-pub that was organically connected to the hotel, and he ate in silence. The meal was surprisingly good. Two young boys played the fruit machine, which leaked artificial light into the glum restaurant. Eddie bought a pint of bitter and a whiskey chaser. A family came in, buoyed by holiday spirits. Their kids argued and sulked and laughed and the mum and dad handled it all like pros.

It reminded Eddie of his brother and his parents and the holidays they used to have. It had been three years since he had spoken to any of them and still he did not understand why. He had cut himself off because of nothing more than a vague feeling of claustrophobia and resentment. Resentment of what he did not know. Now, as usual, he thrust that line of thought brutally to one side. He checked his phone for any message from Martha (there was none) and took the featureless stairs up to the long featureless corridor where he found his room halfway down.

Eddie kicked off his shoes and lay down upon the bed. He felt suddenly overcome with tiredness. Still there was no word from Martha. She would have to wait. He turned off his phone, took off his shirt and lay down on the cold, crisp sheets.

*   *   *   *   *

For many minutes Monte stood by the stone pillars that marked the threshold of Christian Schwarzkopf's property, observing the house as if it were a mystery that could be solved by sight alone. At length he began to walk up the drive. He felt himself in the shadow of something ominous. The door at the top of the steps stood slightly ajar. Monte pushed it wider and entered the hallway.

His feet echoed dully on the marble floor. The place had the trappings of tasteful opulence. Polished wood and gold ornamentation. A large portrait hung upon the wall, the face of a man with strong, aquiline features and streaks of grey in his hair. The man was unsmiling. Monte wondered what it was that drove people to have portraits made of themselves. Much like the modern phenomenon of selfies, he mused, an endless quest to display oneself at one's most attractive. Part of the endless game, made more tangible by social media, to rank oneself in the great order of life. A fool's errand by any meaningful measure.

"My father."

Monte turned. Christian Schwarzkopf was dressed in suit and tie, but there was a ragged looseness about his demeanor.

"I've come to talk."

"You're less grubby than I supposed," said Christian, "one thinks of private investigators as poorly-dressed alcoholics with tobacco-stained fingers."

"It will be better for you if turn yourself in."

Christian smiled. "Now that sounds more like a PI. Turn myself in for what exactly?"

"Murder," said Monte, "and conspiracy to murder."

The billionaire rubbed his forehead. He turned and, seemingly as an afterthought, motioned the detective to follow. The drawing room was spacious and comfortable and decorated in cream and light gold. Christian took a seat. Monte remained standing.

"How much do you want?" said Christian.

"I don't want money."

"Oh come now, mister Boutista. Yes you do. Everybody does. They might pretend otherwise but the truth is that everyone desires what I have."

Monte shook his head.

"It's not a boast," said Christian, "everybody has a price. Do you understand how depressing that is? When you experience that truth of that, what is there left?"

"I don't believe that it is true," said Monte.

"Then you're a fool," said Christian, "or deluded. I've done things to people, Boutisa, that you couldn't imagine. And they let me. Because money is power and power is everything."

"Some would say that love is everything," said Monte.

Christian sneered. "Love," he said, "love is weakness, a mental illness."

"I think that you're wrong about that."

"People like you disgust me. Sentimentality. Yearning. Softness. You want to see strength, Mr. Boutista? Follow me."

The room to which Christian led them was wide and long, with high skylights and no furniture. Along both sides, rows of paintings hung upon the oak-paneled walls.

"Do you know Vorticism?"

"I know of it," said Monte.

"They knew that you had to destroy the old in order to create the new. They embraced the rise of the machine—the cold hard logic that many among mankind are weak and feeble and must be conquered or replaced. To recognise that the only power is that of the individual. That is true strength."

Monte looked at the paintings. "Sounds like plain old fascism to me."

"You disappoint me."

"And yet I can't be bought."

"Can't you? What about the life of your friends? Would you make me a deal for that?"

"You've already threatened my friends," said Monte, "I'm still here. So are they."

"Do you see this painting?" said Christian, turning away, "the bold brutality of the lines. The magnificent vibrancy of the colours. Do you have any interest in art?"

"Music," said Monte, "is my thing."

Christian chuckled. "My father acquired this painting in nineteen-sixty-two. The owner didn't want to sell. My father drove the man's business into the ground, acquired his debts, and took the painting in payment. Do you know what he said to him then?"

"No."

"He said 'next time a Schwarzkopf makes you an offer, you take it'."

"I'm not that man," said Monte, "and you are not your father."

Christian turned. There was a snarl upon his lips. "You don't know anything about me."

Monte took a step forward. "The first time I saw a ghost," he said.

Christian raised his chin. "What?"

"The first time I saw a ghost," said Monte, "I was seven years old. It was a road traffic accident. My father was driving the car. He stopped to help. It was the only time I'd ever seen him do something selfless. I stood by the side of the road and I watched as a woman pumped the chest of a man who lay upon the asphalt. His face was covered in blood."

Christian hooked a finger under his shirt collar. "Why are you telling me this?"

"I saw that man rise up and leave his body behind. He seemed confused at first. He looked around and he saw himself upon the ground. For a moment he was sad but then his face changed to a gentle mask. He saw me and he smiled and at once I knew much that had gone on in his life. I knew his secrets. I glimpsed his soul."

"You think I'm going to fall for some Halloween tale?"

Monte shook his head. "I saw James Robertson. I saw Lucas Grundy. I see you, yet to come."

Christian felt a cold prickle along his spine.

"It is never too late," said Monte, "to turn back."

"To turn back to what?"

"You are not your father."

"You think I am a monster," said Christian, "you think I haven't loved? I have. And yet still I do the things that I do. Where does that leave your precious philosophy?"

"Maria."

"What did you say?"

"Maria Waters. Was it her that you loved?"

Christian licked his lips. His hands clenched into fists. "Get out," he said.

Monte began to speak.

"Get out of my house. I'll see you dead, you understand?" He continued to shout as the detective walked away. "I'll see your blood upon the ground! You think I can't do it? I'm Christian Schwarzkopf, do you hear? You are nobody. Nobody. I'll kill you and all you hold dear."

The words followed Monte as he left the house and walked down the drive. Leaves blew in the breeze. The trees swayed their branches and dark clouds bunched overhead.

*   *   *   *   *

The man who opened the door was younger and more handsome than Martha had expected.

"Hello," she smiled, twisting her hips and shoulders to display herself at what she considered her most alluring angle.

The man smiled but said nothing. His eyes were steel blue.

"I'm a friend of Charles Addington," said Martha, "from Cambridge. Are his parents in?"

"No," said the man, "I'm his brother, Iain."

"I didn't know Charlie had a brother. Will your parents be back soon?"

"I don't think so."

Martha sighed, and made a show of looking up at the rain and pulling her cardigan tighter.

"Would you like to come in?"

"Please," said Martha. "Is it just you here?" she asked as Iain led the way. The hallway was two-floors high, with a sweeping marble staircase at one end, portraits upon the wall and a real elephant's-foot umbrella stand.

Iain opened one of the many doors. It led to a large and stylish living room, with bay windows, comfortable chairs, and a coal fireplace that crackled with small flames. Rain gusted against the panes. Martha held her hands out to the fire.

"Just me," said Iain, "I hope that you're not disappointed."

"Oh, not at all," said Martha, aware of the way in which her wet clothes hung to her figure. A handsome stranger and an empty house were conditions far exceeding her expectations. She coughed lightly.

"Some whiskey to warm you up?"

"Super," said Martha. She removed her cardigan. "I seem to have gotten a little wet, Iain."

She was disappointed that his gaze did not linger but the challenge made it all the more exciting.

Iain poured drinks for both of them, took a seat and crossed one leg over the other. Martha was left standing in the middle of the room, momentarily unsure of what to do and puzzled and somewhat irritated by the man's lack of chivalry.

"What brought you here on such a night?" said Iain, "is your car outside?"

"I took a taxi," said Martha. Determined to take back control of the situation, she set her glass upon the mantelpiece and reached up under her dress. "The trouble with leggings," she said, rolling them down with practiced grace, "is that they do absorb the rain so." Martha draped them upon the mantelpiece, took up her glass and leaned back against the wall. With satisfaction she noticed Iain's gaze flicker down to her bare legs.

"I didn't catch your name," he said.

"Martha Candelbury."

"Charles mentioned you."

"How sweet of him."

"You're a friend of Christian Schwarzkopf also?"

"Yes, that's right." Martha crossed to the sofa and positioned herself upon it, leaning back and, angling her head and looking up at Iain with her lips slightly parted. "And what do you do, older brother?"

The man who called himself Iain sat forward upon the edge of the chair. He put his elbows upon his knees and stared silently at Martha for so long that a thrill of fear and expectation rose inside her. At last he stood up and moved to a low cupboard upon which stood an old-fashioned record player. He slid open the door underneath and began flicking through records.

"You know something, Martha," he said.

"Tell me."

"I think you and I are going to get along famously." Iain stood and turned the record he had picked up over in his hands. "Do you like country music?" he asked, "I'm a big fan."

*   *   *   *   *

There were no lights on in the rustic stone-walled house. Aabira rung the doorbell but no sound could be heard. Harry knocked loudly.

"It might be the wrong place," he said. He glanced back at the car.

"You don't trust Charles?"

"Do you?"

"Let's try round the back," said Aabira.

They followed the path around the side of the house. It took them past the little garden, with its high hedges, un-mown lawn and the long-dead swing. Harry trod on something in the gloom. He bent down to pick it up.

"A teddy bear?" said Aabira. She took it from him. They reached the back door. It was locked. All was quiet and still.

"Give me a hand," said Harry. The top-most pane of the kitchen window stood open. "I need something to stand on."

"You'll never fit," said Aabira, as Harry dragged over a tree stump from the woodpile that stood to one side. "You won't fit," she said again as he reached up. "I'll do it."

Harry paused. "Are you sure?"

"Yes," said Aabira, "just…don't look."

"I'll need to help you up."

"I'll be fine."

Harry turned away and crossed his arms. "Shout if you need me," he said, "I mean it."

"Okay." Aabira dragged the stump a little further forward and climbed atop it. She pulled the hem of her dress up to her waist and tied the whole in place with a makeshift knot. Putting one foot on the sill, she pulled herself up. The window was very wide and she figured she could angle her body through and swing a leg up and over.

"Are you okay?" called Harry.

"Fine," said Aabira, without much conviction.

She managed to get her upper body through, balancing with one arm on the inside frame. It was painful and awkward. Now, she realised, the only choices were to fully commit or to back out entirely. With a deep breath, she swung her left leg up and over, lost her grip, and felt herself falling unstoppably forward.

Harry turned when he heard the bang. Aabira was nowhere in sight. He called her name repeatedly, framing his hands against the glass and peering in. At length he saw a movement beyond the sink. A dark shape that resolved itself into a figure.

"I'm okay," came Aabira's muffled voice, "sort of."

"Is there a key in the door?"

"Hold on."

Harry watched, feeling frustrated and helpless. "It might be in a drawer somewhere," he said, "or in one of those pots. Aabira?"

For a few moments there was silence. "Got it," she called. A lock rattled and the door swung open. Aabira stood nursing her side.

"What happened? Are you sure you're okay?"

"Hit myself on the tap and scraped my knee. I'll live. We're in now. Let's at least have a look around."

Reluctant to turn on the lights or the torches on their phones, they moved in semi-darkness. Unwashed plates lay in the sink. A stack of empty jars, methodically piled into a neat tower, covered one end of the work surface. Aabira opened the fridge, spilling yellow light into the room.

"Look," she said.

A number of trays sat on the shelves, each covered in clingfilm and labeled with a day of the week. There was milk, butter and bread but nothing more. They left the kitchen. The hallway was long and narrow. At the far end was the front door. A carpeted staircase led up. A muffled thump came from behind the nearest door, which was pushed closed.

Harry took the lead, reached out and pushed the door slowly open. It led into a living room which, like the rest, was shrouded in darkness.

There was a lot of old furniture covered in shawls. Shelves, cupboard-tops, mantelpiece and tables contained a bewildering array of cuddly toys. Rabbits, cats, dogs and all manner in between.

"Hello?" Harry's voice sounded shocking as it broke the stillness. "Hello."

The sound came again, a shuffling movement accompanied by a half-human utterance, high-pitched and fearful.

"Turn on the light," said Harry.

Aabira's hand groped for the switch. The room flooded with light. A thousand unseeing eyes looked on.

"It's okay," said Harry, "we won't hurt you."

Aabira could not see. The open door blocked whomever Harry was talking to. He was staring down at something on the floor. Aabira was shaking. She forced herself to circle to the side, next to Harry.

The woman was older than in the photographs Aabira had seen, but the figure huddled upon the floor was undoubtedly Maria. Her dark hair was longer, her face lined and care-worn. She wore a green skirt festooned with sequins and a purple top decorated with beads. Her eyes faced away from the visitors and she was breathing quickly. In one trembling hand she held a kitchen knife against her neck.

"You won't take me," she said, "I'm not going. I'll kill myself first."

"We're not going to take you anywhere," said Harry, spreading his hands wide, "please put down the knife."

Maria half-laughed and half-spat. "You expect me to believe that?" She shook her head and moved the knife closer to her flesh.

"Wait," said Aabira, "just keep an eye on her."

"Where are you going?" said Harry.

"Wait."

She ran back to the kitchen and through the door. It took her a moment to remember where she had placed the teddy bear. Harry had moved back a little by the time Aabira returned. "Please don't do anything stupid," he was saying.

"Maria," said Aabira. The woman did not move her head. Aabira glanced at Harry, and took a step forward. She held out the bear. "I found this," she said, "I think that it's yours." Very slowly she inched forwards. "Is he yours? He's lovely."

Maria's eyes flickered toward Aabira, then away. Aabira sensed that the woman was fighting herself. At last, the knife fractionally lowering, Maria turned, reached hesitantly out and took the toy bear from Aabira's hand. Maria cradled the creature to her chest. Tears rolled down her eyes. She sniffed and wiped her nose.

"Can I have the knife?" said Aabira.

"What do you want?" said Maria, still crying.

"We just want to talk. My name is Aabira. This is Harry. Would you like some water?"

Maria nodded.

"Harry?"

"Don't get too close," warned Harry. With a curse he disappeared into the hallway.

Aabira handed Maria a tissue. "I had a bear once," she said. "I lost him. What's this one called?"

"Freddy."

"Freddy, that's a nice name."

Harry came back with one of the jars full of water. Aabira took it and handed it to Maria, who cupped it with both hands, still clinging on to the knife.

"How long have you lived here?"

It took a long time for Maria to answer. "He told me that you'd come," she said.

"Don't you ever go out?"

"Too dangerous."

"Why is it dangerous?"

"Because they want me. Are you going to take me away?"

"Not unless you want us to."

Maria shook her head. "I can't," she said, "it's too dangerous."

"Does anyone visit you?" said Aabira. "Who cooks those meals?"

Maria bit her lip.

"Someone must come. Who cooks those meals in the fridge?"

"Stop asking me questions. That's rude."

"Don't you want go out and see people?"

"Everyone outside hates me. They'll kill me."

Aabira slowly lowered herself to sit cross-legged upon the floor. "But we're from outside and we just want to be friends."

"That's what you say. You'll change. You're not one of them yet."

"One of who?"

"The aliens."

"Aliens?"

"Don't you know?" Maria began to rock to and fro. "They're everywhere."

"Maria," said Aabira, "who told you that?"

"He..."

"Who?"

Maria lapsed back into silence. She held the cup and the bear and the knife and rocked gently.

"I want to help you," said Aabira, "tell me how I can help you?"

Maria looked into her eyes. More tears welled up. "They want to kill me."

"The aliens?"

"Yes."

"Look at me, Maria. I came here. We came here. I live out there. I've lived out there for years and I would never lie to you. There are no aliens."

The other woman rubbed her eyes.

"There are no aliens," said Aabira, "it's safe out there. Take my hand."

Maria looked at the proffered hand. She swallowed hard.

"You can do it," said Aabira.

The woman's eyes rolled. She clutched the teddy tighter to her chest.

"Please," said Aabira.

"You fucking liar." The force of Maria's cry made Aabira half-fall. Harry grabbed Aabira's arm and pulled her back.

"Fucking liar," shouted Maria, kicking her leg out in Aabira's direction.

"She needs help," urged Harry, "we should go. It's not safe."

"We can't just leave her like this."

"Yes we can," said Harry, "we have to."

Maria was looking away now, rocking back and forth faster and faster.

A car horn sounded urgently from outside.

"We'll come back," said Aabira as Harry guided her from the room, "Maria, we'll come back."

They exited the back door and half-ran to the front. Charles, standing beside the car, was talking with a stout-looking middle-aged woman wheeling a bicycle.

"These are your friends?" said the woman as Harry and Aabira approached. "Who are you? Nobody is supposed to be here."

"What's that it your basket?" asked Aabira. Before the woman could answer, Aabira pulled open the bag. "Food. Do you know who it's for? Do you know what you're doing to her?"

"You let go of that," screeched the woman, "that's none of your business."

Aabira squared up but Harry moved between them. "We just want to know what you're doing here?" he said.

"None of your business," repeated the woman, "I shall phone Mister…"

"Who?" said Harry. "Mister who?"

"This is private property," said the woman.

"Who pays you to come here?" said Harry. "Is is Christian Schwarzkopf?"

Without a word the woman turned her bicycle and made off hurriedly down the slope.

Harry ran a hand through his hair. "We'd better get back to Monte," he said.

"And leave Maria?" said Aabira.

"Well what do you suggest that we do?"

"Call the police."

"And tell them what?"

"Is she okay?" said Charles. "Maria?"

"The best we can do," said Harry, "is to get back to Monte and tell him what happened."

"That woman," said Charles, "will probably tell Schwarzkopf that we were here."

"Then we should move," said Harry, "now."

"What happened in there?" asked Charles, as Harry guided the car at speed down the lane. No one answered. Charles, sensing something important had occurred between the two, sat back and wondered. He took a last look out of the rear window at the house as it disappeared behind the brow of the hill. *I won't live to see the end of this*, he thought to himself with an odd feeling of detachment, *I can't*. He knew in his heart that he could not survive prison. In fact what he feared most was not being able to kill himself, once he were in there. He could not survive prison and he knew now that he could not let Christian Schwarzkopf go unchallenged. What choice that left him was grim and somehow thrilling. As the car drove on through the night, he settled the plan into his mind and sought solace in the reparations it might bring.

*   *   *   *   *

Penny recognised the car as it pulled into the drive. Still, she watched through the spy-hole until the man behind the wheel got out. By the time he reached the door she had opened it, though she was careful to remain hidden from view.

"Richard."

"Penny," Richard smiled. She led him into the kitchen.

"Cup of tea?"

"Herbal, please, if you have it."

Penny rummaged in the cupboard and switched on the kettle.

"How are you?"

"I was about to ask the same? I've been concerned." Richard looked at the open book upon the table. "*The Self-Aware Universe*?"

"I'm trying to educate myself," said Penny.

"How are you getting on?"

"Did you know," said Penny, taking a seat, "Siddhartha Gautama described how matter was made up of invisible microscopic particles two thousand, five hundred years ago."

"Gautama?"

"Better known as Buddha."

"He was a scientist?"

"No," said Penny, "the point is," she stirred her tea, "I believe that the divide between science and religion is a misunderstanding. Quantum physics proves it."

"How so?"

"It points to what mystics have been saying for centuries—that all things are connected, that separateness is an illusion. Every soul is a part of the universal consciousness. If we could understand that then war, poverty, suffering would cease. All would be well."

"I think I'd like to believe that," said Richard. He yawned. "Excuse me."

"When was the last time you took a break?"

"At some point," said Richard, "I'm going to land up in jail. Probably for a few years. I've resolved myself to that. When I come out I'm going to retire, with money that I've hidden somewhere safe."

"Then what?"

Richard shrugged. "I'll live by the sea. Italy maybe. Or somewhere further."

"And what will you do?"

"I've always fancied painting."

"You could take that up now."

"No," said Richard, "painting requires a certain calmness of the…"

"Soul?"

"I was going to say mind," Richard smiled.

"The I-Ching," said Penny.

"Divination," said Richard, "the…uh, Japanese text."

"Chinese. People in the West nowadays think it's a game. Like reading horoscopes in the paper. It's a subtle philosophical and psychological tool. It's not about providing answers, it's about helping you to find them within yourself. These things have been around for thousands of years for a reason."

"And you're suggesting I try it?"

"If you do it properly. I have a set back at the shop. When all this is over…"

"I don't know much about what you're working on," said Richard, "but I've been at this long enough to know that sometimes you have to walk away."

"Monte isn't one for walking away."

"That's what worries me." Richard drained the last of his tea. "Where is he now?"

Penny began to speak but abruptly paused. She took a sip of her drink.

Richard nodded. "Quite right," he said, "you should trust no-one."

"I trust you," said Penny.

Richard frowned. "But you don't want to tell me where he is?"

"Why are you asking, Richard?"

"Like I said. I'm concerned."

Penny nodded.

"Forget I asked," said Richard, "but when you see him, tell him I stopped by as a friend."

"As a friend," said Penny.

After Richard had gone Penny cleared the table and took her tarot deck from her bag. Choosing a basic three-card spread, she thought for a moment and then dealt the cards. She took her time in turning them over, absorbing the meaning and importance of each. The one representing the future she picked up and carried to the window. Holding it up against the grey sky she observed its lines and detail. It was the 'Tower'. Danger. Destruction. Liberation.

"Yes," she said to herself, "that would be it."

*　*　*　*　*

In the taxi Monte turned on his main mobile. Heeding Coy's warning, he had kept it deactivated for a day and a half. There were five messages and two missed calls. One was from an unknown number, the other had been Sumiyyah. His thumb hovered over the call-button, but in the end he turned the phone off and replaced it in his pocket. He took out the burner-phone and dialed Coy's number. It rang for a long time before cutting off.

Monte reached forward and tapped the dividing window. "Hospital instead, please," he said.

By the time they reached Addenbrooke's, darkness had fallen and a thousand yellow rectangles shone into the night. Monte pulled his coat collar up as he crossed the threshold. Hospitals the world over shared the same atmosphere. The mood was subdued, people were hushed, more inclined to smile sympathetically and somewhat sadly. Staff moved purposefully with an easy professionalism. Late night visitors queued politely at the water machines and even the shops seemed to operate at a more respectful pace.

Monte pressed the button for the elevator. It took him a moment to recognize that the patient being wheeled towards him was his sister, Sarrah. He called out her name. The two orderlies wheeling the bed looked up. Sarrah did not stir. There were thick bandages upon her arms and a drip attached to her wrist.

"Sarrah," said Monte again, then to the orderlies: "I'm her brother."

They exchanged glances. "She was brought in this morning," said the first man.

"What happened?"

"I'm afraid you'll have to ask the doctors," said the second.

"Can I come with you?"

"You'll have to talk to the ward nurse, but yes."

The elevator was big enough for them all. It rumbled into life. The orderlies stood in awkward silence. With a kick and a low rumble, the elevator began to move upward.

Monte held his sister's hand. The neon strip-lights began to fade. The walls of the lift melted away. The orderlies darkened to black shadows and disappeared. Monte stood in his sister's room at Highfields. The half-light of dawn crept through a crack in the curtains, casting the scene in subdued colours. Sarrah sat propped up in the bed in her white-and-blue-striped nightgown. With skeleton-thin hands she was working at something. Monte moved closer.

Sarrah held a pencil-sharpener and was working at its screws with the blunt edge of a kitchen-knife.

She pried the little blade loose and leaned back, exhausted from the effort. She reached out to drop the knife and sharpener upon the bedside table. Her hand flickered and paused upon an envelope that stood there. It had Monte's name upon it. With a sigh she sat back, her eyes still fixed upon the note. At length her eyes closed and her head turned.

Moments passed. Sarrah's eyes slowly re-opened. She turned her hands palm-up and looked at them. Between her right thumb and forefinger she gripped the little blade, slowly cut into the flesh of her left wrist and began dragging it across. Her features contorted with the pain and her breath came faster. Blood poured from the wound at an alarming rate, staining her nightgown and blossoming in dark stains upon the bed sheet. Shaking and gasping, Sarrah transferred the blade to her left hand and repeated the cut on her right wrist.

Then she lay her ravaged arms upon the bed, watching the thick, dark liquid pool and run.

A wave of horror and revulsion assailed Monte. It wasn't Sarrah's act itself that shocked him. It was the look of peace upon his sister's face as she lay dying.

*   *   *   *   *

Agent Jerry Buchanan took the call on a secure line at the agency safe house, a three-floor Victorian terrace in what he had been told was the exclusive end of town. "The situation is," he told the voice on the other end of the line, several thousands miles away, "we've started a clean-up. The hunter is in the field, but nothing's in the bag yet."

"I don't know, Jerry…" came the voice.

"What don't you know?" Buchanan pulled another grape from the bowl in front of him and popped it into his mouth.

"I'm getting a lot of heat," said the voice, "from further up the ladder. People are starting to wonder if this isn't getting out of hand."

"Look," said Buchanan, "protecting assets is what we do. We take care of the inner circle. Three kids and one dead-beat, who cares?"

"Are you sure that's going to be enough?"

"They're the only ones who have direct information on our man. These four are loners. No one's going to miss them. At least not enough to cause a problem."

"I don't know, Jerry."

"Will you stop saying that," Buchanan fished a pip from his mouth and threw it onto the carpet, "you know what our guy is worth." There came no reply. Buchanan banged the receiver sharply down upon the desk then picked it up. "Are you there?" he said into it.

"All I'm saying," said the voice, "is if the heat gets too hot, Jerry, we're going to have cash in our asset."

Buchanan shook his head. "You can't do that."

"We can, and we will. If we have to."

"No, no, no. This is my operation."

"You've put a lot of work in, Jerry. I respect that."

"Screw your respect. We need this. You know that I need this. I want my seat back at the table. I deserve it."

"It might not come to that," said the voice, "but you know how this works. We cannot compromise our position with the Fountainhead."

"I'm doing this *for* the Fountainhead," said Buchanan, "and I need you to promise me that you'll do everything you can to keep this operation live."

"I promise, Jerry."

"You owe me," said Buchanan, and hung up.

He leaned back and rubbed his temples. The trouble with the Fountainhead, he thought to himself, is that nobody had any balls. One sniff of danger and the fat pigs went cowering for the undergrowth, desperate to save their flesh from the cooking pot. They needed a real man back on the board. *Someone like me*, he thought wryly and laughed.

He tapped his fingers upon the arm of the chair, picked up the phone and began to dial.

*   *   *   *

Monte switched on his old phone and made the call standing outside the doors to the ward. "Richard," he said, "I can't really talk but I may need more help. Can you meet me tomorrow morning at the time and place we discussed? Great. Thanks. I'll see you then."

He hung up and switched off the phone. A middle-aged woman with glasses and long dark hair stood across the corridor leaning against the window. She gave Monte a smile. "Visiting someone?" she asked.

"My sister."

"My daughter's boyfriend," she said, "I needed to get out for a bit."

Monte nodded. He closed his eyes and took a deep breath. "I hope she's okay," he said, as he walked away from the ward, back towards the lift area.

"He," the woman called out.

"He, yes. I'm sorry."

Monte took the lift up to the fifth floor. The hour was late and there were few people about. The neon strip-lights caused a dull pain behind his eyes. The police constable on duty outside Coy's door sat in a plastic chair, his legs and his arms crossed. He eyed the approaching detective suspiciously.

Monte held out his passport. "Monte Boutista. I'm on the list."

The policeman nodded. He stood up and thumbed the radio at his shoulder. "Monte Boutista," he said, "here to visit." He put a finger to the receiver in his ear and cocked his head. "If you could just wait here a moment sir."

Monte crossed to the window and looked out into the night. Far below lay the lit car park, sparsely populated. A bus idled at its stop. A dozen passengers slumped in its seats, most connected to their smart phones. One read a book—a dying breed. Monte observed the policeman's reflection. He stood with is hands behind his back, looking pointedly to one side.

"I'll come back later," said Monte. He turned away. From the corner of his eye he saw the constable reach for his radio and put out a hand. The flimsy swing-doors further along pushed open. He recognized the Detective Sergeant—Hardacre. Karen? Another uniformed policeman was with her, tall and thin, with dark close-set eyes.

"Mister Boutista," said Hardacre, "we'd like to ask you some questions."

"I'm afraid I don't have time right now."

"This isn't a request," said Hardacre, "I need you to accompany me to the station."

"Am I being arrested?"

"Not unless we have to."

Monte looked from one officer to the other. "I'll come."

Hardacre led the way. Back to the lifts, down to the ground floor and through the labyrinthine interior. They passed the main reception area. The two women manning the desk followed them with their eyes. Monte wondered what they speculated he had done. The wide exit corridor let out into the cool night air through automatic sliding doors. Monte saw the dark-haired woman he had spoken to outside the ward. She was leaning against a concrete pillar, smoking. The tall policeman put a hand on Monte's shoulder, guiding him left. He briefly met the woman's eyes. She gave him a look of surprise and concern.

Funny, thought Monte as they headed towards the car park, how quickly we can make connections. Just a few words and you are no longer a suspicious stranger. You become a potential ally worthy of concern.

The walked on. The squad car glowed white under the high-pillared lights. "Ill take it from here," said Hardacre, "you'd better go back and relieve Frederickson. I'll make sure someone picks you up at shift change."

"Ma'am." The policeman gave Monte a last look. He opened the rear side door and Monte climbed in. The detective knew from experience that there were no inside handles in the back. The doors could not be opened except by the driver. He settled into his seat as the slamming of the door cocooned him from the night.

Hardacre switched on the engine and guided them out onto the main road. Monte wondered if he should delete his phone messages but decided against it. If Hardacre was going to charge him, she would have done so by now and he was no stranger to this game. Client privilege would buy him some yardage. In order to coerce him, the police would have to prove he had direct knowledge of a crime and Monte doubted they could do that. Not yet.

He had to focus on bringing down Schwarzkopf, that was all. Whatever legal comeback he was due was a problem for another day. Outside the window, the city rolled past. He looked out at familiar shadows, buildings transformed by the dying of the sun. Places wore a different cloak at night. The commonplace could be transformed into the magical, or the fearful.

Monte leaned forward to speak through the wire mesh that separated the passenger seats from the front of the car. "This isn't the way to the station," he said. Hardacre did not speak or turn her head. Monte sat back. The nighttime traffic, looking ghostly and disconnected in the yellow light from the street lamps, rolled and raced and crawled—the inexorable movement of civilisation.

They cruised along the edge of the city centre. The streets were full. It was the hour when pubs disgorged their patrons out into the artificial light, to stagger home, warmed against the chill by a bellyful of alcohol, or onwards in search of watering holes and clubs that would stay open for another three or four hours yet.

Groups of women in heels and dresses, men in shirts despite the cold, hands thrust into their pockets and hunting in packs. Workers buzzed between them, couriers on motorcycles or mopeds. Suited bouncers in twos and threes, neon bands around their arms, occupied small patches of pavement with disinterested authority.

Monte did not know Hardacre well. He did know that there was a chance he was heading for extreme danger. He put his hand in his pocket, found the power button on his old phone by touch and pressed it until he felt it vibrate.

They left the city centre behind. Monte caught Hardacre's gaze briefly in the rear view mirror. Soon they were in the land of cut-price shops, residential estates and late-night newsagents. The streets were quiet here, the houses slumbering with their lids drawn shut. They took a turning from the large roundabout, heading out toward an area Monte knew fairly well.

Hardacre took a turn that Monte had driven down countless times. She stopped the car at the end of the quiet cul-de-sac, a stone's-throw from Donald Coy's house. Monte waited in silence as Hardacre got out and opened the passenger door. Monte got out. Hardacre began to walk toward the entrance to a little alleyway, almost hidden by foliage overflowing from the gardens on either side.

Monte followed. As they entered the alleyway, Hardacre glanced back at him and slowed her pace. "Donald and I," she began, "Donald and I were close once. Very close." She looked at Monte for reassurance that he had understood.

"I didn't know that," the investigator said.

They continued walking.

"When I was a little girl," said Hardacre, "I used to see things. Things that nobody else could. My parents sent me to a psychologist. He told them it was perfectly normal but I don't think he liked me. I think that he thought I was…wrong."

Monte said nothing. He pushed some overhanging branches out of their way.

"That was one subject we bonded over," said Hardacre, "Donald and I. An interest in the supernatural. A belief in the existence of things we can't see or always understand."

They reached the end of the alley. It opened up onto a small field fringed by tall trees. An area on the ground was marked out by police tape tied to metal pegs forced into the earth.

"Donald told me about you," said Hardacre, not looking Monte in the eye.

"This is where he was attacked?"

Hardacre turned. "Rivers ordered me to take you in."

"For what reason?"

"Withholding information. I think he's just making a point." She took a deep breath. "Will you take a look? See if there's anything you can pick up?"

"Are you taking me to the station afterwards?"

She shook her head.

"How are you going to square that with Rivers?"

"I'll think of something."

Monte looked up to the stars. It was a clear night and they stood out beautifully here, away from the light pollution of the centre. He walked to the taped-off area, lifted one leg over and then the other. He looked back at Hardacre—her features were in shadow, though she only stood a few paces away.

Monte crouched down and put his naked palm upon the earth. The peculiar black, choking touch of violence which he had 'felt' as far back as the alley was much stronger here. It was a sensation one could never prepare for, like the smell of rotting meat. However much one experienced it, the feeling was always overwhelming. He had attempted to describe it several times, and had always fallen short. The closest he could get was to illustrate it as a feeling of *wrongness,* a primal warning blasted so loudly at the 'freshest' scenes that it altogether overwhelmed the senses.

As he concentrated, the light from the stars began to dim and the dark ground grew blacker. Abruptly the scene flickered to a blank whiteness, a parody of daylight, like a broken computer screen. The vista adjusted slowly, taking on form and gradations of grey. Then all was very sharp focus—a black-and-white movie in super high definition, although marked by a peculiar 'flatness'. He saw Coy's face, close enough to pick out the hairs on the unshaven part of his cheek, a drop of sweat rolling from his forehead.

Monte took a step back and the scene lurched again. Now he could see the whole of Coy, standing with his arms raised. The policeman held a baton in one hand. For a metre around him, all was clear, but everything beyond was brilliant white. Monte took another backward step and more earth seeped into view beneath his feet.

He looked up and for the briefest of moments the entire field flickered into view. A half-dozen masked figures were moving swiftly towards Coy. Monte's foot hit something solid and he stumbled, the world whirling dizzyingly. Lurching to his feet as the ground seemed to slide beneath him, Monte saw Coy swinging the baton and flailing with his arm as the figures attacked.

Monte fell to his knees, planted both hands upon the ground, wrenched his head up and stared determinedly at his friend. He saw a man hit the ground, saw another with a knife, the blade of which burned whitely as it entered Coy's side. Monte heard himself call out. Coy collapsed to the ground.

The knife-wielder stood over the stricken policeman. The attacker, breathing hard, pulled his balaclava up from his face and spat upon his foe. Gripping the knife, he made to plunge it into the wide target of Coy's back. Something stopped him. His head whipped round. He pulled his balaclava back down and then the figures were running, disappearing into the blank ether.

Monte crawled towards Coy. Everything faded to a darkness so complete it was unnatural. When the night reappeared he was lying flat out upon the grass, looking up at the stars. He rolled onto his front, breathing hard. Hardacre knelt over him. She helped him to sit up as his senses gradually recalibrated back to the real world.

"Is it always this bad?" said Hardacre. "I didn't know. I'm sorry."

Monte shook his head. "Just give me minute." He closed his eyes and took a series of slow, deep breaths. "I'm okay." He planted a hand upon the ground and, with Hardacre's support, got to his feet.

"The man who held the knife," he said, "has a spider's-web tattoo, here, on his neck."

Hardacre nodded.

Monte leaned forward with his hands on his knees.

"Take your time," said Hardacre, "what you just said—the tattoo. It makes sense."

"Good to know," said Monte, still leaning over, "that it wasn't all for nothing."

They waited a minute or so in silence, until Monte, signaling that he was sufficiently recovered, stood up and they began to retrace their steps.

"I don't know what evidence you have on Schwarzkopf," said Hardacre.

"Not enough," replied Monte, "not yet."

"If you do get anything, then bring it to me."

"You know Coy suspects that Rivers is protecting Schwarzkopf? Do you know why? If MI6 are involved then he's possibly an informant, right?"

"I don't know anything," said Hardacre, "but if I had to guess I'd say that you're correct."

"The bigger picture," said Monte.

"It might be that they're right to do so," said Hardacre, "we don't know what's going on."

"Even if it means shielding whoever tried to murder Donald?"

"I'm already sticking my neck out a long way. I could get into serious trouble for this."

"I'm sorry," said Monte, "that was unfair. I know that you care about Don very much."

They reached the car. "Can I drop you somewhere?" asked Hardacre.

"No," said Monte, "I'm good."

"Whatever you're going to do," said Hardacre, as she opened the door, "go and do it. I'll cover you for as long as I can."

As the car pulled away Monte's phone began to ring. It was Penny.

"How much do you trust Richard?" she said.

"Richard?" said Monte. "I trust him."

"He was at the safe house earlier tonight. He wanted to know where you were. Now there's a white van parked a little up the road and it doesn't look friendly."

"Where are the others?"

"Still on the road."

"Okay," said Monte, "I want you to get a taxi…"

"I'm already gone," said Penny, "I went out the back way and left some lights on."

"Where are you now?"

"On a bus on the way to Agatha's. I'll be fine."

"I'm sure you will."

"I texted Aabira," said Penny, "but I've had no reply."

"I'll phone them."

"Let me know when you get through."

"I'll be turning my regular phone off soon. I'll update you tomorrow morning."

"Look after yourself."

It began to rain. Shielding his phone with his hand, Monte hung up and dialed Aabira's number.

*   *   *   *   *

Harry turned on the wipers as they glided through the nighttime city. "What did he say?"

"Not to go back to the safe-house," said Aabira, "turn off our phones until tomorrow at six and tell nobody where we're going."

"Where *are* we going?" asked Harry.

"I have an idea," said Charles.

"What about Penny?"

"She's gone. She's safe," said Aabira, "what's your suggestion Charles?"

"We need more evidence, right? I think I know where we might find it."

"Where?"

"London. Knightsbridge. Schwarzkopf has a place there."

Harry shrugged. "So?"

Charles sat forward. "I know the fellow who looks after it. I can get us in."

"Even if you can, what then?"

"I've been there. There's a room that Christian always keeps locked. There's got to be something important in there."

"What do you think?" said Aabira.

Harry shook his head. "I guess it makes as much sense as anything."

At the next roundabout he took the second exit and guided them towards the M11.

"We'll need to find a place to stay," he said.

Aabira hesitated. "I guess it's okay to use my phone for five minutes."

"Sure, and after that you should try and rest. It's going to be a long night."

*   *   *   *   *

Karen Hardacre guided the police car into the station lot. She was just climbing out when Rivers appeared from the rear entrance. He was moving purposefully.

"Sir," she began, "I didn't bring Boutista back to the station because…"

Rivers gave her a look. She noted the anxiety on his face. For the first time she became aware that he was carrying a hold-all and a small cardboard box. He walked straight past, heading for his car. Hardacre followed after.

"I took a decision not to bring him in."

Rivers opened the boot. "What are you talking about?" he said.

"Have you not read the log updates?"

Rivers slung the bag into the car and shoved the box in behind it. "Sir?"

"I don't want to know." Rivers slammed down the boot. "I'm no longer in charge here. I'm nothing to do with this."

"What do you mean?"

"You're to report to…" Rivers covered his eyes with his hand "… Davies. Rupert Davies. He'll be here sometime tomorrow."

"Where are you going?"

"I've retired," said Rivers, "I've handed in my notice. Today. I'm owed time."

"What about James Robertson? What about DIC Coy."

"Look," said Rivers, waving a finger, "this is nothing to do with me anymore. Do you understand?"

Hardacre nodded. "I think I understand, sir."

Rivers opened the driver's door. "You're a good officer Hardacre," he said, "don't get involved. That's my advice and you ought to take it."

Hardacre watched the car pull out of the station. If a man like Rivers was willing to sacrifice his career, she considered, then things must be very bad indeed.

*   *   *   *   *

By the time Eddie woke it was almost nine. He cursed, rolled out of bed, and checked his phone. Nothing. He showered and dressed in haste but on his way downstairs his sense of urgency slackened. Martha had surely conned her way into staying the night, and god knew what else. She would be fine, he thought. She was always fine, and why the hell should he care anyway.

They were still serving breakfast in the restaurant. Eddie ordered a full English and coffee and took his seat from the previous night. The place was almost empty. All the families had no doubt gotten their brood up early, navigated tantrums and arguments, and scuttled off out to wherever they were going for the day.

A man in his thirties, dressed in shirt and tie, was eating alone. He sat up straight and read from the *Financial Times*. An expensive gold watch was upon his wrist and his tie bore a silver pin. He sipped his coffee with an air of detached importance. Once he looked in Eddie's direction, eyes flickering up and down before turning back to his paper. Threat assessed and dismissed.

A young couple entered, laughing and smiling, their hands all over one another. They sat and giggled and whispered as the waitress handed them a menu. The woman was pretty and blonde and had an accent. Dutch? The man was English. Heavy-set, with almost a mono-brow.

Eddie wondered why he found them all so distasteful. Was it because, for all their mundanity and predictability, they represented a normality of existence that was closed to him now, forever? Or was he bitter? Bitter and resentful because he knew, in truth, that in this life he was alone. Had made himself alone and burned all his bridges to the way back.

He would take it, though. Power, money. By whatever means he could acquire it. And then he could do what he damn well pleased. Irritated, Eddie looked at his watch, his plain, silver watch, and pushed his plate away with a clatter that made the other occupants look round. Eddie got to his feet, stared them down one by one, and left.

The drive did not take him long and he felt a mean edge rising within as he left the city behind, whipping past forlorn fields and stubborn hedgerows, the weak light from the sun trying its last as the world slipped from its grasp into the short, cold days of winter.

The house of Charles' parents looked even more magnificent by day. Eddie cruised past. He could not see any signs of life and no cars were parked outside. He turned in the lane, drove back and pulled into the drive, coming to a halt in the gravel near the imposing entrance with its stone-pillared roof. He killed the engine and got out.

Eddie was confident that Martha would be able to explain his person and presence away. That was one thing she was very good at. Two if you counted the other. The front door stood slightly ajar. Eddie paused, uncertain. He pushed it softly open. "Hello?" There came no reply.

The hallway he stepped into was of the type only seen in stately homes or the movies. It bore an aura of stillness that suggested the whole house was empty and had been for some time. Eddie called out again, louder. He walked further in and looked around. The dead eyes of portraits, heavy with the weight of history, stared back.

Eddie took the door directly opposite. It let to a narrow wooden hallway lined with cages of stuffed birds and animals. Beyond was a bright and spacious kitchen, contrastingly modern, with marble worktops, an island and all manner of implements neatly arranged, but no signs of life. Beyond the windows lay a garden so large and featureless you could have set up a full-size football pitch on it. Crows hopped upon the grass, cawing loudly.

Another door led into a sumptuous living room, with a large marble fireplace. An empty glass stood upon the coffee table. Near the chair next to it, beside the corner of the fireplace, a black garment lay upon the floor. Eddie picked it up. They were a woman's leggings, damp. Eddie could guess to whom they belonged, and how they had ended up on the floor. He shook his head.

Deciding that the bedrooms would be the best places to check, he took the marble staircase to the upper floor. More paintings hung here, and a chandelier, shaped like some futuristic floating city, filled the vaulting space with its graceful towers and chains.

A door, standing half-open at the end of the long hallway drew his eye. The room beyond was bright and the very edge of a white curtain rippled into view and back again. Eddie moved toward it, his feet sinking deep into the plush carpet. Pushing the door open a little more, the expansive bathroom opened out before him.

An old-fashioned bathtub stood in the centre of the tiled floor, its curved bronze feet supporting the sweeping white lines of its form. The back of a woman's head rested against the nearest edge of the tub, her brown hair cascading wildly over its side. The water level was high. A pale knee broke the murky liquid like a barren island. One arm lay resting, its hand dangling languidly over the side. The rest of her form was submerged.

"Martha," said Eddie, then he repeated the name as the woman did not stir.

Eddie sighed and moved forward. His foot caught something that sprang and rattled, hitting the half-open door and rolling back. He bent down to pick it up. It was an almost-empty pill bottle. One or two oblong orange shapes were left at the bottom.

He walked to the far end of the tub and stood looking silently. Martha's sightless eyes were open. Her face was inhumanly pale. Her mouth hung wide. She bore an expression of confusion or bewilderment. It looked unreal and unnatural, like a discarded rubber Halloween mask.

Eddie swallowed hard. Somewhere, in another part of the house, a record began to play. The music crackled like an old 78. A man's voice mixed with a gentle lolloping rhythm floated up in muted tones. It was a sentimental song, disquieting and somehow eerie. It reminded Eddie of old cowboy movies on interminably long Sunday afternoons.

Eddie walked out onto the landing. He followed the music to the top of the stairs and looked down. Not a soul was visible in the hallway. The song came from the open door to the sitting room, the one where he had discovered Martha's clothing.

Mechanically placing one foot below the other, Eddie descended the stairs, his hand sliding along the reassuringly solid banister. The voice continued its song, crooning with wry regret.

The man who stood in the sitting room, next to the record player, was tall, broad-shouldered and handsome, like a catalogue model. He wore a light grey suit and a white shirt with no tie. He looked at Eddie with his head cocked to one side, as if appraising a possible acquisition.

"What's your name?" he said.

"Eddie."

"Hello Eddie. What are you doing in my house?"

"This isn't your house."

The man smiled thinly. "You're a clever one," he said. "My name is Bradley. I killed your friend Martha."

"Why?"

"You like country music?" Bradley held up a record sleeve. "Faron Young. He was a big star. An icon. Girls chasing him. A string of hits, but, as the world moved on and turned to new things, the industry left him behind. The once big star was forgotten. He took his own life. He shot himself."

"Who are you?"

"You know," said Bradley, "it's funny. She didn't give you up.

Didn't say a word. But I knew she didn't come here alone."

"Did Christian send you?"

Bradley blew air from his mouth. He carefully picked up the needle from the record. "Take a seat," he said.

Eddie did not move.

"Don't make this difficult," said Bradley. "You're going to die, Eddie. You have to, and I think that you know that. I can be your friend in this. I can make it easy. Struggling will only make things worse."

Eddie slowly drew back his right foot, shifting his balance and turning a little side-on.

"It's just that you know too much. Like Martha. Like Charles. But it's your choices that led you here. We need to talk first, Eddie. Then I'll make it quick and painless. Are you religious?"

"Let's do this," said Eddie. He clenched his hands into fists, turned further side-on and brought his arms up.

"Let it go," said Bradley, "just rest. I can see it in your eyes, Eddie. I can see that you've had enough. Why not let me help you? We can be friends."

"Shut up," said Eddie, "shut the fuck up."

Bradley raised his eyebrows and shook his head. He put down the record and took a step forward.

Eddie was fast but Bradley was faster. He ducked under the younger man's jab and caught him smartly in the ribs with a punch that made the air explode from Eddie's lungs. Eddie knew all was lost. He fell to his knees, unable to breathe. Bradley put a foot upon Eddie's shoulder and sent him reeling onto his back on the carpet before the fire.

Bradley sat astride Eddie's chest, pinning Eddie's legs with his knees. "That was spirited," he said, "you've given it your best shot now. That's all a man can do. Now I need you to breathe."

Eddie gasped. The pain in his side was excruciating. He closed his eyes, then looked up at the ceiling. His vision was blurred. The weight of the other man upon his chest was unbearable. Eddie strained with his arms.

"Relax," said Bradley, "you'll never be able to breathe if you don't relax."

Eddie lifted his head and banged it down hard against the floor. Grimacing, he concentrated hard on breathing in and out. In shallow gasps he could manage it, though every intake triggered terrible stabbing pains in his side.

"That's good," said Bradley, "that's good." He reached down a hand and smoothed Eddie's hair away from his eyes. "That's very good." There was a husky quality to his voice.

"What are you doing?"

"I told you I could be your friend," said Bradley. He ran the backs of his fingers over Eddie's cheek. "The girl wasn't yours was she? I know. You're too refined for that."

Bradley swallowed hard. His chest heaved. Slowly he lowered his face towards Eddie's. "This is going to happen," he said, "it's up to you how."

Eddie's eyes widened. Bradley turned his head as it descended, seeking Eddie's lips with his own. Eddie resisted the first wet press.

"Shhh," said Bradley. He began to plant light, tender kisses. Then they grew more urgent and forceful. Eddie opened his mouth in response, returning the kiss. Bradley moaned. Eddie opened wider and forced his tongue into the other man's mouth. Bradley cradled Eddie's head, paused for a moment, and then stuck his own tongue between Eddie's lips.

Eddie waited until Bradley's tongue was all the way in before biting down as hard as he could. He felt his teeth sink into flesh and tasted blood. Bradley wailed, an inhuman, terrible cry, and tried to pull away. Eddie let go his bite and heaved his legs upward, sending Bradley tumbling towards the fireplace.

Eddie rose unsteadily to his feet. Bradley was on all fours, blood pouring from his mouth onto the floor. Holding onto furniture for support, Eddie made for the door. He was halfway out when a blast of sound split the air and a searing hot pain slashed across his right thigh.

Eddie threw himself into the hallway and across to the front door. He pulled it shut behind him and fell backwards upon the gravel.

Scrambling to his feet, Eddie lurched towards his car. He heard the front door open and cried out as he forced his legs to propel him around to the driver's side. He ripped open the door, leaped in and turned the key. Bradley, standing upon the steps, raised his gun. Eddie slammed the stick into first and stamped on the gas. He ducked low, roaring out into the road and skidding left.

Wrenching the car back under control he checked the rear view and switched up to second. His hand felt sticky and wet and liquid ran down his right leg. The taste of blood was still in his mouth.

*   *   *   *   *

Monte awoke feeling rough. Cobwebs from the night before clung to his mind. He prayed, showered, shaved, made himself a coffee and took it up into his study. The Stan Kenton record still lay upon his desk. He returned it to the correct place on the shelf, pulled out "Interstellar Space" by John Coltrane, set the record up ready to play but did not start it.

Down in the street, the great twice-daily migration had begun. Workers running against their nine o'clock deadline hurried to and fro, minds taken up with thoughts of the day ahead, these thoughts jostling with a hundred other fears and worries and hopes and dreams, regrets, ambitions, primal urges and unrecognised prejudice.

Monte dialed the number. It was a long time before Coy answered. He sounded groggy.

"Did I wake you up?"

"What time is it?"

"Nearly nine."

"What's new?"

"I came to see you last night," said Monte, "they wouldn't let me in. Hardacre had orders to take me to the station."

"What did you tell them?"

"I didn't. She took me alone in the car and let me go."

"Good for her. Where are we with the case?"

"We found Maria Waters, alive and living in a place set up by Schwarzkopf. At least that's my guess. Aabira says that her mental health is not good."

"Did you take her in?"

"Where? Donald, we have Charles. We know where Maria is. Those two together ought to be enough to sink Schwarzkopf. So how do we get around MI6?"

"We don't."

"That's not very helpful."

"There's one more thing you can do," said Coy, "Coroner Leigh Farmoor-Dawley."

"Go on."

"He was on the Lucas Grundy case and he's a friend of Schwarzkopf. He fudged the evidence to make it look like suicide. If you can get him to talk it ought to push the balance. A mentally ill woman and a confessed murderer won't make for great witnesses. Call it a last throw of the dice."

"So how do I get this coroner to talk?"

"Mention the Twenty-Two club. Let him think that you bugged it. Tell him it's going to come out one way or another. Tell him anything you like."

"I'll give it a shot."

"Do it today. The longer you sit on Charles and the woman, the more trouble you're going to be in."

"I'll keep you updated," said Monte, "rest up."

"That's all that they let me bloody do."

"Don't try and tell me you don't enjoy all those nurses running round after you."

"This is twenty-eighteen," said Coy, "half of them are male and they're all wearing trousers."

"Who are you trying to convince?" said Monte. "I'll call you later."

"Watch your back."

Call ended, Monte put down the phone, started the turntable, lowered the needle and sat down, placing his feet up on the desk. As the gentle beginning of the music filled the room, he sat and he thought, rehearsing in his head conversations that were yet to come. It was now nine-fifteen. John Coltrane and Rasheed Ali were whipping up a storm it was difficult to believe could be created by just two musicians. Through the seeming chaos and the waves of sound, a mighty and majestic beauty shone forth.

Monte drained the last of his herbal tea, closed his eyes, and allowed himself a few minutes of pleasant abandon.

*　*　*　*　*

When Aabira awoke it took her a few seconds to adjust to her surroundings. They were in an anonymous Travel Lodge hotel room. It had one twin bed and one single, upon which she was lying. The blinds were half-turned, letting a little light into the room. Wind gusted against the panes and what was visible of the day was gloomy and grey. Aabira checked her watch. The double bed was empty. Charles sat in a chair by the little counter, drinking tea and facing away from her.

Aabira sat up. Charles turned toward her. "Good morning," he said.

"Good morning. Where's Harry?"

"He was up early. Said he needed some air."

Aabira's hand went automatically to her head scarf. She had slept fully clothed. It had been an uncomfortable night.

"Would you like some tea?" asked Charles. "There's one bag left."

Aabira shook her head.

Charles stood up. "I'll give you some space."

"It's okay Charles, you don't have to go. I can get ready in the bathroom."

Charles nodded and sat back down.

"Harry doesn't like me," he said, "he doesn't trust me. It's okay. I know I don't deserve anyone's trust."

"You took a wrong path," said Aabira, "and you did something very bad. That doesn't mean that your life is over."

"It should do," said Charles, "it should do."

"Don't despise yourself. There is always hope. Only Allah can judge what is right and what is wrong."

"Some people," he said, "live with worse things inside them. I don't think that I can."

"You can. You have to. You're already doing the right thing, by helping us."

"I think I'll wait downstairs after all. Don't worry, I'm not going anywhere."

After Charles had left Aabira washed and showered, dressed and prayed. She remained prostrate for longer than usual, reciting passages she considered especially appropriate. When she had finished she sat in silence for a time, looking out of the window at the gathering storm.

*   *   *   *   *

It was an hour before Eddie felt safe enough to stop. He was driving through the high, hilly trails on the edge of the Peak District. Finding a lay-by that was little more than a flattened piece of ground by the side of the road, he pulled over and killed the engine.

With shaking hands he pulled at the material of his jeans where it had split at the side of his right thigh. It was soaked in dark blood and he could not see the bullet hole. Eddie opened the door and slid out. Moving gingerly on one leg, he rounded the back of the car and opened the boot. He pulled Maria's bag forward, unzipped it and began rummaging through the contents. He found what he had hoped to—an unopened bottle of vodka.

Eddie moved round to the passenger side, away from the road, opened the door and sat with his legs out. With difficulty he unbuttoned his jeans and slid them down. His right leg was slick with blood. He twisted the cap off the bottle and poured out a generous splash of alcohol. The pain was worse than the films made out.

It was some moments before he could unclench his teeth and open his eyes. There was a long, lateral gash on the outside of his thigh, open to perhaps a quarter of an inch in the middle. He could see no hole. The bullet must have skimmed the very edge. A wave of relief washed over him, but then, in a sudden panic, Eddie hastily checked his other leg and the rest of his body. He poured more vodka to clean the blood from his hands and checked again. When he was sure that there were no further wounds he sat back and allowed himself a few moments rest.

After that he looked again at the wound. Maybe it was not so bad after all. He took off his shirt, wadded the main part together and, using the arms, tied it around his leg, pulling as tight as he could. Eddie's heart leaped at the sound of an approaching engine. He twisted round in time to see a red Land Rover cruise past. The driver was a blonde woman in sunglasses. Eddie collapsed back.

"Fuck," he said to himself, "get it together now. Get it together." With a grunt he struggled upright. Using the frame of the car for balance, he shut the boot, moved back to the driver's side and carefully pulled himself in. Testing his leg he found it was painful to press down on the accelerator, but not unbearably so.

*   *   *   *   *

Monte took an Uber to the park, arriving forty-five minutes before the appointed time. At this hour on a weekday it was quiet, with just a dog-walker or two and the parking lot nearly empty. Waiting till no one was in sight, he pushed through the bushes until he found a suitable spot, dense enough to be hidden but with a fair line of sight back the way he had come. Sitting cross-legged upon the ground, he took out the compact binoculars and tested the view. Satisfied that he could see clearly, he unscrewed his Thermos, poured himself a cup of green tea, and waited.

It was a long time before the sound of an engine caused him to sit up and reach for the lenses. It was Richard's car. It pulled in and parked, about a hundred metres away. Monte watched carefully. The man was alone. Richard got out, looked around him and then leaned back against the boot, arms crossed.

A movement at Monte's side made him turn but it was nothing more than a blackbird, a twig in its beak. The little creature appeared to look at him quizzically before hopping back into the undergrowth. The investigator turned his attention back to his quarry. Richard waited unmoving, apart from a sweep of his head from side to side. After thirty minutes Richard got back in his car, took out his mobile and dialed. The call was answered and lasted for some time. It seemed to Monte that his friend was uncharacteristically agitated. When the call ended, Richard started the car and drove off.

Monte waited another thirty minutes before rising. He walked away from the lot, across the park and out the other exit, called an Uber and stood out of sight until it neared.

*   *   *   *   *

Christian Schwarzkopf sounded his car's horn again and nudged closer to the Mini Metro in front. "Go, dammit, go." At last the car began to move. Schwarzkopf put his foot down, sending his vehicle lurching forward. At the first opportunity he swung out and overtook. Braking as late as possible for the roundabout, he swung round smoothly and accelerated. Normally he would take pleasure in the deep throbbing of the engine, the satisfying pull of gravity, forcing him back into the padded leather seat as the car leaped and growled. Like all of Christian's possessions, it represented the pinnacle of luxury and status.

Right now all he could think about was reaching his destination, reaching Maria. He drove with one hand, biting a nail, cursing. The call had come in last night, but he had only listened to the recorded message that morning. He could still recall the imbecilic woman's voice.

"Mister Schwarzkopf," she had stuttered, "I've just been up to the house to do the cleaning and…well there were some folks there. Strangers. I didn't tell them a thing. Not a thing. I think they'd been inside and they were asking me all sorts of questions and one of them was one of those Muslims and I didn't tell them a thing but I thought I should tell you."

It could have been the police. Or it could have been Buchanan or the private detective, but none of them knew. None of them. He had been so clever. Buchanan thought he knew everything but he did not. Until now, whenever he visited Maria, Schwarzkopf had always taken a taxi, booked in another name, or had Spider drive him. Spider. Had he gone to the police? Had he ratted him out?

Schwarzkopf braked hard, the wheels squealing. The car he had not seen beeped and flashed its lights. Schwarzkopf swore, wrenched at the wheel and gunned his car forwards. It began to rain. He switched on the wipers but did not slow down. When the top of the cathedral towers came into view he felt himself relax the slightest degree. Calmly he navigated the pedestrian district. *It will be fine*, he thought to himself, Buchanan will do nothing to you, *the police can do nothing to you*. He had an army of lawyers at his beck and call. Spider may have gone but others remained.

It was a pity about Eddie. Giving him up to Buchanan had pained him. Eddie was smart, but then again *too* smart. Perhaps it was all for the best. There would be no shortage of new recruits. Finding people with the right balance of awareness and ambition was the key. As he guided the car out of the town and into the quieter lanes, Schwarzkopf thought of his paintings. His beautiful paintings. They were his evidence. Evidence that progress lay in destruction and reinvention. That tomorrow was all that mattered and those trampled under foot were the bricks and mortars that built the palaces for people who deserved them. People like him.

As he guided the car up the wooded slope and pulled to a stop outside the stone house his confidence deserted him. As ever, the spectre of his father came unbidden into his mind. "I don't understand you," his father had said to him once. "I tell you exactly what to do and you cannot do it."

Cannot do it. But Christian had saved Maria. Hadn't he saved her? Hadn't he cherished her and given her a safe place to hide away from the world? He got out of the car. Did she understand that he loved her? Did she know what that cost him, that weakness? And it would cost him, he knew, somewhere deep down in his gut. She was his Achilles' heel. So many people wanted to bring him down.

He took the chain from around his neck. It held the key to the front door, which he unlocked and pushed open. The house was silent save for the quiet voice of Maria. She was half-humming and half-singing a tune that Christian had heard her recite a thousand times. "You Are My Sunshine," it was called.

Christian walked to the doorway. Maria, dressed in a long, flowing brown top and nothing else, sat upon a stool with the easel before her. She held a long brush in one hand and in the other a palette of colours. There was paint in her hair. Abruptly she stopped singing. "Is it you?" she asked without turning around.

"Yes," said Christian, "it's me."

He was glad he that he could not see the reaction upon her face.

"What are you painting?" he asked.

She stood and turned, hiding the canvas from view. The shirt that she wore was wrinkled and stained. Her unkempt hair hung down past her shoulders in a great tangle. Christian thought that he had never seen her more beautiful. She walked slowly towards him, reached up to cradle his face and kissed him deeply upon the lips.

Later, as they lay naked upon the bed, her head resting upon his chest, Christian gazed upon her body. The angular slopes and curved edges pleased him greatly. Being here with her brought a foggy calmness to his mind. Her slender hand reached up to cover his eyes. He laughed.

"Sleep," said Maria, "rest my love."

Christian inched his head down till it lay comfortably upon the pillow. A great wave of weariness came upon him. He looked up at the ceiling through her fingers. "Sleep," she said again. He closed his eyes, relaxed his shoulders and sighed. He could feel Maria's weight shifting next to him. She was reaching for something. The springs of the bed shifted. Christian wondered idly what she was doing, but he was reluctant to break the spell.

He would never know what it was that made him open his eyes at that instant. The knife, its wicked blade shimmering in the light, was already descending. He screamed and threw up his arms, blocking her wrist, and at the same time lurched to one side, rolling off the bed and scrambling to his feet.

Maria was charging towards him, knife in hand, eyes impossibly wide. Christian brought his hands up and stepped back. His calves hit against something hard and he fell, Maria tumbling on top of him. Desperately he grabbed at the hand holding the knife, but she twisted it free. Christian brought his knees up between them and kicked with all his might, sending the still-naked woman sprawling backwards.

"What are you doing?" he shouted, "Maria, stop."

She was on all fours, panting like an animal, the knife still in her hand. "You lied to me." Her voice was low and guttural.

Christian shook his head. "I never lied," he said, pushing himself back into the corner beneath the window. He looked around for a weapon but there was none. "I never lied."

"You said they were out there. You said that they wanted to kill me."

"Maria," said Christian, slowly getting to his feet, "you know me. You know I would never hurt you."

Maria appeared to waver. She moved into a crouch, the knife held low at her side.

"Come on now," said Christian, regaining something of the usual authority in his voice, "don't be stupid. Put down the knife."

"No," said Maria.

"Put it down."

"No."

"I said put it down."

"No." She sprang at him wildly, the blade flashing through the air. They came together in a whirl of limbs and curses. The world spun around. They crashed to the ground, writhing. Christian got his left hand around the woman's wrist. He screamed as the blade sliced down, narrowly missing his head, pushed with all his might and swung his legs. Her fingers dug into his face. He punched her hard and the knife clattered to the ground. They both scrambled for it but Christian was faster. He scrambled astride Maria as she flailed and scratched at his face with her nails.

Christian brought the knife down hard and felt it sink into flesh.

The next that he knew he was sitting slumped against the door, looking across at where the woman lay, the handle of the knife sticking obscenely and almost comically straight up from her chest. Blood began to seep out from the wound, trickling down her side and across her belly. Christian wiped his face and stood up.

Then he collapsed upon the bed and began to weep.

*   *   *   *   *

When Eddie pulled in at the services his leg was aching abysmally and nausea was rising in his stomach. Parking in the corner furthest away from the stores, he reached back and pulled his rucksack from the rear seat. A clean shirt was the first thing he put on. Then he untied the one around his leg and gingerly and with difficulty pushed off his jeans. Blood was smeared over his thigh but at least the wound appeared to have mostly stopped bleeding.

Biting and tearing, Eddie succeeded in ripping material free from his remaining T-shirt and bound it around the cut. Pulling on the new pair of jeans was difficult and painful but at last he was able to sit back and rest. After a few moment's recovery, he stuffed the bloody clothing out of view under the passenger seat and started up the car.

He found an empty space very near to the entrance. Walking as naturally as possible (which meant very slowly), he made it to the gents, which mercifully was empty. Eddie was startled to discover that the image in the mirror had spots of blood on its face. He washed himself in haste, rinsing red from around the basin and swallowing several handfuls of water.

He was drying himself off with blue paper towels when the cleaner came in. Eddie threw the towels away, nodded a terse greeting and left. On the way to the diner he checked his thigh for signs of blood coming through but there were none. Ordering a full English breakfast, tea and Coke, he took a seat by the window to wait, awkwardly lifting his injured leg under the table so that it could rest on the vacant chair facing him.

He thought about Martha, lying dead in the bath. His chest felt cold and empty. Had the whole thing been a setup? Is that why Spider had sent them? There were no places left to go. Back to Cambridge meant death. He had a little money saved. Enough to lay low in a hotel for a month or two. His passport was in his apartment. Christian's apartment.

The waitress smiled as she placed down his order. She was a young girl. Blonde, pretty. Her whole life ahead of her. Eddie forced himself to eat. A black SUV with tinted windows rolled past. It seemed to Eddie it was moving too slowly. He froze, ice forming in his stomach. The car drifted past, turned left and pulled into a lot thirty metres off. Eddie watched, adrenaline coursing through his body. It seemed an eternity before the doors open and a middle-aged man and a woman got out.

Eddie slumped forward, resting his head in his hands. He unscrewed the Coke, took a hefty swig and tried to focus his thoughts on what to do next.

*   *   *   *   *

By the time Agent Buchanan finally found the wooded lane leading to the house it had ceased raining. He pulled to a stop behind Christian's car, got out and walked slowly across the gravel to the open front door. He found Christian sitting in the kitchen in his shirtsleeves, holding a glass of whiskey, one leg crossed over the other.

"Buchanan," he said, "drink?"

"Why am I here?"

Christian sniffed. He took another gulp of the whiskey.

Buchanan looked around. On the easel behind Christian stood a large canvas. The painting upon it was of a woman's face, smiling and pretty. The woman wore a hijab and a band of golden-yellow like a halo surrounded her head, separating it from the dark featureless background.

"Upstairs," said Christian, "it was an accident. I'm afraid," he giggled, "I'm afraid I've been a bad boy." The laugh abruptly ceased. He put down the drink. "It was an accident. She attacked me. I didn't mean to do it."

Buchanan was gone for some minutes. Christian heard his footsteps upon the stairs and in the rooms above. Christian opened the back door and stood in the fresh air. He lit a cigarette and held it loosely.

"Who was she?" said Buchanan from behind him.

"Her name was Maria Waters. She has no family. No one knew she was here."

"What do you expect me to do?"

"I expect you to do your job," said Christian, "you're a cleaner." He took a deep drag on the cigarette, exhaled and flicked ash upon the concrete, "that's what you do."

"Jesus Christ, Christian."

"Don't pretend that you can't?"

Buchanan was quiet for a long time. "Get out," he said, "go home. Not Cambridge. London. Go to your apartment and stay there."

Christian threw the cigarette upon the ground. Without looking at the other man he brushed past and left the house. Not long after Buchanan heard an engine start and a car pull away.

Buchanan sat and looked at the painting. He felt old and tired. After a while he picked up his phone and dialed. "About our last conversation," he said, "you're right. We need to retire our asset. We need to do it now."

"Do you want me to make the arrangements?"

"No," said Buchanan, "I'll see to it myself."

He hung up and dialed another number. One he had memorised. "We have a change of plan," he said, "I'll send you the order by the usual means. Where do we stand on the others?"

He listened.

"What's wrong with your voice?" he asked , and listened again, his eyes squeezed tight shut. "Okay, clean up the witness and forget about the rest. This new one is all that matters."

Buchanan hung up. He stared at the painting. He stared at it for a long, long time.

*   *   *   *   *

From behind the wheel of the parked van, James Reynolds looked out at the house. It was day, but a few lights were on and some of the curtains were drawn. It was just as it had been the previous evening. He heard noises in the back of the vehicle. Steadman poked his head through into the cab. "Any change?"

James shook his head. "I don't think they're coming back."

"Let me try ringing Spider."

"His phone's off," said James, "I already tried. Christian said to keep watching."

Steadman shook his head. "What are we supposed to do anyhow? Kill them all in broad daylight."

"Just shake them up a bit."

"Thought we'd already done that."

"Well," said James, "evidently not enough."

"You got any blues?"

James fished the plastic bag out of his pocket.

"Thank you sir," said Steadman. He climbed through to the front and took a seat. "Seen Martha lately?"

"Not for a while."

"I heard she's gone off with Eddie. Some secret mission. I didn't think Eddie liked her."

James took a swig of water and passed the bottle to his friend. "Everyone likes Martha," he said.

Steadman smiled. "Jim," he said, "do you ever worry about all this? Things seem very shaky lately."

"We'll be alright with Christian."

"Charles wasn't."

"Charles was a fool," said James, "he didn't do what he was told."

"I liked him," said Steadman, "at the start," he added hastily.

James watched Steadman take the pill and wash it down. "Hey," he said, "you remember that weekend in Blackpool?"

"God," Steadman grimaced, "what a filthy chavvy hole."

"Do you remember that restaurant we trashed?"

"They were screaming for the police," said Steadman, laughing, "but they changed their minds when we started throwing cash in their faces."

"And you remember those girls we picked up?"

"How could I forget? You said that you liked foie gras and that tart thought it was a type of perfume."

They both laughed, loud and from the belly, until tears came to their eyes.

"They were ignorant animals," said James, once they had recovered, "with no breeding. You have to choose where you stand, you see, "he said, "there are only two sides. We're with Christian. You need to remember that."

Steadman paused, "Yes," he said, nodding, then "yes," again with more fervor.

A fist banged on the window. So unexpected was it that Steadman jumped and lost his grip on the bottle. James turned round sharply. Another bang sounded further back. A siren wailed. "This is the police," shouted a voice.

A figure came into view through the windscreen. The officer held a pistol in both hands. It was pointing straight at them. Shouted commands seemed to issue from every direction. Steadman looked with panic at his friend. "What do we do?"

The door was wrenched open. James threw his hands into the air.

"Get down," shouted the officers, "down on the ground. Down on the ground. Now."

James knelt on the concrete. Something shoved him hard in the back, sending him sprawling face-first. His hands were yanked painfully behind his back. A wire was wrapped round them and pulled tight.

"Knife," someone shouted as hands roughly searched him. "Clear."

As the shouting died down, a pair of feet approached James. They were shod in brown leather brogues. Absurdly, James' first thoughts were to admire them. The owner of the shoes knelt down. He looked into James' eyes. "Read him his rights, Constable Paulsen," he said, "then get him into the van. And don't be too gentle about it."

Inspector Maddocks stood up, took out his phone, and dialed Hardacre's number. She was en route to Birmingham, he knew, but he was certain she would want to hear the good news straight away.

*   *   *   *   *

Park Tower stabbed into the overcast sky. A cylindrical finger of light, twenty or thirty floors high. Charles, Harry and Aabira stood across from it. The bustling wind chased litter along the pavement. Cars jostled by like animals.

"This is a hotel," said Aabira, "I thought you said Schwarzkopf had an apartment?"

"He rents one all year round. Room one-two-five on the fifteenth floor."

"So we just walk in there?" asked Harry.

"Let me go first," said Charles, "If Anthony is in there, I'll talk to him. When he goes out I'll signal and you can come up."

"What with?" said Harry, "the bat-sign?"

"Fifteenth floor," Charles pointed, "count up. It's just to the left of centre, straight above the entrance. When I flash the light on and off, you come up."

"Are you sure he's going to be friendly?" said Harry.

"No."

"And what if he's not home?"

"Then I'll come back." Charles waited for a gap in the traffic and set off, hands deep in his pockets against the cold.

"You don't trust him?" said Aabira.

"Do you?"

"I think so."

They waited for fifteen minutes. Aabira went to get coffee and returned with two steaming cups.

"Thank you," said Harry.

"I guess you got more than you bargained for," said Aabira, "joining the team."

"Are you telling me it's always like this?"

She laughed. "I don't think I'd be here if it was."

"Oh I don't know," said Harry, "I have a feeling you don't quit something easy."

Aabira was warming her hands on her cup. "Is that so?"

"I'm good at reading people," said Harry.

"So what else have you learned about me?"

"That you're a better person than I am. If it had been you that found Tony, I think he would still be alive."

Aabira put a hand on his arm. "Don't torture yourself," she said, "it was an accident. Even the police said so."

"Yeah, well. I'm not sure I can forgive myself that easily."

"There is a Buddhist saying," said Aabira, "that Monte is fond of. It goes: you yourself, as much as any other being in the universe, is deserving of your love and compassion."

Harry sipped his coffee and stared at the building.

"The lights," said Aabira, pointing up.

The interior of the hotel was the definition of luxury—gleaming polished marble floor, extravagant pot-plants, columns, artworks and dark oak. Aabira felt as if she were stepping into a film set. No one seemed to pay them much heed and they found the lifts without difficulty. Charles was waiting at the door of apartment one-two-five. The room inside were just as lavishly decorated and spacious. One entire wall of the sitting room was taken up with floor-to-ceiling windows. The view across the city was breathtaking.

"Anthony isn't here," said Charles, "he's away for two weeks. A girl called Mary-Ann let me in. She doesn't know anything."

"And where is Mary-Ann?" said Harry.

"On her way back to Cambridge. I convinced her to leave me the spare key."

Harry looked around. The glass coffee table had two lines of white powder upon it. A wooden bowl nearby held tubes and devices that he half-recognised as drug paraphernalia. There were also two or three sealed plastic bags containing syringes.

"Where is this locked room?" said Aabira.

Charles led them into the cavernous bedroom. Harry inspected the door. "It's triple-bolted," he said. "There's no way we're opening this without a key. Or an axe."

Aabira crossed the room and pulled out a drawer on the bedside cabinet. "It might be here somewhere," she said, "we should search everything."

Harry and Charles exchanged glances, and followed suit.

*   *   *   *   *

Donald Coy received the call just as the orderly had left his breakfast. Eggs, toast, beans, and a plastic cup of orange juice with bits in. Coy did not like bits in his juice. "What's the latest in the free world?" he grumbled into his phone.

"How are you feeling?" shouted Hardacre, over a large amount of unidentifiable background noise.

"Like I've been stabbed in the side and confined to a hospital."

"We picked up two students in the same van that was outside Boutista's shop." Hardacre strained to make each word distinct. "They were watching the house where he's staying."

"Who put you on to that?"

"Monte did."

"Ah," said Coy, "he told me you had a little chat. Did you get them to talk?"

"I'm not at the station," shouted Hardacre, "but I had Maddocks put the fear of god into them. One of them had a knife."

"Good old Maddocks. What about Rivers?"

"Rivers is gone."

"Gone where?"

"I think that someone put the fear of god into *him*."

"Ha," said Coy, "those boys are bound to clam up and wait for their lawyer."

"I'm not so sure…" Hardacre's voice deteriorated into static for a second, "…falling apart."

"Where the hell are you?"

"I'm in a helicopter."

Coy raised his eyebrows. "Adventurous. The obvious next question is why?"

"...Moony..." came Hardacre's voice through the static, "...Colin Moony."

"Our friend with the spider-web neck."

"I'll phone you later."

The signal broke off. Coy put down his phone and regarded his breakfast. "Go get 'em," he said, picked up the juice and, reluctantly, drained it down.

*   *   *   *   *

It was a gamble that had paid off. Monte had been waiting outside the coroner's office since mid-day, on a nearby bench with a good view of the door, sipping from his Thermos and reading, with a touch of irony, the satirical magazine *Private Eye*. It was chilly, but not too much. The sun, appearing in brief waves, cast warming yellow light upon his face.

At round about twelve-forty, Coroner Leigh Farmoor-Dawley emerged from the building. Dressed neatly in suit and tie, he held a small paper bag in his hands. The coroner crossed the road and walked almost straight past Monte, without giving him a look. Monte waited a suitable amount of time, rose, and began to follow. He had a fair idea where they were headed.

The park was a picturesque square of green, half a mile or so across town. A small river ran parallel to one side; tall trees abounded, and a dozen benches spread out along the concrete walkways. Coroner Leigh took a seat, tucked his tie into his shirt, opened his bag and began to eat.

Monte approached him head on. "Coroner Dawley?"

The man looked up. "Farmoor-Dawley," he said.

"My name's Monte Boutista. I'd like to ask you a few questions."

"Are you police?"

"No." Monte handed over his card. The coroner took it uncertainly. "A private investigator," he said.

"It's about an old case. Lucas Grundy."

Farmoor-Dawley attempted to hand back the card but Monte did not take it.

"I'm not talking to you about anything."

"I think that you should."

"How dare you," said the coroner, standing up, "how did you find me? Did you follow me? I'll call the police."

"I know about the Twenty-two Club," said Monte, "I know that you are a friend of Christian Schwarzkopf. I need to know if somebody paid you to alter your report on Lucas Grundy. I need to know anything you have on Schwarzkopf that can help me."

"Rubbish," said Farmoor-Dawley, "you're insane. Get out of my way."

"Do you have a daughter?" said Monte. "Did you know that Schwarzkopf kidnapped a young woman and kept her prisoner?" Something flickered at the edge of Monte's sight. A thing that he knew was not of the physical world. The coroner began to walk away. An image became superimposed upon Monte's vision, a frame in black and white. He struggled to make it out. A man and a young woman. The wing of a plane glimpsed from a window. Blue skies and mountains and a shimmering lake. A hospital. A name. A voice was whispering a name.

"Elizabeth," he called out.

The coroner turned. "What did you say?"

"Elizabeth. She died. You took her abroad and she died."

"How did you know that?"

Monte sat down upon the bench, rubbing his eyes. "She was very ill. You took her abroad."

Farmoor-Dawley walked slowly back to stand in front of the investigator.

Monte looked at him. "Schwarzkopf gave you the money."

"You don't understand."

"And in return you doctored the evidence."

"What do you expect from me?"

"He's killed people," said Monte, "or had them killed and he'll do it again. I don't think that you really want to be a part of that. You have a chance now to do something about it."

The coroner shook his head.

"You must have loved her very much."

Farmoor-Dawley sat. "My wife."

"Will you help?"

"I can't go to prison."

"It will be better if you give yourself up."

The coroner took out a handkerchief and wiped it across his forehead.

"Go home," said Monte, "all I'm asking is that you consider."

He watched Farmoor-Dawley walk away. Monte felt tired and sick and sorry. Sorry for all the bad things that people did. Sorry for the victims and sorry for the perpetrators. Life, he considered, as he looked up at the grey sky, could at times feel like an ocean of unbridled desires, so overpowering that all you could do was ride it like a fishing boat at the mercy of the squall.

*   *   *   *   *

When the door to Christian Schwarzkopf's Cambridge home swung open, the man standing there was Richard Bowers, the secretary.

"Is he in?" said Eddie.

Bowers looked him up and down. A bead of sweat trickled down his forehead, despite the cold.

"Is he in?" said Eddie again.

Bowers nodded. "Yes." He stood back. "Mr. Schwarzkopf is in the gallery room."

Eddie limped forward. In a strange way he was growing used to the pain in his leg. He had not bothered to rehearse what he was going to say, or even to think about what he hoped to achieve. He simply knew it was something that had to be done.

The ceiling lights in the gallery room were off. The sole illumination came from the soft spotlights focused on each canvas. They were a special sort of fitting, Eddie recalled, designed not to damage the paint. Schwarzkopf stood at the far end, facing away, his head bowed. Eddie walked towards him.

"Martha's dead," he said, simply, "did you know that?"

There was no change in the other man's poise.

"He nearly killed me too. Did you send him?"

Still there was no reaction.

"Why would you do that? You didn't have to do that, you god damn son of a bitch."

"I'm sorry Edward," the man turned. His voice was oddly slurred.

It was not Christian Schwarzkopf.

"Some things are just bigger than you and me." Bradley Crawford took a pair of latex gloves from his pocket and began to pull them on. "If it's any consolation," he said, "you did well. No one has gotten away from me before." He pointed towards his mouth. "You should not have let go. If you'd bitten my tongue off I would have bled to death."

Eddie sighed. He felt a great weight drain from his soul. Eddie closed his eyes. He heard a rustle, a click, and then nothing more.

*   *   *   *   *

"It's probably not even here," said Harry, surveying the room, hands on hips.

Aabira sat on the floor, sorting through the contents of a removed desk drawer that was in front of her. She looked up. "We can't give up."

"I think Harry's right," said Charles, "Christian is too careful to leave the key here."

"Then this whole idea was a waste of time," said Harry.

"I'm sorry," said Charles.

Aabira stood. "Look, Monte said to turn our phones on again at six and he'd check in with us." She looked at her watch. "It's half-past three now. Why don't we get something to eat and wait."

Harry sighed. "Okay. I'll go and pick something up."

"I'll come with you," said Aabira, "I need some things from the shops. Charles?"

Charles shook his head. "I'll stay here."

After they had left Charles walked to the window. The endless city was cloaked in gloom. Somewhere out there was his family. At some place across the miles was Christian. Eddie too. Martha. Monte. And a billion other people, totally unaware of his life. Many would be going through struggles of their own. Some worse. Some trivial. Charles longed for trivial problems. He wished for the time when all he had to deal with were his studies and a broken heart. She was out there too. Somewhere. Living a new life. Charles wondered if she were happy and if she ever thought about him. He hoped so on both counts.

Crossing back to the desk he took out the writing pad and pens he had found. Sitting down at the small table before the window, he paused with pen held over page, took a deep breath, and stirred himself to write.

Thunder rumbled in the sky.

*   *   *   *   *

Colin Moony checked his ticket for the fifth time. He stood in the cavernous Heathrow check-in, a vast white space with curving vaulted roof, hundreds of neon spotlights and thousands of travellers. Along one side stood ten-foot-high digital billboards. There were endless rows of desks, each demarcated by a letter upon large glowing-yellow rectangles. Before each of these were the queues.

Moony hated queues, but he liked the bustle and excitement of the airport, the thrill of a new adventure beckoning. It had begun to rain outside. Newcomers trailed wet tracks across the shiny floor like snails. The line moved forward a few inches. Moony thought of Christian. Perhaps there was no danger. Maybe he had misunderstood. But no, Christian had given that man his name for a reason. And that man did only one thing.

Someone was arguing at the desk. A foreign woman shouting in… he did not know what the language was. Moony had never loved Christian but there was a bond between them as deep and entwined as any he had ever felt. That Christian had given him up hurt Moony but it did not surprise him. The man was a survivor to the core. He would throw everyone and anything to the wolves if it bought him a minute's more life. Except perhaps for the woman and his precious paintings. He seemed to regard them both in the same way.

A backpacker pushed his way in front of him, his bulky rucksack catching Moony on the shoulder. "Sorry, mate," mumbled the man without stopping. Moony clenched his fists. He looked up at the board. Finally the line was moving forward again. It seemed an age before it was his turn at the desk.

He handed over his passport, hefted his luggage onto the belt and stood waiting. The blonde woman behind the desk seemed to be taking an age. "Problem?" asked Moony. She ignored him, flicking through his passport again, turning the pages with what seemed to Moony an agonizing slowness.

"Is there a problem?" he asked again.

"Colin Moony?" a man's voice spoke from his side.

The check-in woman glanced up for an instant and quickly averted her eyes, sliding free of the stall and back a few paces. A tall man in the same uniform came from the back to stand beside her. In that very moment, Moony understood that the game was up.

"Colin Moony," said the voice again.

Four uniformed policemen stood around him. They wore stab-vests and fluorescent jackets and one of them had his hand on a radio.

"What is it?" said Moony.

"You need to come with us, sir."

Moony complied without argument. With an officer on every side, they steered him further down the concourse, past staring travellers into a side door. Then it was down an anonymous carpeted corridor that smelled of cleaning products, and into a small featureless room where a female officer sat behind a plastic desk. There was a grey-haired overweight man at her side. He wore a suit and had a clip-on badge upon his tie.

"Sit down Colin," said Hardacre.

"Couldn't stay away?" said Moony, but he did not feel his usual swagger. He sat. "Can I have some water?"

The big man nodded to one of the officers. "You're in a lot of trouble, Colin," he said.

"Who are you?"

Hardacre picked up a piece of paper. "James Reynolds and Iain Steadman," she read.

"Who?"

"We arrested them both this morning. They had a knife and a gun in their possession, along with a quantity of class-A drugs. We also recovered balaclavas and other clothing. My team is searching their houses as we speak."

"What's that got to do with me?" asked Moony. He crossed his legs and put his hands behind his head. "Are you going to let me get on my flight?"

"They're scared young men," said Hardacre, "they've already started to talk."

"Good for them."

"I suggest that you do likewise."

Moony shook his head. "You haven't a thing on me."

"Edward Dankworth. Martha Wainright. Charles Addington. These are three of the names that James Reynolds supplied us."

"So?"

"Edward Dankworth's body was discovered this morning at the home of Christian Schwarzkopf by his secretary. Martha Wainwright was found dead at a house belonging to the parents of Charles Addington. Addington himself is a missing person."

Moony uncrossed his leg and lowered his hands.

"I think you're in more trouble than you know," said Hardacre.

An officer handed Moony his water. Moony took a sip. "I want to make a deal," he said.

Hardacre and the big man exchanged a look.

"We'll talk about that later," said Hardacre, and gestured to the officer at the door.

*   *   *   *   *

Monte ended the call, turned his phone off and walked back into the hospital concourse. Halfway down he stopped, put his head in his hands and stood motionless. After a few seconds he felt a hand upon his arm. "Are you alright?" said a voice.

Monte opened his eyes. It was the woman he had met earlier outside the ward. He smiled. "I'm fine now," he said, "thank you."

The woman nodded. "I hope your sister's okay," she said, "I have to go. My Uber…"

"Thank you again," said Monte, "good luck."

This time he had no problem getting in to see Coy. The officer on the door was polite. Coy sat propped up reading a book, his glasses halfway down his nose.

"You look better," said Monte.

"It's this healthy food they're force-feeding me." Coy put down the book. "Hardacre picked up the occupants of the van that was watching your safe-house."

Monte took a seat next to the bed.

"She picked up Colin Moony too. All three are tripping over each other to point the finger."

"I thought Moony was lawyered-up."

"There have been some deaths. I think someone is trying to clean house. I guess they got nervous."

"Simple as that," said Monte.

"Simple as," said Coy. "I think it's time you bring Charles Addington in now. Hardacre's done the best she can. Kicked up enough dust that it will be difficult for anyone to keep a lid on it. I can't make any promises but…"

"…but we've done everything that we can?"

"We have."

Monte checked his watch. "I'm checking with Aabira at six. I'll have them bring Charles back right away."

"Let him come in on his own," said Coy, "it'll look better. Any chance he'll neglect to mention being shielded by a private investigator for three days?"

"I want to keep Harry, Penny and Aabira out of it. If he needs to use my name, well I guess I'll deal with that when it happens. My worry now is for the safety of my team."

Coy scratched his chin. "You'll be alright," he said. "Luckily you have friends in the right places."

"And Schwarzkopf?"

"Hardacre will pick him up. Shame. I'd have liked to be there for that one."

"It was Colin Moony," said Monte, "who stabbed you."

Coy nodded. "Hardacre told me that too."

"This doesn't feel very neat," said Monte, "what if none of it hangs together?"

"All will be well," said Coy, "and all manner of things will be well." He tapped the book.

"Julian of Norwich," said Monte.

"She was a very wise woman."

Monte checked his watch again. "If you don't mind," he said, "I ought to go and see Sarrah."

"Of course," said Coy, "how is she?"

"I didn't get a chance to tell you," said Monte, "she's here. Two floors down. She's having a bad time."

"Monte," said Coy, "I'm sorry. Give her my best. Go."

When Monte reached his sister's room, before he said anything, he gave her a big hug.

"Hey, brother," she said, "you missed me that much?"

"Always."

She brushed his hair back from his face.

"You're looking better," he said.

"You're not," said Sarrah, "you look wrecked."

Monte smiled. "I've had a lot to think about."

"I'm sorry."

"No," said Monte, "it's not you. I mean of course I've been worried, but…I've been involved with a case. A long, hard case."

"Want to talk about it?"

"Later. I think the last of it is playing out without me. This is where I need to be now. I just have to make a phone call in a few minutes, okay?"

Sarrah nodded. "You're a good human," she said, "a good human. Don't you ever forget that."

Monte thought of James Roberston and Tony Perkins and Lucas Grundy, of Harry and Aabira and Penny. He thought of Christian Schwarzkopf and Maria Waters and he thought of Charles. Somehow, out of everyone, he felt worst about Charles.

"I hope that I am," he said to Sarrah, "I hope so."

*   *   *   *   *

The first thing Christian Schwarzkopf saw upon entering his

apartment was Charles Addington. Charles sat at the desk before the window that let out into the night. When Schwarzkopf entered Charles looked up, his right hand, which was holding a pen, paused.

Christian gave a short laugh and crossed to the drinks cabinet. He busied himself with a bottle of whiskey and a glass. "You're impudence," he said, "is breath-taking."

Charles did not move or look up.

"This is how you repay me?" said Christian, glass in hand. "You break into my apartment and sit there, using my paper, at my desk. Who are you writing to? Is it the police?"

For the first time Charles looked at Christian.

"I gave you everything," said Christian, "and you sneak around like a rat."

"You gave me nothing."

"What?" Christian leaned against the back of the sofa. "Oh this is priceless," he said.

"You used me," said Charles, "and then you were going to kill me."

"I used you?" said Christian, "Really Charles? And how did I do that? Was anybody twisting your arm? On the night that you stabbed a man in the neck?"

"You were going to kill me, weren't you?"

Christian drained his glass. "Don't give me your sob story," he said, "you were very happy to take my money, my drugs. I gave you a life you'd never even dreamed of."

"It was a life I never wanted."

"But you took it," said Christian. He threw the glass at Charles. It missed by a good distance, hit the window with a dull thud and dropped onto the carpet. "You took it," he said again.

Charles' gaze fell. Christian moved to stand over him. "I was never going to kill you," he said. "Charlie." His hand went to Charles' arm. "You were my favourite, didn't you know that? You have a courage none of the others did. Not even Edward. It's not too late, you know." Christian moved back to the cabinet. "Let me get you a drink. We can start again, you and I."

"It's too late," said Charles.

Christian paused. "It's never too late."

"Why me?" said Charles, "why did you pick me?"

Christian finished pouring. "Edward picked you," he said. "You want to know why? Truthfully? Because he knew you could be manipulated."

"Don't take it the wrong way," he continued, crossing back and holding out the glass, "in a way it's a complement."

"What's in your locked room?" asked Charles.

Christian set the second glass down on the desk. He took a seat.

"Why do you want to know that?"

"You want me to help you?" said Charles, "Show me."

"*You* help me?"

"Yes."

Christian smiled thinly. Putting down his drink he took a key out from his wallet. "Alright," he said, "I'll show you." He stood up and walked to the corner door in the next room. Charles followed. Christian paused with the key in the lock.

"You want to know," he said, softly. He turned the key and opened the door. A light flickered on automatically.

"I don't understand," said Charles.

Schwarzkopf wasn't listening. He was looking. For the first time in a long, long while, a tear came to his eye.

To Charles' eye the paintings stacked inside were far from masterpieces. There was a certain quality to them but they were undeniably naïve, crudely rendered and in some instances little more than amorphous swirls of colour.

"Are they valuable?"

"Valuable?" Christian turned. His face was wet. He began to laugh, an awful, unhinged sound. He took a pace back, leaned against the wall and slid down it until he sat, his hands lying limp upon the floor.

"Turn yourself in," said Charles.

Christian looked up. The buzzer sounded. Charles walked to the door. "Don't," said Christian, "wait."

Charles looked through the spy-hole, and opened the door.

*　　*　　*　　*　　*

"What do you think Charles would like?"

Harry shrugged. "Let's just get a bit of everything."

They stood in the brightly lit interior of an upmarket eatery a couple of streets down from Park Tower. "Is everything in here vegetarian?"

"There's fish," said Aabira.

"I mean proper meat."

Aabira picked up another tray to add to her collection. "It's healthy food, it'll do you good."

"Doesn't it worry you?" said Harry, "us being in Schwarzkopf's apartment. Anyone could turn up."

"Charles thinks that it's safe."

"Charles."

"It's not long till six," said Aabira, "we'll talk to Monte and make a plan."

They waited in the queue.

"How did you get involved in the first place?"

"Alison Perkins," said Aabira.

"No," said Harry, "I mean the agency. It just doesn't seem like your sort of thing."

"What does seem like my sort of thing?"

"You know what I mean."

Aabira stacked the trays on the counter. "Monte isn't just any investigator," she said, "the cases he takes on are important."

"That still doesn't answer my question."

"No," said Aabira, taking the bags, "it doesn't."

"Like that is it?" said Harry, he took both the bags from Aabira.

"Maybe I'll tell you one day."

"I'll look forward to that."

They walked back in silence. Night had taken hold. Cars cruised through the dark. Tired commuters thronged the streets. A rumble of thunder sounded. By the time they had reached the atrium, rain had begun to fall.

*   *   *   *   *

Tens of miles away, Coroner Leigh Farmoor-Dawley rested his hands around the comforting warmth of his mug of tea. He sat in the old armchair, his feet up on a stool, his long legs stretched out before him. A little black cat made a puddle of warmth in his lap. Old English folk music played upon his stereo.

In front of the cat lay an open book of photographs. They had been taken a long time ago. The faded colours and lack of definition did not diminish their potency. They were wedding photos. Leigh had not looked at them for a long time. His heart ached with sadness and with joy remembered. At length, he shook the cat gently off his lap, closed the album and stood up. The tea had grown cold in its cup.

Leigh picked up the phone and stood looking from the window into the night, waiting for an answer. When the answer came he paused just for an instant, then: "This is Coroner Leigh Farmoor-Dawley," he said, "I'd like to speak to an Inspector. I have a confession to make."

*   *   *   *   *

There was something about London that Bradley disliked. He thought perhaps it might be the associations that rose unbidden to his mind. Bradley's father had been a war historian, and consequently Bradley had grown up with the city eternally fixed in his mind in black-and-white; gnarled old men in string shirts and old women in curlers, struggling over heaps of collapsed buildings. Babies crying.

School children in gas masks. Air raid wardens and blackouts, wailing sirens and the sound of V2 rockets. Your country needs you.

Whey did it make him feel so…morose? That was not the word. Not quite. It was something subtler, darker and stronger that tugged at the edges of his psyche. Bradley thought of the man he had just killed. His tongue hurt still and he could not tolerate coffee or tea, which irked him greatly.

By the time that he reached the tube station it was rush hour. Bradley stood his ground. His size, build and demeanor generated respect. Man is still an animal, Bradley understood, and there was no shame in being an Alpha.

He got off on Knightsbridge and when he emerged onto the street the relatively fresh air was welcome. He was glad that the mission had changed. Just one last target and then he would be away. Tonight. Heading back for the land of his birth, the greatest, the only truly free country in the world, so long as they could keep the liberal threat at bay.

And they would.

Thunder rumbled in the dark sky. Bradley followed the flow of the crowd, moving steadily and easily. A shop front caught his eye, an eatery, the bright light from its windows spilling out onto the street. He knew he should walk on but found himself entering through the wide open door. He was thirsty and he needed to take another does of painkillers.

The diner was full of London's fashionable elite. They sat on long benches before communal tables and ate with chopsticks. The food was a mix of sushi and exotic vegetarian dishes. Bradley picked out a glass bottle of water and lined up for the counter.

He became interested in the couple in front of him in the queue—a tall blonde Englishman and a dark-skinned woman in a hijab. He wondered what their story was. The man had an athletic build not dissimilar to his own. He carried himself like a sportsman. They were buying a lot of food to take away.

Bradley saw them again as he journeyed the final half-mile to Park Tower. The man carried their bags and they walked in silence. The Tower itself pointed like a lit finger up into the night. The couple preceded him into the atrium and across to the elevator. They must have money. Perhaps the woman was Saudi. It could be, thought Bradley, with a sudden spark of interest, that the blonde man was her bodyguard. He followed them into the lift, took a place in the corner and all three, the sole passengers, rode up in silence to the fifteenth floor.

Keeping a suitable distance, Bradley followed them along the corridor. They stopped at apartment one-two-five and the blonde man pressed the buzzer. Bradley was about to walk past when Charles Addington opened the door. Over Addington's shoulder Bradley caught sight of Christian Schwarzkopf. It was a split-second decision. Bradley followed the couple in, pulling out his gun as he did so.

Charles, seeing the intruder raise his weapon, yelled out and threw himself forward. Bradley shoved him back hard. Charles fell. Schwarzkopf himself seemed frozen, his mouth hanging open and his hands out before him, pleading. Bradley raised the gun. On the fringe of his vision, he saw the punch coming and leaned back just in time to avoid the full force of the blow. Nevertheless it exploded forcefully against his chin. He staggered sideways into a cabinet. There was the sound of smashing china and the gun fell from his hand.

Bradley kicked out and felt his foot connect. Harry fell back onto the carpet. Schwarzkopf, seizing his chance, bolted through the door and into the corridor. Charles followed. The gun had flown several feet onto the carpet. Bradley walked calmly across to retrieve it. He heard, rather than saw, the blonde man and the girl flee the apartment.

Harry pushed Aabira in front of him. "Go," he shouted, "go."

"This way," Charles was standing twenty feet further on. He was holding open an access door. Harry, glancing behind, saw the man with the gun emerge into the corridor. Harry pushed Charles and Aabira before him, through the access door and into a brick-walled stairwell. Charles began to run up the echoing iron steps.

"What are you doing?" shouted Harry, "go down."

"Schwarzkopf," called Charles, his footsteps clanging above.

Aabira started after him.

"Down," said Harry, "Aabira we have to go down."

"We can't leave Charles," she called back.

Harry cursed and followed.

Christian burst through the door onto the roof and out into the night air. Wind tore at his clothes and rain pricked at his face. He kept running wildly, gasping for breath, only slowing as he reached the low-fenced edge. The entirety of the city spread before him. Miniature cars, far below, raced through the streets. Christian began to laugh. The door he had emerged through clanged open and Charles came out. Christian ran a hand through his wet hair. He turned to grasp the railing, closed his eyes and tilted his head back to the storm.

"Christian."

Schwarzkopf opened his eyes and turned. "We're here, Charles," he said, holding his arms out wide, "we're here."

In the stairwell Harry and Aabira rushed on, curve after curve. Through the gaps in the steps they could see the assassin moving swiftly after. "Faster," said Harry, "go." Aabira thought that her heart might burst. She was torn between looking up and looking down. The stairs seemed endless. Round and round they went at dizzying speed, Harry pushing her on.

Harry cried out. Aabira turned. He had stopped running. He was leaning against the wall, his hand to his chest, his face drained of colour. "Harry," she cried, running back down, "we can't stop. What's wrong?"

Harry couldn't answer. He felt as though his chest was being constricted by a giant vice. Feeling the strength drain from his legs he slipped down. The world tilted. It seemed to Harry that he was looking out from a telescope, a long way off. The edges of his vision were blurred. He could see the concern on Aabira's face as she knelt over him, but he could not quite hear her words.

Aabira turned as the assassin rounded the corner. She threw herself over Harry's limp body, glaring up at the hit man, breathing hard. Bradley looked down at her. He did not pause for more than a moment before rushing past, bounding up the stairs two at a time. The rain was coming down fast when he emerged onto the roof. Charles and Schwarzkopf stood across from him at the rail. They both turned to look. Bradley checked his gun as he walked towards them. A flash of lighting lit up the sky. Thunder followed.

Charles turned, grabbed Christian in a bear hug, and pushed hard with his legs, toppling them both over the edge and into the night.

Bradley walked to the lip and looked down. Nothing of the pavement could be seen through the rain. He stood for a while, feeling the water run down his face, around his neck and onto his hands. When he turned the woman and the man stood behind him, not far from the door. His arm was around her shoulders and she was struggling to support his weight.

Bradley holstered his gun. He looked them both in the eyes as he walked past, and then he was gone, moving swiftly down the stairwell and out of sight.

*   *   *   *   *

It was a cold November morning and the world seemed drained of colour. Monte stood next to Donald Coy in the churchyard as the coffin was lowered into the ground. He looked across to where Harry and Aabira stood, next to the parents of Charles Addington. The reading was short, and Charles' father was the first to bend down and throw a handful of dirt into the hole.

"Seems like this is where we came in," said Penny, as they walked back towards the car park. "Excuse me a moment," she patted Monte's arm, "I'm going to go and speak to the parents."

Monte caught Harry's eye and they exchanged a nod as he and Aabira came over. Harry smiled grimly.

"How are you feeling?" asked Monte.

"Just fine," said Harry, "considering."

"I'm going to drive Harry home," said Aabira, "do you want a lift?"

"Thank you, no," said Monte. "I'm going to get a taxi back with Don."

He watched them walk away. Before they had gone too far, Harry turned. "Hey boss," he called back, "I'll see you on Monday."

Monte nodded, smiled, and waved.

"Kids got guts," said Coy, moving slowly to Monte's side.

"He's not the only one," said Monte. He looked at the walking stick. "Glad to see you're not being completely pig-headed over that."

"Do you have time for a walk?" asked Coy. "Just to the bench across the road. I can make it that far."

They sat for a while looking out across the park.

"Hell of a case," said Coy.

Monte nodded.

"Feel like jacking it in?" asked Coy.

Monte looked at his friend. "Do you?"

In the park joggers ran, couples walked, a group of kids played football, and autumn leaves fell softly upon the ground.

"I have a client this afternoon," said Monte, looking at his watch.

"Anything interesting?"

"Could be," said Monte. "You ready to go?"

"Not yet," said Coy, "this fresh air is good for me."

They stayed for an hour longer, and talked about everything and anything but work.

And across the city of Cambridge, life went on as normal.

Mostly.

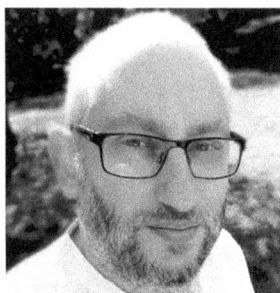

ABOUT THE AUTHOR:

Chris Wheatley is a writer and musician from Oxford, U.K. He has too many records, too many musical instruments, and not enough cats.

If you enjoyed reading this book,
please consider writing your honest review
and sharing it with other readers.

Many of our Authors are happy to participate in
Book Club and Reader Group discussions.
For more information, contact us at info@encirclepub.com.

Thank you,
Encircle Publications

For news about more exciting new fiction, join us at:

Facebook: www.facebook.com/encirclepub

Twitter: twitter.com/encirclepub

Instagram: www.instagram.com/encirclepublications

Sign up for Encircle Publications newsletter and specials:
eepurl.com/cs8taP

Lightning Source UK Ltd.
Milton Keynes UK
UKHW010633140721
387149UK00001B/209